99 Days

Also by Katie Cotugno

How to Love

99 Days

KATIE COTUGNO

Quercus

First published in 2015 by Balzer + Bray, an imprint of HarperCollin's Publishers
10 East 53rd St, New York, NY10022

First published in Great Britain in 2015 by

Quercus Publishing Ltd
Carmelite House
50 Victoria Embankment
London EC4Y 0DZ

An Hachette UK company

alloyentertainment

A CIP catalogue record for this book is available
from the British Library

PB 978 1 78206 002 4
EBOOK 978 1 78206 003 1

10 9 8 7 6 5 4 3 2

Printed and bound in Great Britain by Clays Ltd, St Ives plc

This one's for the girls

DAY 1

Julia Donnelly eggs my house the first night I'm back in Star Lake, and that's how I know everyone still remembers everything.

"Quite the welcome wagon," my mom says, coming outside to stand on the lawn beside me and survey the runny yellow damage to her lopsided lilac Victorian. There are yolks smeared down all the windows. There are eggshells in the shrubs. Just past ten in the morning, and it's already starting to smell rotten, sulfurous and baking in the early summer sun. "They must have gone to Costco to get all those eggs."

"Can you not?" My heart is pounding. I'd forgotten this, or tried to, what it was like before I ran away from here a year ago: Julia's reign of holy terror, designed with ruthless precision to bring me to justice for all my various capital crimes. The bottoms of my feet are clammy inside my lace-up boots. I glance over my shoulder at the sleepy street beyond the long, windy driveway, half expecting to see her cruising by in her family's ancient Bronco, admiring her handiwork. "Where's the hose?"

"Oh, leave it." My mom, of course, is completely unbothered, the toss of her curly blond head designed to let me know I'm overreacting. Nothing is a big deal when it comes to my mother: The President of the United States could egg her house, her house itself could *burn down*, and it would turn into not a big deal. *It's a good story*, she used to say whenever I'd come to her with some little-kid unfairness to report, no recess or getting picked last for basketball. *Remember this for later, Molly. It'll make a good story someday.* It never occurred to me to ask which one of us would be doing the telling. "I'll call Alex to come clean it up this afternoon."

"Are you kidding?" I say shrilly. My face feels red and blotchy, and all I want to do is make myself as small as humanly possible—the size of a dust mote, the size of a speck—but there's no way I'm letting my mom's handyman spray a half-cooked omelet off the front of the house just because everyone in this town thinks I'm a slut and wants to remind me. "I said where's the *hose*, Mom?"

"Watch the tone, please, Molly." My mom shakes her head resolutely. Somewhere under the egg and the garden I can smell her, the lavender-sandalwood perfume she's worn since I was a baby. She hasn't changed at all since I

2

left here: the silver rings on every one of her fingers, her tissue-thin black cardigan and her ripped jeans. When I was little I thought my mom was the most beautiful woman in the world. Whenever she'd go on tour, reading from her fat novels in bookstores in New York City and Chicago and L.A., I used to lie on my stomach in the Donnellys' living room and look at the author photos on the backs of all her books. "Don't you blame me; I'm not the one who did this to you."

I turn on her then, standing on the grass in this place I never wanted to come back to, not in a hundred million years. "Who would you like me to *blame*, then?" I demand. For a second I let myself remember it, the cold, sick feeling of seeing the article in *People* for the first time in April of junior year, along with the grossest, juiciest scenes from the novel and a glossy picture of my mom leaning against her desk: *Diana Barlow's latest novel,* Driftwood, *was based on her daughter's complicated relationship with two local boys.* The knowing in my ribs and stomach and spine that now everyone else would know, too. "Who?"

For a second my mom looks completely exhausted, older than I ever think of her as being—glamorous or not, she was almost forty when she adopted me, is close to sixty now. Then she blinks, and it's gone. "Molly—"

"Look, don't." I hold up a hand to stop her, wanting so, so badly not to talk about it. To be anywhere other than here. Ninety-nine days between now and the first day of freshman orientation in Boston, I remind myself, trying to take a deep breath and not give in to the overwhelming urge to bolt for the nearest bus station as fast as my two legs can carry me—not as fast, admittedly, as they might have a year ago. Ninety-nine days, and I can leave for college and be done.

My mom stands in the yard and looks at me: She's barefoot like always, dark nails and a tattoo of a rose on her ankle like a cross between Carole King and the first lady of a motorcycle gang. *It'll make a great story someday*. She *said* that, she *told* me what was going to happen, so really there's no earthly reason to still be so baffled after all this time that I told her the worst, most secret, most important thing in my life—and she wrote a best-selling book about it.

"The hose is in the shed," she finally says.

"Thank you." I swallow down the phlegmy thickness in my throat and head for the backyard, squirming against the sour, panicky sweat I can feel gathered at the base of my backbone. I wait until I'm hidden in the blue-gray shade of the house before I let myself cry.

DAY 2

I spend the next day holed up in my bedroom with the blinds closed, eating Red Vines and watching weird Netflix documentaries on my laptop, hiding out like a wounded fugitive in the last third of a Clint Eastwood movie. Vita, my mom's ornery old tabby, wanders in and out as she likes. Everything up here is the same as I left it: blue-and-white striped wallpaper, the cheerful yellow rug, the fluffy gray duvet on the bed. The *Golly, Molly* artwork a designer friend of my mom's did when I was a baby hanging above the desk, right next to a bulletin board holding my track meet schedule from junior year and a photo of me at the Donnellys' farmhouse with Julia and Patrick and Gabe, my mouth wide open mid-laugh. Even my hairbrush is still sitting on the dresser, the one I forgot to take with me in my mad dash out of Star Lake after the *People* article, like it was just waiting for me to come crawling all the way back here with a head full of knots.

It's the photo I keep catching myself looking at, though, like there's some kind of karmic magnet attached to the back of it drawing my attention from clear across the room. Finally, I haul myself out of bed and pull it down to examine more closely: It's from their family party the summer after freshman year, back when Patrick and I were dating. The four of us are sitting sprawled on the ratty old couch in the barn behind the farmhouse, me and all three Donnellys, Julia in the middle of saying something snarky and Patrick with his arm hooked tight around my waist. Gabe's looking right at me, although I never actually noticed that until after everything happened. Just holding the stupid picture feels like pressing on a bruise.

Patrick's not even home this summer, I know from creeping him on Facebook. He's doing some volunteer program in Colorado, clearing brush and learning to fight forest fires just like he always dreamed of doing when we were little and running around in the woods behind his parents' house. There's no chance of even bumping into him around town.

Probably there's no good reason to feel disappointed about that.

I slap the photo facedown on the desktop and climb back under the covers, pushing Vita onto the carpet—this room has been hers and the dog's in my absence; the sticky layer of pet hair has made that much abundantly clear. When

I was a kid, living up here made me feel like a princess, tucked in the third-floor turret of my mom's old haunted house. Now, barely a week after high school graduation, it makes me feel like one again—trapped in a magical tower, with no place in the whole world to go.

I dig the last Red Vine out of the cellophane package just as Vita hops right back up onto the pillow beside me. "Get out, Vita," I order, pushing her gently off again and rolling my eyes at the haughty flick of her feline tail as she stalks out the door, fully expecting her to turn up again almost immediately.

DAY 3

Vita doesn't.

DAY 4

Imogen doesn't, either. When I was staring down my summer-long sentence in Star Lake, the idea of seeing her again was the only thing that made it feel at all bearable, but so far my *hey, I'm back* and *let's hang out* texts have gone resolutely unanswered. Could be she hates me, too. Imogen and I have been friends since first grade, and she stuck by me pretty hard at the end of junior year, sitting beside me in the cafeteria at school even as everyone else at our lunch table mysteriously disappeared and the whispers turned into something way, way worse. Still, the truth is I didn't exactly give her a heads-up before I left Star Lake to do my senior year at Bristol—an all-girls boarding school plunked like a missile silo in the middle of the desert outside Tempe, Arizona.

Absconded under the cover of darkness, more like.

By the next day it's been a full ninety-six hours of minimal human contact, though, so when my mom knocks hard on the bedroom door to let me know her cleaning lady is coming, I pull some clean shorts out of the pile of detritus already accumulated on my floor. My T-shirts and underwear are still in my giant duffel. I'll have to unpack at some point, probably, although the truth is I'd almost rather live out of a suitcase for three months. My old sneakers are tucked underneath the desk chair, I notice while I'm crouched down there, the laces still tied from the last time I wore them—the day the article came out I remember suddenly, like I thought I could somehow outrun a national publication. I had sprinted as hard and as fast as I could manage.

I'd thrown up on the dusty side of the road.

Woof. I do my best to shake off the memory, grabbing the photo of me and the Donnellys—still facedown on the desk where I left it the other night—and shoving it into the back of the drawer in my nightstand. Then I lace my boots up and take my neglected old Passat into Star Lake proper.

It's cool enough to open the windows, and even through the pine trees lining the sides of Route 4 I can smell the slightly mildewy scent of the lake as I head for the short stretch of civilization that makes up downtown: Main Street is small and rumpled, all diners and dingy grocery stores, a roller rink that hasn't been open since roughly 1982. That's about the last time this place was a destination, as far as I've ever been able to tell—the lakefront plus the endless green stretch of the Catskill Mountains was a big vacation spot in the sixties and seventies, but ever since I can remember Star Lake has had the air of something that used to be but isn't anymore, like you fell into your grandparents' honeymoon by mistake.

I speed up as I bypass the Donnellys' pizza shop, slouching low in my seat like a gangbanger until I pull up in front of French Roast, the coffee shop where Imogen's worked since we were freshmen. I open the door to the smell of freshly ground beans and the sound of some moody girl singer on the radio. The shop is mostly empty, a late-morning lull. Imogen's standing behind the counter, midnight-dark hair hanging in her eyes, and when she looks up at the jangle of the bells, guilty, awkward panic flashes across her pretty face in the moment before she can quell it.

"Oh my God," she says once she's recovered, coming around the counter and hugging me fast and antiseptic, then holding me back at arm's length like a great-aunt having a look at how much I've grown. Literally, in my case—I've put on fifteen pounds easy since I left for Arizona—and even though she'd never say anything about it, I can feel her taking it in. "You're here!"

"I am," I agree, my voice sounding weird and false. She's wearing a gauzy sundress under her French Roast apron, a splotch of deep blue on the side of her hand like she was up late sketching one of the pen-and-ink portraits she's been

11

doing since we were little kids. Every year on her birthday I buy her a fresh set of markers, the fancy kind from the art supply store. When I was in Tempe I went online and had them shipped. "Did you get my texts?"

Imogen does something between a nod and a headshake, noncommittal. "Yeah, my phone's been really weird lately?" she says, voice coming up at the end like she's unsure. She shrugs then, always oddly graceful even though she's been five eleven since we were in middle school. Somehow she never got teased. "It eats things; I need a new one. Come on, let me get you coffee." She heads back around the counter, past the rack of mugs they give people who plan to hang out on one of the sagging couches, and hands me a paper to-go cup. I'm not sure if it's a message or not. She waves me off when I try to pay.

"Thanks," I tell her, smiling a little bit helplessly. I'm not used to making small talk with her. "So, hey, RISD, huh?" I try—I saw on Instagram that that's where she's headed in the fall, a selfie of her smiling hugely in a Rhode Island School of Design sweatshirt. As the words come out of my mouth I realize how totally bizarre it is that *that's* how I found out. We told each other everything—well, *almost* everything—once upon a time. "We'll be neighbors in the fall, Providence and Boston."

"Oh, yeah," Imogen says, sounding distracted. "I think it's like an hour, though, right?"

"Yeah, but an hour's not that long," I reply uncertainly.

It feels like there's a river between us, and I don't know how to build a bridge. "Look, Imogen——" I start, then break off awkwardly. I want to apologize for falling off the face of the earth the way I did—want to tell her about my mom and about Julia, that I'm here for ninety-five more days and I'm terrified, and I need all the allies I can get. I want to tell Imogen everything, but before I can get another word out I'm interrupted by the telltale chime of a text message dinging out from inside the pocket of her apron.

So much for a phone that eats things. Imogen blushes a deep sunburned red.

I take a deep breath. "Okay," I say, pushing my wild, wavy brown hair behind my ears just as the front door opens and a whole gaggle of women in yoga gear come crowding into the shop, jabbering eagerly for their half-caf nonfat whatevers.

"I'll see you around, okay?" I ask, shrugging a little. Imogen nods and waves good-bye.

I head back out to where my car's parked at the curb, pointedly ignoring the huge LOCAL AUTHOR! display in the window of Star Lake's one tiny bookstore across the street—a million paperback copies of *Driftwood* available for the low, low price of $6.99 plus my dignity. I'm devoting so much attention to ignoring it, in fact, that I don't notice the note tucked under my wipers until the very last second, Julia's pink-marker scrawl across the back of a Chinese take-out menu:

dirty slut

The panic is cold and wet and skittering in the second before it's replaced by the hot rush of shame; my stomach lurches. I reach out and snatch the menu off the windshield, the paper going limp and clammy inside my damp, embarrassed fist.

Sure enough, there it is, idling at the stoplight at the end of the block: the Donnellys' late-nineties Bronco, big and olive and dented where Patrick backed it into a mailbox in the fall of our sophomore year. It's the same one all three of them learned to drive on, the one we all used to pile into so that Gabe could ferry us to school when we were freshmen. Julia's raven hair glints in the sun as the light turns green and she speeds away.

I force myself to take three deep breaths before I ball up the menu and toss it onto the passenger seat of my car, then two more before I pull out into traffic. I grip the wheel tightly so my hands will stop shaking. Julia was my friend first, before I ever met either one of her brothers. Maybe it makes sense that she's the one who hates me most. I remember running into her here not long after the article came out, how she turned and saw me standing there with my latte, the unadulterated loathing painted all over her face.

"Why the fuck do I see you everywhere, Molly?" she demanded, and she sounded so incredibly frustrated— like she really wanted to know so we could solve this, so it wouldn't keep happening over and over again. "For the love of God, why won't you just go away?"

I went home and called Bristol that same afternoon.

There's nowhere for me to go now, though, not really: All I want is to floor it home and bury myself under the covers with a documentary about the deep ocean or something, but I make myself stop at the gas station to fill my empty tank and pick up more Red Vines, just like I'd planned to.

I can't spend my whole summer like this.

Can I?

I'm just fitting my credit card into the pump when a big hand lands square on my shoulder. "Get the fuck out of here!" a deep voice says. I whirl around, heart thrumming and ready for a fight, before I realize it's an exclamation and not an order.

Before I realize it's coming from *Gabe*.

"You're *home*?" he asks incredulously, his tan face breaking into a wide grin. He's wearing frayed khaki shorts and aviators and a T-shirt from Notre Dame, and he looks happier to see me than anyone has since I got here.

I can't help it: I burst into tears.

Gabe doesn't blink. "Hey, hey," he says easily, getting his arms around me and squeezing. He smells like farmer's market bar soap and clothes dried on the line. "Molly Barlow, why you crying?"

"I'm not," I protest, even as I blatantly get snot all over the front of his T-shirt. I pull back and wipe my eyes,

15

shaking my head. "Oh my God, I'm not, I'm sorry. That's embarrassing. Hi."

Gabe keeps smiling, even if he does look a little surprised. "Hey," he says, reaching out and swiping at my cheek with the heel of his hand. "So, you know, welcome back, how have you been, I see you're enjoying your return to the warm bosom of Star Lake."

"Uh-huh." I sniffle once and pull it together, mostly—God, I didn't realize I was so hard up for a friendly face, it's ridiculous. Or, okay, I *did*, but I didn't think I'd lose it quite so hard at the sight of one. "It's been awesome." I reach into the open window of the Passat and hand him the crumpled-up take-out menu. "For example, here is my homecoming card from your sister."

Gabe smoothes it out and looks at it, then nods. "Weird," he says, calm as the surface of the lake in the middle of the night. "She put the same one on my car this morning."

My eyes widen. "Really?"

"No," Gabe says, grinning when I make a face. Then his eyes go dark. "Seriously, though, are you okay? That's, like, pretty fucked up and horrifying of her, actually."

I sigh and roll my eyes—at myself or at the situation, at the gut-wrenching absurdity of the mess I made. "It's—whatever," I tell him, trying to sound cool or above it or something. "I'm fine. It is what it is."

"It feels unfair, though, right?" Gabe says. "I mean, if you're a dirty slut, then I'm a dirty slut."

I laugh. I can't help it, even though it feels colossally weird to hear him say it out loud. We never talked about it once after it happened, not even when the book—and the article—came out and the world came crashing down around my ears. Could be enough time has passed that it doesn't feel like a big deal to him anymore, although apparently he's the only one. God knows it still feels like a big deal to me. "You definitely are," I agree, then watch as he balls up the menu and tosses it over his shoulder, missing the trash can next to the pump by a distance of roughly seven feet. "That's littering," I tell him, smirking a little.

"Add it to the list," Gabe says, apparently unconcerned about this or any other lapses in good citizenship. He was student council president when he was a senior. Patrick and Julia and I hung all his campaign posters at school. "Look, people are assholes. My sister is an asshole. And my brother—" He breaks off, shrugging. His shaggy brown hair curls down over his ears, a lighter honey-molasses color than his brother's and sister's. Patrick's hair is almost black. "Well, my brother is my brother, but anyway, he's not here. What are *you* doing, are you working, what?"

"I—nothing yet," I confess, feeling suddenly embarrassed at how reclusive I've been, humiliated that there's virtually nobody here who wants to see me. Gabe's had a million friends as long as I've known him. "Hiding, mostly."

Gabe nods at that. But then: "Think you'll be hiding tomorrow, too?"

I remember once, when I was ten or eleven, that I stepped on a piece of glass down by the lake, and Gabe carried me all the way home piggyback. I remember that we lied to Patrick for an entire year. My whole face has that clogged, bloated post-cry feeling, like there's something made of cotton shoved up into my brain. "I don't know," I say eventually, cautious, intrigued in spite of myself— maybe it's just the constant ache of loneliness, but running into Gabe makes me feel like something's about to happen, a bend in a dusty road. "Probably. Why?"

Gabe grins down at me like a master of ceremonies, like someone who suspects I need a little anticipation in my life and wants to deliver. "Pick you up at eight," is all he says.

DAY 5

Gabe's right on time, two quick taps on the horn of his beat-up station wagon to let me know he's outside. I hurry down the stairs faster than I've done much of anything since I've been here, the noisy clunk of my boots on the hardwood. My hair's long and loose down my back.

"You going out?" my mom calls from her office. She sounds surprised—fair enough, I guess, since my social circle up until now has pretty much consisted of Vita, Oscar, and the little Netflix robot that recommends stuff based on what you've already watched. "Who with?"

I almost don't even tell her—the urge to lie like a reflex, to keep myself from winding up fodder for Oprah's Book Club one more time. Then I decide I don't care. "With Gabe," I announce, my voice like a challenge. I don't wait for her response before I walk out the door.

He's idling in the driveway with Bob Dylan in the CD player, low and clanging and familiar. His parents were both giant hippies—Chuck wore his hair to his shoulders until Patrick and Julia were five—and we both grew up listening to that kind of stuff on the stereo in his house. "Hey, stranger," he says as I climb into the passenger seat, in a voice like I'm not one at all. "Wreck any homes today?"

I snort. "Not yet," I assure him, rolling my eyes as I buckle my seat belt. It's not until I let out a breath I hadn't quite known I was holding that I realize I've been nervous about this moment all day long. I didn't need to be, though, of course I didn't need to be—it's just Gabe, who I've known since I was in preschool; Gabe, my literal partner in crime. "But, you know. It's early."

We drive fifteen minutes outside of town to Frank's Franks, a hot dog truck in a parking lot off the side of the road where his mom and dad used to take us all when we were really small. The perimeter's strung up with Christmas lights, picnic tables gone tacky with the humidity and too many layers of glossy paint. Families eat ice cream in noisy clusters. A baby fusses in a stroller; a boy and a girl play on a jungle gym in the last of the deep blue twilight. Gabe's arm brushes mine as we wait in line to pay. *He's gotten handsomer*, I think, broader in his back since the last time I saw him—two full years ago, before he left for Notre Dame. He's almost startlingly tall now.

We sit on top of a free table instead of at one, my boots

and Gabe's preppy leather flip-flops lined up side by side on the bench. He gets a giant paper boat full of onion rings, the smell of fried batter and grill smoke hanging in the air. His body's warm next to mine, the closest I've been to a boy since Patrick told me he never wanted to see me again. In Tempe, I didn't exactly date. "So, what are you doing back here anyway, huh?" Gabe asks.

I take a sip of my soda, swat idly at a mosquito hovering near my bare knee. "School's out," I tell him, shrugging a bit. "Nowhere to go after graduation. Could run, I guess, but . . ."

"Can't hide," Gabe finishes, an echo of our conversation at the gas station yesterday. I smile. We sit in comfortable silence for a minute—it's strange to be with him like this. I was least close to Gabe out of all the Donnellys before everything happened. He wasn't the person I told my secrets to—at least, not until things fell apart so hard with Patrick. He was never the one who knew my every tell and shudder. Maybe it's fitting he's the only one who'll have anything to do with me now.

We eat our hot dogs, and Gabe tells me about school in Indiana, where he's a bio major, how he's hanging out this summer and working at their pizza shop to help his mom.

"How's she doing?" I ask, thinking of Connie's thick gray ponytail and easy smile, how instead of folding in on herself like an origami swan after Chuck died, her spine only ever got straighter. Chuck had a heart attack at their kitchen table one night when I was fourteen and over for dinner, right in the middle of an argument between Gabe and Patrick over whose turn it was to hose down their motorboat, the *Sally Forth*. Connie sold the boat the following summer. She manages the shop by herself.

"She's good," Gabe tells me now, and I smile. We talk about dumb stuff: a costume party he went to a couple of weeks ago where all the dudes dressed up as their mothers, and what we've been watching on TV. "Wow." Gabe laughs when I let loose with some truly scintillating facts I've gleaned about Prohibition and the Transcontinental Railroad from all the documentaries I've been mainlining. "You really are starved for human contact, huh?"

"Shut up," I tell him, and he offers me the last of his onion rings with a guilty grin. I make a face but take them anyway—after all, it's not like he's wrong.

"Well," Gabe says, still smiling. His eyes are a deep, lake-water blue. Across the lot a car hums to life and pulls out onto the parkway, headlights cutting a bright swath through the summer dark. "For what it's worth, Molly Barlow, I'm really glad you're back."

DAY 6

"I'm sorry, are you *smiling?*" my mom asks the following morning, looking at me incredulously across the kitchen island.

I grin into my coffee cup and don't reply.

DAY 7

I wake up early in the morning with a long-lost, instantly identifiable itch in my body; I lie there under the duvet for a while, waiting to see if it will pass. The sun spills yellow through the window. The air smells cool and Star Lake—wet. I snooze for ten minutes. I reassess.

Nope. Still there.

Finally, I get out of bed and pull an old, ratty pair of leggings out of the bottom dresser drawer, wincing when I realize how tight the waistband is now, cutting into the soft, mushy skin of my midsection. I grimace and set about untying the knots in the laces of my sneakers that are literally a full year old.

I'll probably drop dead after a quarter mile, wind up lying there like a fat, flattened raccoon on the side of the road.

But I want to run.

My mom's drinking coffee in the breakfast nook when I come downstairs but—wisely—decides not to comment on my sudden emergence from the third-floor tower, watching wordlessly as I clip Oscar's leather leash onto his collar. "Be easy on him, will you?" is all she says, probably the first time she's asked anyone to be easy on anyone else in her entire life. "He doesn't get much exercise."

"Don't worry about it," I mutter, sticking my headphones into my ears and making for the back door. I wave at Alex, who's trimming the rhododendrons, and head down the driveway toward the street. "Neither do I."

I ran track all through middle and the first three years of high school; sophomore year Bristol tried to recruit me for their track team, which is how I found out about them to begin with. By the time I actually went to Tempe after everything happened, though—the longest, fastest run of my whole life—I was finished. I spent senior year parked on the bleachers, mostly motionless. Now I feel like a pale, doughy Tin Man, creaking stiffly back to life.

I make my way along the rocky bike path that's parallel to Route 4, which eventually narrows and becomes Star Lake Road. Patrick and I used to run this route all the time—when it was warm like this but also in the winter, the edges of the lake frozen over and snow coating the delicate-looking branches of the pine tree overhead. He got a bright green pullover for Christmas sophomore year and I remember watching him as we hoofed it through the

25

drab gray landscape, standing out like some exotic bird. I watched him all the time, his fast elegant body—Patrick and I were both serious enough runners back then, I suppose, but mostly our treks around the lake were an excuse to be alone. We'd been dating since the previous fall, but everything still felt new and exciting and secret-amazing, like nobody had ever lived it before us.

"Gabe told me he and Sophie Tabor went skinny-dipping out here in the fall," he told me when we were done with the loop one afternoon, his bare hand reaching for my gloved one.

I tucked both our hands into the pocket of my jacket to get warm. "They did?" I asked, distracted by the feeling of having him so close. Then I wrinkled my nose. "Don't you think *skinny-dipping* is a gross phrase? There's something about it that's, like, off-putting to me. Like *moist*."

"Or *panties*."

"Don't say *panties*," I ordered.

"Sorry." Patrick grinned at me, bumping his shoulder against mine as we followed the frozen curve of the lake. A weak halo of sunlight peeked through the winter clouds. "We should try it, though."

"What?" I asked blankly. Then: "Skinny-dipping?" I looked at the hard crust of snow covering the ground, then back at him. "We should, huh?"

"Well, not now," Patrick clarified, squeezing my hand inside my pocket. "I'd like to get to graduation without my junk freezing off, thank you. But when it gets warmer, yeah. We should."

I looked over at him in the chilly white light, intrigued and curious; a shiver skittered through me. So far all we'd done was kiss. "This summer," I agreed, and popped up onto my toes to peck the corner of his mouth.

Patrick turned his head and caught my face between two hands. "Love you," he said quietly, and I smiled.

"Love you back."

I don't know if it's the memory or the physical exertion that knocks the wind out of me, but either way it's less than one wheezy mile before Oscar and I have to stop and walk a bit. The roads are woodsy and winding back here, only an occasional car rolling by. The trees make a canopy over the blacktop, but still I'm sweating inside my V-neck T-shirt; the morning air's beginning to warm. When we pass the turnoff for the Star Lake Lodge, I tug the leash on a whim, making my way down the familiar gravel pathway toward the clearing where the old resort slouches, the Catskills in the distance and the lake itself glittering at their feet.

I worked at the rumpled Lodge for three full summers before I left here, handing towels out lakeside and manning the register at the tiny gift shop off the lobby—a lot of people from school did, waiting tables in the dining room or teaching swim classes at the pool. Patrick and Julia would come visit between their shifts at the pizza place; even Imogen temped here for a few months sophomore year, when French Roast was closed for renovations. It was fun in a shabby kind of way, all faded cabbage-rose carpet and an old-fashioned elevator that hadn't worked since before I was born. The whole place was perpetually on the verge of closing, and it looks like that's exactly what finally happened: The main parking lot is deserted, and the front lawn is speckled with goose poop. The rocking chairs on the sagging front porch sway creepily in the breeze coming off the water. There's a light on inside, though, and when I try the main door it swings wide open into the empty lobby, full of the same faded, floral-print furniture I remember.

I'm about to turn around and get out of here—it's spooky, how abandoned this place seems—when a little boy in light-up sneakers darts through the lobby like something out of *The* freaking *Shining*, bouncing off one of the brocade sofas before careening away down the hallway that leads to the dining room. I gasp out loud.

"Fabian! Fabian, what did I *just* say to you about running in here?" A tall, thirtyish woman in skinny jeans and an NYPD T-shirt strides into the lobby, stopping short when she finds me hovering in the doorway like a lurking freak. "Oh. Are you the new assistant?" she asks me, glancing over her shoulder toward the hallway Fabian ran down. She sounds irritated. A riot of tight, springy curls surrounds her face. "You're late."

"Oh, no." I shake my head, embarrassed. It was weird of me to come in here. I don't know what I keep doing since I got back, showing up one place after another where I'm not

28

wanted. It's like my new hobby. "I'm sorry; I used to work here. I didn't realize you were closed."

"Reopening this summer," the woman tells me. "Under new management. We were supposed to open Memorial Day, but that was a fantasy if ever I've had one." I watch her take in my sweaty clothes and sneakers, my damp ponytail, my blotchy red face. "What did you do?"

For one insane second, I think she's talking about Gabe and Patrick—that's how knee-jerk the guilt is, like even this total stranger can smell it on me—but then I realize she means when I worked here, and I explain.

"Really," she says, looking interested. "Well, we're hiring. Personal assistant to the new owner. Actually, we hired one, but she's late, and here you are. I'm gonna take that as a sign. That's a thing I do now, I take signs. It makes my kids really nervous."

I smile, I can't help it. I definitely wasn't looking for a job—especially not one where it's entirely possible I'll run into a whole glut of people who hate me—but there's something about this lady that's winning, that kindles the same lick of anticipation I felt when I ran into Gabe at the gas station the other day. "Who's the new owner?" I ask.

The woman grins back, bright and wry like she's got a secret and really likes to share it, and she's glad that I'm here so she can. "Me." She sticks one smooth brown hand out and shakes mine, confident. "Pennsylvania Jones. Call me Penn. Can you start tomorrow?"

DAY 8

My first shift as Penn's assistant consists mostly of locating and compiling the fourteen hundred to-do lists she's made and then lost all over the entire property, scribbled on cocktail napkins at the bar and taped to the stainless steel fridge in the kitchen. I find one that just says *CHLORINE* scrawled on the activities chalkboard by the pool. By the time I'm pretty sure I'm found them all I've filled seven pages of old Star Lake Lodge stationery, back and front.

"Oh, for God's sake," Penn says when I knock on her office door and hand them over, her desk buried under a jumble of purchase orders and receipts. There's a trace of New York City in her exasperated voice. She and her kids—six-year-old Fabian plus a little girl named Desi who can't be more than four and said not one word the entire time I was in the room—moved here from Brooklyn last spring, she told me this morning. She didn't say anything about their dad, and I didn't ask. "Okay. I'll look at these after the staff meeting, all right? Come on, I told everyone two in the lobby. I meant to get donuts. Did I say that to you, or did it just languish in my brain all day?"

"You told me," I promise, following her out the door of the office and down the dim, wood-paneled hallway. "I ran out and picked them up at lunch."

"Oh, you're good," Penn says, but I'm not quite listening anymore, frozen in the tall arched doorway to the lobby. A couple dozen people are crammed onto the chairs and couches around the big stone fireplace, faces so familiar that for a moment I literally can't move—Elizabeth Reese, who was student council secretary three years running; Jake and Annie, who I've known since pre-K and who have been dating just about that long. She nudges him when she notices me, her immaculately tweezed eyebrows crawling clear up to her hairline. She makes a big show of turning away.

I think of the note on my windshield—*dirty slut*—and feel my skin prickle hotly, imagining everyone here somehow saw it, too, or wrote it or is thinking it even if they didn't do either of those things. This is what it was like before I left. Julia once called my house phone and left a message, pretending to be from Planned Parenthood saying my STD test had come back positive, and I remember being grateful to her when it happened because at least nobody witnessed that one but my mom. I deserved it, maybe, the way everybody seemed to turn on me as soon as the book and the article came out, like I had some kind of social disease that was catching. But that doesn't mean I want to go through it again.

If Penn notices people noticing me—and they are: a restless kind of weight shifting, a girl from my junior English class whispering something behind her hand—she doesn't let on. "Did everybody get a donut?" she begins.

It's a fast meeting, *welcome to the new Lodge* and how to use the ancient time clock. I look around to see who else is here. There's a middle-aged chef and his younger, friendlier sous, who I met this morning as they were prepping the kitchen, and the housekeepers who've been airing the guest rooms, the old windows flung open wide. A trio of Julia's cheerleading friends are perched on the leather sofa all in a row like birds on a wire, three identical French braids draped over their skinny shoulders. I work to keep my spine straight as I stand there in the corner, not to wither like an undernourished plant at their triplicate expressions of casual disdain: The one on the left looks right at me and mouths, very clearly, the word *skank*. I cross my armst, feeling totally, grossly naked. I want to slither right out of my skin.

Afterward, I take my donut outside to the back porch overlooking the lake, picking at the sprinkles and trying to pull myself together. There's a girl about my age in shorts and sneakers hosing down the lounge chairs, her red hair in a messy bun up on top of her head—she startles when she sees me, alarm painted all over her face. "Crap," she says, checking her watch and looking back up at me, pale eyebrows furrowing. "Did I just miss the meeting? I totally just missed the meeting, didn't I. *Crap*."

"I—yeah," I tell her apologetically. "It's probably okay, though. And I think there's still donuts left."

"Well, in that case," she says, dropping the hose and climbing the steps to the porch, holding her hand out. Her skin is alabaster pale underneath the pink flush of sunburn. "I'm Tess," she says. "Head lifeguard, or I guess I will be once there's anybody to swim here. For now I'm just a hose wench." She wrinkles her nose. "Sorry, that sounded a lot less filthy in my head. Did you just start?"

I laugh out loud—the first time all day, and the sound is sort of startling to me, unfamiliar. "First shift," I tell her. "Well, sort of. I'm Molly, I'm Penn's assistant." I explain how I used to work here, that I moved away and I'm just back for the summer. I take a big, self-conscious bite of my donut when I'm through.

Tess nods. "That's why I didn't recognize you, then," she says. "I've only lived here, like, a year. I came in as a senior." She gestures at my donut. "Are there really more of those inside?"

"There are," I promise, opening the flimsy screen door and following Tess back into the cool, dark lodge. "Bear claws, even."

Tess snorts. "I've got that going for me, at least," she says as we head through the old-fashioned dining room, hung with half a dozen dusty brass chandeliers. "I don't know if I thought this was going to be glamorous or something, working at a hotel? My boyfriend's gone for the summer, though, so I was basically like, 'Give me all the hours you can, I'll just work all the time and have no social life.'"

"That's pretty much my plan, too," I agree, glancing around for Julia's coven of nasty friends and leaving out the part where the whole *no social life* thing isn't exactly a choice. I like Tess already; the last thing I want to do is identify myself—or worse, have somebody *else* identify me—as her friendly neighborhood adulteress and family-ruiner. "Where's your boyfriend?" I ask instead.

The lobby's cleared out by the time we get back there; Tess picks a glazed chocolate donut out of the box and takes a bite. "He's in Colorado," she tells me with her mouth full, reaching for a napkin and swallowing. "Sorry, I'm rude. He's doing some volunteer firefighter thing. I think he saw a Lifetime movie about smoke jumpers or something. I don't even know."

She's joking, but I don't laugh this time; my heart is somewhere in the general vicinity of the faded dining room carpet. Whatever's replaced it is cold and slimy and wet inside my chest.

He didn't see a Lifetime movie, I think dully. *He's wanted to fight fires since we were little kids.*

"Is your boyfriend—" I start, then break off, unable to

say it. She can't—there's no way. There's no *way*. "I mean, what's his—?"

Tess smiles at me, easy and careless. There's a bit of donut glaze on her upper lip. "Patrick Donnelly?" she says, the affection palpable in her voice, the way you talk about your favorite song or movie or person. "Why, you know him?"

He was my best friend. He was my first love. I had sex with his big brother. I broke his fucking heart.

"Yeah," I say finally, reaching for another donut and forcing a weak, jellyfish smile of my own. "I do."

There's a moment of silence, Tess still smiling but her eyes gone cloudy and confused. Then I watch her figure it out. *"Molly,"* she says, like my name is the answer to a pie-piece question in a tied game of Trivial Pursuit, like she'd known it somewhere at the back of her head but hadn't been able to come up with the word in time. Like she lost. "Wow, hi."

"Hi," I say, executing the world's most awkward wave even though she's standing a foot away from me. Jesus Christ, why do I insist on leaving my house? "I'm sorry; I wasn't trying to be a weirdo. I didn't realize—"

"Yeah, no, me neither." Tess swallows the rest of her donut like a shot of Jameson, wrinkling her nose and setting the balled-up napkin down on an empty side table. For a second neither one of us talks. I imagine her calling Patrick in Colorado. *I met your trashy ex-girlfriend this morning.* I purposely don't imagine what he'll say in response.

"It was nice to meet you," I tell Tess finally, wanting to get out of this lobby like I haven't wanted anything since I got here. I wonder if she's made friends with Julia. I wonder if she helped egg my house. It was stupid, to feel hopeful like that for a second. It was stupid of me to take this job at all. "I . . . guess I'll see you around."

"I guess so," Tess says, nodding, raising one hand in an awkward wave of her own as I head toward the hallway that leads to the kitchen. I imagine I can feel her behind me the rest of the whole afternoon.

I'm sitting at the reservations desk in the lobby near the end of my shift, making a list of magazines and websites for us to advertise with, when the front door to the Lodge swings open and Imogen walks in. "Uh, hey!" she says when she spies me, clearly startled—she's got that same look from the coffee shop the other morning, like I've surprised her and not in a good way. "Are you working here again?"

I nod, tucking my wavy hair behind my ears and trying for a smile. I hate how colossally awkward it feels between us, like puzzle pieces that got wet and warped and don't fit correctly at all anymore. Imogen never treated me like a pariah before I left. "Grand opening in a couple weeks," I try anyway. "Games and fireworks. You here to sign up for the three-legged race?"

Imogen shakes her head, smiling the kind of tolerant smile you'd use on a little kid who just asked if your refrigerator was running. "I'm actually supposed to pick up my friend Tess." Her dress has buttons up the front and is printed with tiny leaves. "She works here, too. We were gonna get food and maybe drive over to Silverton and see a movie."

I bite the inside of my cheek—of *course* they're friends, of course they would be. For a second I think meanly of that movie *All About Eve* that my mom likes, where the young actress takes over the other woman's whole identity. "I met Tess," I say. I'm dying to ask Imogen if she and Patrick are serious—if they've been together ever since last September, if he loves her more and better than he ever loved me. "She's nice."

"You want to come with?" Imogen asks now, her voice high and uncertain. "We're probably just going to the diner or something, but you could . . . come with?"

God, that's a non-invitation if ever I've heard one. "I've got some stuff to finish up here," I tell Imogen, shaking my head. I miss her, though. I can't deny that. When we were little we always wore our hair exactly the same. "But maybe we could get dinner sometime, just you and me, catch up? I'll get cake, you could do my cards?" Imogen's mom has been crazy for tarot for as long as I've known her; Imogen got a deck of her own for her thirteenth birthday. She used to read for me all the time, laying out the spread slow and careful on my fluffy duvet, the quiet flipping sound as she turned them over: four of swords, seven of pentacles. The

hanged man. The sun. I always repaid her in German chocolate cake from the diner on Main Street, which I maintain
is dry and crumbly and gross—cake and diner both—but
which Imogen loves beyond all others.

She shrugs at the invitation, though, blunt bangs swinging as she shakes her head. "I'm not really doing that so
much anymore," she tells me. "Cards, I mean. But sure, let's
get dinner, absolutely."

I'm about to suggest a day when we both spot Tess coming in across the lobby, holding a piece of watermelon.
Imogen's gone so fast I don't get a chance to say good-bye.

"I gotta go," she calls over her shoulder. The door to the
Lodge thuds shut.

DAY 9

I'm wiped when I get back from the Lodge the next after-noon, having spent the better part of my shift helping clear the old furniture out of the dining room so the ugly old carpet can get ripped out in the morning—work I liked a lot, actually, because it meant nobody could talk to me. All I want is a shower followed by a face plant directly into my bed, but my mom's in the kitchen, cutting up lemon slices to float in the iced green tea she drinks by the gallon whenever she's working on a book, wearing jeans and a silky tank top, barefoot on the hardwood. She grew up in this house, has walked these same creaking, wide-planked floors since she was a baby. She was born in the master bedroom upstairs.

I was born in a county hospital in Farragut, Tennessee, to a couple younger than I am now who couldn't keep me: *The night Molly came home* was a staple bedtime story when I was a kid. "I chose you," my mom liked to tell me, both of us tucked under the duvet, my small feet brushing her knee-caps and my hair a tangled mess over the pillows. She never was much for braids or bows. "I chose you, Molly baby. All I wanted in the whole world was to be your mom."

Diana Barlow, if nothing else, has never lacked the imagination to craft a tall tale.

Okay, *possibly* I'm editorializing a little. Still, for some-body who wanted a baby so badly, it's always been kind of funny to me how emphatically not maternal my mom is. Not in an ice-queen, TV, *Flowers in the Attic* kind of way—she was never mean or cruel, she always told me she loved me, and I believed her—but in a way where she was just kind of *bored* by kid stuff, Patrick and Julia and me yelling our heads off in the yard all day long. It was like she'd woken up one day to find some foreign storybook creature living in her house with her and she wasn't entirely sure what to do with it. Maybe that makes sense, though—after all, she wanted a *baby*.

And that baby turned into—well. Me.

"You're filthy," she observes now, dropping the lemons into the pitcher and sticking the whole outfit into the refrig-erator. "What do they have you doing over there, huh?"

"Hog wrestling, mostly." My muscles are aching. I prob-ably smell. I fill a glass of water at the tap, waiting for it to run cold as I can get it. She's done work on the kitchen since I left, different appliances and countertops, and I pull the peanut butter from the pantry with its new sliding barn door. My mom hadn't written a book in five years when she stole my worst secret and turned it into a best seller. The novel she put out before that, *Summer Girls*, was a giant flop. Not writing made her angry, had her stalking around the house like a zoo animal in a too-small cage; I remember how glad I was when she disappeared into her office again my junior year, how happy she seemed to be back at work. "I cleared the block!" she crowed, toasting me with her coffee cup one morning over breakfast. I had no idea she'd used me as the dynamite to do it.

"Oh, you're funny," she says now, shaking her head and smirking at me a little. "I mean it; I thought you were doing a personal assistant thing over there, not physical labor."

I shrug, taking a big gulp of my water and fishing a spoon out of the drawer. "I do whatever she needs me to do."

"You don't have to be doing it at all, Molly." My mom turns to look at me. "You don't have to spend this summer working, I told you that. It's your last summer before college; you should be spending it relaxing, not making hotel beds for ten dollars an hour."

"I'm not making hotel beds," I argue. "But even if I *was*—"

"You don't have to work at *all*," she counters, and I have to make an actual effort not to roll my eyes at her. She used to ring this bell all the time when the book came out and all holy hell broke loose, as if somehow her cannibalizing my darkest secrets was some generous act she did for my benefit. It never seemed to occur to her that the last thing I wanted was her payoff. "That money is *yours*."

"That money is Emily Green's," I shoot back angrily. Emily's the heroine in *Driftwood*, some effortlessly beautiful sap caught in a dumb, turgid love triangle—a horrifying fun-house version of me, gross and distorted but still completely recognizable to anyone who cared enough to look. "I don't *want* it."

Vita scampers out of the kitchen at the sound of our raised voices; I set the water glass down on the countertop hard enough that both of us flinch. "I don't want it," I repeat, more quietly this time. My mother shakes her head. I take a deep breath, smelling pine trees and lake water through the open window. I try to remember if this place ever felt like home.

DAY 10

I'm running some errands for Penn the next day on my lunch break, singing along to a Joni Mitchell CD I'd forgotten I had. It's nice out—iced coffee weather—so I park outside of French Roast to grab a latte on my way back. I'm already out of the car when I spy Gabe in a pair of shorts and a Yankees cap, holding court on one of the benches outside on the patio, and I stop short without meaning to, because he's drinking mocha chillers with Elizabeth Reese from the Lodge.

I freeze in the middle of the sidewalk for a second, awkward and stung and right away telling myself it's ridiculous to be. Clearly, he can drink mocha chillers with whomever he likes. Elizabeth was a year ahead of me and Patrick and Julia at school, which put her a year behind Gabe; she did student government with him and always wore a long row of bracelets up one arm, silver and jingling. She goes to Duke now, I think. She's pretty.

On the wooden bench she laughs and punches Gabe in one sinewy bicep, her smooth ponytail swishing—there's nowhere to walk but right past them and sure enough, Gabe sees me and waves. "Hey, Molly Barlow," he calls easily, tipping his cup in my direction. Elizabeth doesn't say anything at all, just purses her glossy mouth and looks away.

I mutter a quick, embarrassed "Hey" before I slip into the dark, temperature-regulated safety of the coffee shop.

Imogen's not working today, but I linger inside anyway, cheeks flaming, hoping the two of them will have disappeared by the time I clear out. I'm fifty-percent successful—Elizabeth's gone, but Gabe gets up and follows me all the way to the curb. "Hey," he says, reaching out and curling his fingers around my upper arm, gentle but insistent. "Molly, wait up."

"I'm *working*." I'm overreacting is what I'm doing—I *know* that I'm overreacting—but I feel close to tears anyway, tired and frustrated and so lonely all over again. Even Gabe is a lost cause to me now. It's my fault, it's my own stupid fault; I made my choices. But the truth is it doesn't feel fair.

"You got time for lunch?" Gabe asks, undeterred by the poisonous cloud I feel sure is hanging low around me, heavy as cigarette smoke. "I'm thinking about lunch."

44

I check my watch like a reflex. "Not really, no."

"We'll make it quick," he promises. "You gotta eat, right?"

I shake my head. "Gabe . . ." What the hell? I feel sour and cranky, and I can't even articulate why, exactly: if it's the sting of catching so much more blowback than Gabe has seemed to or just the interested way he was looking at Elizabeth when I drove up to French Roast. It's insane to feel jealous—I don't even know what I'm jealous *of*, like maybe I'm just some horrifying green-eyed monster guarding the one person who's seemed glad to see me since I got back here, or if maybe I possibly liked his attention in a different, more serious way. "Quick," I warn after a moment. "And not at the pizza place."

Gabe grins at that. "Not at the pizza place," he says.

We walk a block over to Bunchie's, a diner with greasy burgers in red plastic baskets and one of those claw-prize machines ringing loudly in the corner, a staple for families on vacation in town. "Can I ask you something?" I begin once we've ordered. It's half past noon and the diner is noisy, the clink of cheap silverware on heavy white plates. I can hear Loretta Lynn on the stereo, line cooks calling to one another in the back. I take a breath. "Not that this is any of my business, and not that I'm, like, assuming anything, but are you dating Elizabeth Reese?"

Gabe smiles at that—he looks surprised now, himself, thick eyebrows arcing just the slightest bit. His eyes are very,

very blue. "No," he says slowly, a dimple I'd forgotten he had appearing in the crease of his cheek. He's stupidly cute, Gabe is. All the girls used to say so, but I never saw it until the moment I did. "I . . . *definitely* am not, no. Why?"

"Just wondering," I hedge, taking a bite of my burger. Then, once I've swallowed: "You know, in the interest of avoiding further scandal, how it follows me everywhere I go and all."

"Yup." Gabe smirks. "Everywhere you and me go together, you mean?" He nods over his shoulder, just subtle: By the plate-glass window is a gaggle of Julia's friends staring like we're Bonnie and Clyde fresh off a bank robbery, shotguns still smoking in our hands.

"Uh-huh," I say, the itchy prickle of shame creeping down my backbone one more time. God, what am I even doing here? I hunch my shoulders defensively, imagining Gabe's hand splayed out flat on my naked rib cage. Remembering the press of his warm mouth on mine. I think of the look on Patrick's face when he found out about us, like a thousand years of solitude was preferable to ever seeing me again, and I push my plate to the side.

"Ignore them," Gabe advises, swapping my fries for some of his onion rings, his tan arm brushing mine as he reaches across the table for the squeeze bottle of ketchup. Then, changing the subject altogether: "I don't know what you're doing this week, but a buddy of mine's having a party if you wanna come hang out," he tells me, voice so casual

46

that for a moment I can't tell if it's put on or not. "Meet some new people."

"I don't know." I flinch at the spray of laughter coming from the table by the window—it's one of the girls from the Lodge, Michaela, plus two girls I only recognize by face. You don't have to know me to hate me in this town. I don't want to *do* this again, how it was before I left for Bristol, conversations stopping abruptly whenever I walked into a classroom, and *Molly Barlow can't keep her legs closed* written in sparkly lip gloss on the bathroom mirror at school. "Are there new people to meet in Star Lake?"

Gabe nods, like *fair point*. "Probably not," he admits. He's still got his hat on plus a green Donnelly's Pizza T-shirt, the tawny hair on his arms catching the sunlight pouring in. "But there are some cool ones."

"Oh yeah?" I raise my eyebrows. "That so?"

"That's so." Gabe smiles. "His place is right on the lake; you can bring a suit if you want. It'll be fun."

I'm opening my mouth to tell him thanks but no thanks when somebody kicks the back of my chair leg, hard enough to jostle my arm into the plastic French Roast cup I brought inside. It's empty but the leftover ice spills all over the table; my gaze snaps up just in time to see Michaela heading for the doorway, tossing a casual wave over her shoulder in my direction. "Oops," she coos, sweet as crumble-topped pie laced with DDT.

Watch out, I want to snap, but Michaela's already through

47

the doorway; Gabe swears and reaches for a napkin to mop up the ice. I can taste the iron muscle of my heart, like I bit my tongue without realizing it.

I'm humiliated.

But I'm also totally pissed.

I shut my eyes and when I open them I find Gabe watching closely, like he's ready to take any cue I want to give him. Like he's ready to let me lead. I take a deep breath, let it out again. "So, hey, when's that party?" I ask.

DAY 11

The TVs in the Lodge rooms are all huge monstrosities from the 1980s with bunny ears and dials on the sides, so I spend the morning calling around to price out new ones—never mind the fact that the budget Penn gave me to work with is barely even enough to have somebody come haul our old ones *away*. I'm trying to figure out the best approach for me to sell her on abandoning the idea altogether *(Back to nature! Commune with your family away from the harsh glare of consumerism! Hipsters don't own TVs, and neither do we!)* when I look up and find Desi hovering in the doorway of the office like a specter, her small skinny body pressed against the dark wooden frame. I've got no idea how long she's been waiting. More than a week here, and I've never heard her speak.

"Hey, Des," I venture quietly, voice cautious like I'm trying not to scare a baby deer. Her hair is done in a million tiny, careful braids all over her head. She's a beautiful kid, Desi. Her eyes are dark and huge. "You looking for your mom?"

Desi shakes her head, but doesn't say anything. Her T-shirt's got a picture of Dora the Explorer. She's got her hands knotted in its hem, tugging like she's bored or unhappy, but I have no earthly idea what she's after.

"You wanna come color?" I try next—there's a sixty-four-count box of Crayola crayons on the bookshelf for just this purpose, along with a stack of activity books and a couple of board games—but that earns me another silent no. We look at each other. I think. Finally, I reach into my purse and pull out a package of Red Vines, hold them out in her direction like an offering.

Desi grins.

DAY 12

Gabe's buddy Ryan is a friend of a friend he knows from college, an early-twenties trust-fund burnout type who lives in a possibly illegal camper on the far side of Star Lake. Gabe's got to work the dinner rush at the shop, so he texts me to meet him at the party, and I go late on purpose so I don't show up before he does. It's close to nine-thirty by the time I park the Passat and the air has that night-water smell about it, murky and mysterious. There's a bonfire blazing on a sandy patch of shore.

"Hey," Gabe calls, weaving through the crowd once he sees me. He's holding two red Solo cups, and he hands one over when he's hugged me hello, wavy hair curling down over his ears and a look on his face that might or might not be worried; it's hard for me to tell. I can hear some clang-y, fratty music coming from somebody's tinny iPod speakers, Vampire Weekend maybe. "You made it."

"I did." I smile at the half-surprised look on his face. "Thought I'd bail?"

Gabe shrugs and taps his plastic cup against mine, grinning. "Maybe."

"Well," I tell him, trying to sound more confident than I feel, "here I am." I swig a big, sour gulp of my beer. It's noisy, way more people than I was expecting—girls in shorts and bikini tops, guys in flip-flops. There's a group of dudes playing beer pong on an old door laid horizontally across two sawhorses.

I'm about to ask where all these people came from when a shirtless guy in a cowboy hat I'm assuming is ironic slings his arm around Gabe's shoulders. "Angel Gabriel," he intones in a voice like the Bedtime Magic DJ on a lite FM radio station. "Who's your friend?"

"Angel Gabriel, seriously?" I snort, putting my hand out to shake his. "That . . . is really something."

"What's more embarrassing is that he answers to it," the guy says good-naturedly. "I'm Ryan, this is my hobo palace. Come on, kids, there's food."

"There's food," Gabe echoes wryly, like *how can we possibly say no to that amazing offer*, and we follow Ryan across the yard toward the grill. The whole affair is kind of cheerfully sketchy, Christmas lights rigged up across the yard and the faint reek of pot every time a breeze comes through. Gabe slips his hand into mine so I don't get lost as we make our way through the crowd, and I try not to shiver at the contact. His palm is warm and dry.

52

I was wrong, that there's nobody new to meet in Star Lake: The crowd here is a little bit older—kids who would have been seniors back when I was a freshman, and were off at college by the time the *Driftwood* debacle hit school like a hurricane. I was a sophomore when Gabe and I slept together; he left for Notre Dame that summer, and I spent all of junior year back with Patrick, trying so hard to pretend nothing had ever happened between me and his brother that some days I almost forgot anything had.

Everyone here seems to know Gabe, one eager voice after another calling out his name, everyone wanting his attention. He weaves me through the crush of people, one easy hand on the small of my back, introducing me to a long-haired guy studying horticulture at Penn State and a girl named Kelsey with giant gauges in her ears who works at a trendy gift shop in town. "What're you going to major in?" she asks when she finds out I'm headed to Boston at the end of the summer.

I'm about to explain to her that I don't really know when Gabe bumps my arm with his, friendly, and motions to where Ryan and a guy whose name I think is Steve are splashing around in the lake like a couple of lunatics. "What do you say, Molly Barlow?" he asks, raising his eyebrows. He's had a couple more beers than me, I think. He looks as mischievous as a little kid. "You wanna get in?"

"Uh, no," I tell him, smirking. Even if there *were* a snow-ball's chance in hell I'd wear a bathing suit in front of a bunch of strangers looking like I look right now, I didn't bring one. "I'll pass, thanks."

Gabe nods. "You sure?" he asks, teasing, inching closer. "You need some help getting there, maybe?"

Oh, there's no way. "Don't you dare," I manage, taking a step backward, laughing a little. It's been a long time since somebody flirted with me.

"Sorry, what's that?" Gabe asks. "I couldn't hear you. It sounded like you were saying you wanted me to pick you up and throw you off the dock."

"I'll murder you," I warn him, just as Kelsey says, "Uh-oh!" and then Gabe's just doing it, scooping me up and tossing me over his shoulder like I don't weigh anything at all. "A violent death!" I promise, but the truth is I can hardly get the words out with how hard I'm laughing. I smell smoke from the bonfire and the clean cotton of Gabe's T-shirt as he strides toward the dock. Steve and Ryan are hooting at us from the lake, somebody clapping. Everyone's looking, I'm sure of it. The weird thing is, in this moment I don't even mind. "Lots of pain!"

"Sorry, what's that?" Gabe asks. "I still can't hear you."

"With a hammer!" I declare, pounding my fists on his back. I don't actually think he's going to do it, but I'm about to smack him on the ass anyway when he stops super-abruptly and puts me on my feet all at once.

"The hammer scared you off, huh?" I say, out of breath from giggling, my hair all crazy messy and hanging in my face. When I lift my head to look at him, though, Gabe isn't laughing back. I follow his gaze and that's the moment I spy Tess watching us in the light of the bonfire, orange sparks flying through the air.

And Patrick—*my* Patrick—is by her side.

For a minute we only just stare at each other across the sandy, scrubby distance, his smoke-gray eyes locked on mine from yards and yards away. He's taller than he was last time I saw him. There's a livid purple bruise across one sharp cheek. I open my mouth and then close it again, feeling like I left my heart on the side of the road somewhere, blood-red and beating. My chest has closed up like a fist.

Patrick looks from me to Gabe and back again, shakes his head ever so slightly. "Are you *kidding* me right now?" he asks. From the look on his face before he turns away you'd think he was seeing something truly disgusting, a rotting corpse or a puddle of human vomit.

Or me.

The instinct to run is physical, as if some kind of rabid animal is snapping at my heels; I make for my car as fast as I can without breaking into an all-out sprint and calling even more attention to myself. I twist my ankle on a tree root anyway, trip a bit before I catch my balance. All I want is to get out of here without talking to another breathing soul. I had a hoodie at some point, I think vaguely; I don't know what happened to it. I'm jabbing at the UNLOCK button on my key ring over and over, frantic, when Gabe catches up to me. "Molly," he says, catching my arm and tugging gently until I turn to face him, his handsome face painted dark with worry. "Hey. Wait up."

"Are you *kidding* me?" I gape at him, echoing his brother without meaning to—I can't believe what just happened here, that I just walked into it so completely blithely. I feel like a moron. I feel like what people are probably calling me. I feel like a dumb slut. "You think for one second I'm going to *stay* here?"

Gabe takes a step back, like he suspects I'm about to rip his throat out. "Okay," he says, holding up both hands in surrender. "That was bad. But just listen to me for a second, okay?"

"Uh-uh," I manage, breathing hard. The jagged edge of my car key is digging into my palm. "That was shady. You knew he was here, obviously you knew he was here, and you just—you *set me up*, Gabe. Like, I don't understand—why—"

"I didn't set you up," he says, shaking his head, looking wounded that I'd think that about him. "Molly, hey, come on, it's me. I wouldn't do that. I knew he was home, okay, but I didn't think he was going to show up here. And I knew if I told you, you wouldn't have come out."

"You're right," I tell him flatly. "I wouldn't have."

"But I wanted you to."

"So you *lied*?" There's something about that that really doesn't sit right with me. Patrick used to complain about it all the time, I remember suddenly—that Gabe was the nicest guy in the world as long as he's getting his way. I don't like seeing that side of him turned in my direction. "You wanted me to come, so you lied?"

Gabe's forehead wrinkles. "I didn't lie," he argues. "I was going to tell you at the end of the night, I swear. I just, we were having a good time, *you* were having a good time, and I knew—"

"Yeah," I cut him off, wrapping my arms around myself and caring a little more about my missing hoodie now, how I feel so absurdly exposed. "That's still a bullshit excuse, Gabe."

Gabe lets a breath out, rubs a bit at the back of his neck. "You're right," he says after a minute. I can still hear the sound of the party through the trees, people laughing. "Okay. You're right. I screwed up. I'm really sorry. It was stupid of me. Look, why don't we get out of here, go get a coffee or something? I don't know what's even gonna be open now, but let me make it up to you."

I shake my head, holding myself a little bit tighter. I keep picturing the totally disgusted look on Patrick's face. "I just wanna go," I tell him quietly. "I just—I'm done for tonight, okay?"

Gabe exhales again, but he doesn't argue. "Text when you're home," is all he says. I don't tell him I have no idea where that is.

DAY 13

I re-up my supply of Red Vines and spend the next day learning about the intricacies of General Sherman's march to the sea, courtesy of Ken Burns's *The Civil War* documentary, wearing sweatpants and a long-sleeved shirt even though it's seventy degrees outside the house. I get all the way to 1864 before I even leave my room to pee. I was never into documentaries before I went to Bristol, but my roommate, this ferrety brunette named Karla who hung a sheet from the ceiling around her bed to disguise whatever the hell she was doing in there, was surprisingly generous with her Netflix password—probably because she thought it would keep me from doing anything crazy like trying to strike up a conversation. That was when I started working my way through one after another, a chorus of soothing, mostly British narrators explicating the details of various terrifying oddities, both natural and not: the Alaskan frontier, Steve Jobs, the Aryan Brotherhood. The knowledge felt like power, a little. It felt like a way to keep control.

Today I wait until I hear the crunch of my mom's wheels receding down the gravel driveway before I creep downstairs for some avocado on toast. I've been living mostly on corn syrup and red 40 since I got here. I can feel a zit sprouting on my cheek. I fiddle with the fancy coffeemaker and stare out the window at the yard while it gurgles away on the granite counter. Oscar sighs noisily on the black-and-white tiled floor. Used to be when I had a sulk on Patrick would tell me stupid jokes until I snapped out of it: *What did the buffalo say when he dropped his kid off at school? (Bye, son)* and *What's green and has wheels? (Grass, I lied about the wheels)*.

I think of his face the first time he ever kissed me. I think of his face when he saw me last night. I take my coffee and my toast and get back under the covers with my laptop, and I do my best not to think at all.

DAY 14

I'm not sure if Patrick's working his old shifts at the shop now that he's back in Star Lake for the summer, but I can't get it out of my head that I have to see him, so the next afternoon I find him parked behind the ancient register just like two years ago, ringing a middle-aged lady up for three large extra-cheese pies.

Donnelly's Pizza is sandwiched between a grubby laundromat and a clog-heavy shoe store on Main Street, has been for as long as I've been alive: Connie and Chuck were high school sweethearts, and started up the shop the year after they got married. It was always Chuck's dream to own a pizza place, and Connie, whose maiden name was Ciavolella, taught him how to cook. The building is cheerfully scruffy, a big plate-glass window emblazoned with curling yellow script and a roof of unpainted wooden shingles, what's probably the one working pay phone in the entire state of New York mounted on the wall outside the bathrooms. Red-and-white checked oilcloth covers all the tables. Photo collages of sports teams from the high school paper the walls.

Patrick doesn't notice me right away, sharp face bent over the register and his curly hair falling into his eyes. When we were in first and second grade, all the girls used to try and touch it. It used to make Patrick nuts.

For a second I only just watch him—outside of the party the other night we haven't shared space since the day more than a year ago when the *People* article came out. Julia was the one who showed it to Patrick to begin with—she loves any and all things having to do with celebrity, or at least she used to. She had subscriptions to *People* and *Us Weekly* and *Life & Style*, and strong opinions about the veracity of the information contained in each. I woke up to fourteen missed calls from her that morning on my cell phone, plus a series of texts so garbled by disbelief and anger and copious *WTF*s that I had to read them all twice before I figured out what the hell had happened.

What had happened was that I'd finally been caught.

When Patrick turned up later that day it was with a page yanked from Julia's magazine, the edges ragged and torn. There was a crease in the middle of the photo of my mom in her office, a fold running right down the center of her face.

"Is this real?" Patrick asked me, and his voice was so quiet. The Bronco was still running in the driveway of my house. It was raining, a pale cold drizzle. Exhaust huffed out into the misty gray air.

"Okay," I said, voice shaking, hands flat and out to try and soothe him. I'd seen the article that morning, and had been hiding in my room all afternoon. I knew what was coming. I should have gone to him first thing and faced the inevitable. Instead I'd been a coward and made him come to me. "Okay, can we just—"

"Mols." Patrick looked ripped open, like shrapnel had exploded inside him. He looked like someone who'd come home and found a crater where his house used to be. "I said, is it true? Did you—" He shook his dark, curly head, so baffled. "I mean. With my *brother*?"

"I need you to listen," I said, instead of replying. "Will you—"

"I'm listening." Already Patrick's voice was dangerously cold, like somewhere inside him he knew what was coming and wanted to brace for it. His eyes had turned the flat gray of steel. "Yes or no, Mols?"

"Patrick," I said, and I couldn't even answer him. "Please."

Patrick took a step back then, like I'd physically struck him. There was rainwater collecting on his eyelashes and in his hair. "Okay," he said slowly, then, fast, like a rubber band snapping: "I need to—yeah. I need to not be here."

"Patrick," I said again, curling my fingers around his arm to try and stop him; he shook me off and swung himself into the truck in one long fluid movement, slamming it into reverse and taking off like someone who hadn't expected to be here very long at all. I stood on my lawn in the rain and I watched him recede into the distance, my heart and my history gone gone gone.

Now I hold my breath as I wait for him to see me, scanning the shelves underneath the counter for Red Vines. Connie used to order them specifically because she knew I was obsessed with them, but I don't see them tucked between the Sour Patch Kids and the Mars bars, where they used to be. I'm looking around to see what else is different in here when the lady takes her pizza boxes and walks away, and then it's just the two of us, me and Patrick, staring at each other like we're on opposite sides of the lake.

"So, hey," I try now, my voice coming out in a sandpapery croak, like maybe I haven't talked since the party. "Heard any good gossip lately?"

Patrick doesn't smile, just shakes his head and reaches under the counter for a fresh roll of register tape. He wouldn't speak to me at all after the article came out, wouldn't even come near me, and it was the horrifying loneliness of losing him even more than it was everyone else's nastiness that sent me to Bristol in the end. "What do you want, Molly?" he asks, opening up the printer and setting it inside. The bruise underneath his eye has mostly faded, just a sickly yellow green.

"What happened?" I ask instead of answering, tucking my hands into the pockets of my shorts and chancing half a step closer.

Patrick shrugs and finishes with the receipt paper, slamming the lid shut and ripping off the colored edge with finality. "I hit somebody," he tells me flatly. "Then I got hit back."

That surprises me: Never, in all the years I've known him, has Patrick ever gotten in a physical fight. Connie and Chuck were practically the poster parents for nonviolent conflict resolution. Growing up, they made us work out our arguments using handmade felt puppets. "Is that why you came home?" I ask.

"Yup," Patrick says, without elaboration. "That's why."

"Okay." I nod and wonder who he is now, to toss something he wanted for so long like it didn't even matter. I wonder if somehow I made him that way. "Look, Patrick. I just—there's nothing going on with me and Gabe, okay? I just want you to know that. I came home for the summer, and I was being pathetic and so he invited me to that party, but it isn't—we're not—" I break off, unsure how to keep going. When we were twelve and thirteen, Patrick always talked about serious stuff sitting back-to-back, like it made it easier if we didn't have to stare at each other. I wonder what would happen if I asked him to do that with me now.

Instead, he holds up a hand to stop me. "Look, Mols," he says, echoing my tone exactly. It's the nickname he's had for me since we were little kids in pre-K, the same one his dad used to use. "Here's the thing: You can whore around with my brother every day of the week if you want to. I really don't care."

I take a step back like Patrick's hit *me* this time, like tomorrow morning I'll wake up and find both my eyes swollen shut. My whole body goes prickly and hot. Patrick's calm as the woods in dead winter, though, turning his full attention to the young family coming through the door, a practiced indifference like maybe I never interrupted him to begin with. Like maybe I was never here at all.

DAY 15

"Done for the day?" Penn asks me at quitting time, both her kids trailing her down the staff hallway toward the exit that leads to the side parking lot. Fabian takes karate twice during the week and once on Saturday afternoons, and is skipping across the linoleum in his immaculate white *gi*. Desi follows silently, her tiny hand tucked into her mom's.

"All done," I tell her, spinning the combination on my locker—the ones lining the hallway are small, like the kind at gyms and skating rinks, big enough to hold my canvas purse and emergency cache of Red Vines and not much else.

"Any luck with the TVs?"

"Not yet." I shake my head. "But I'm working on it. Oh, also, remember you've got that meeting tomorrow with the guy from—" I break off suddenly, staring at the contents of my locker. Big enough for my purse and not much else, right—the *not much else*, at this particular moment, being a long strip of a dozen foil-wrapped condoms that I definitely didn't put there myself.

Penn stops a few feet away and turns to look at me, quizzical. "Meeting with the guy from . . . ?" she prompts.

"Oh! Uh," I say, shoving the condoms into the bottom of my purse before I take it out, praying that Penn—or, God forbid, the kids—don't get a glimpse of them. I blink at the vents on my locker door, just wide enough for somebody to slide the foil strip inside. "With the glass guy, about the cracked windows on the second floor. I called to confirm yesterday afternoon."

"Good girl," Penn says, still looking at me a little uncertainly. Then: "You coming?"

"Yup," I manage. Fabian flings his tiny body against the PUSH bar on the door, sunlight leaking into the hallway. "Let's go."

I wave good-bye to Penn and the kids, and cross the blacktop to my car—it's sitting right under a pine tree where I left it this morning, exactly the same save a long, jagged scratch along the side.

Someone's keyed my driver's door good, leaving a deep white scar clear across the body.

Not someone.

This is all Julia.

"*Damn* it," I say out loud, slamming my palm down

hard against the window, loud enough that Penn and the kids, climbing into their spaceship-like minivan, look up in alarm.

"You swore," Fabian calls out cheerfully from the back-seat, sneakered legs kicking. Penn clicks the remote and shuts both kids inside.

"You lose your keys?" she calls, crossing the lot in my direction. "Molly?"

"No, it's—" I shake my head, ashamed and embar-rassed, not wanting her to come any closer. I hate the idea of Penn seeing, like she'll be able to figure the whole sordid story just from a fistful of condoms and one stupid scratch on my car.

In the end, I'm pretty sure it's my face that gives me away more than the damage to the Passat. "Yikes," Penn says, looking from me to the gouge and back again. "Molly. You know who did that?"

I think of Julia's hands all of a sudden, her knobby knuckles that she hates and how she always has a neon manicure, hot pink or electric yellow. She used to like to paint mine, too. I remember the chemical smell of the nail polish hanging low and heavy in her room—back when the rule in the Donnelly house was that I could still sleep over as long as I crashed with Julia, the two of us piled head-to-toe in her twin bed, her chilly ankles brushing my arm. "Oh my *God*, this mattress is not big enough for the both of us," she complained one night, rolling onto her side and whacking her elbow on the nightstand. The tiny bottles of polish rattled in protest. Julia swore.

"I said I'd go get the sleeping bag!" I protested.

Julia sighed theatrically. "No, it's fine," she said, then made a goofy face so I knew she wasn't actually irritated. "Just hurry up and marry my brother so you can crowd him instead, will you?"

My eyebrows arced, surprised to hear her say the words out loud. Not even Patrick and I talked like that, *forever*s and *when*s. Possibly we were both too afraid. "Oh, is that the plan?" I asked teasingly.

"That is the plan," Julia confirmed, stretching her arms up over her head so her fingertips brushed the head-board. "You guys are going to give me a million nieces and nephews, and gross everyone out with the story of how you met when you were fetuses, and it's going to be totally vomi-tous but also nice. The end."

I snorted.

"What?" Julia propped herself up on the pillows and peered at me in the dark, her voice gone oddly serious. "You don't think it'll happen?"

Julia was funny that way, one-half full of kerosene and one-half hopeless romantic, but I hadn't really thought she was serious before now. Of *course* I thought about Patrick and me long term. We were already long term, the two of us. "No, I'm not saying that at all, I just—"

"Relax, you big weirdo." Julia grinned then, flopping

back onto the pillows and pulling the quilt up around her shoulders. Her hair fanned out across the mattress, a blue-black storm. "I don't have, like, a creepy binder full of cut-outs from wedding magazines for you guys. I'm just glad Patrick has you, is all I'm saying. I'm glad you guys have each other."

I thought of the good-night kiss Patrick had pressed behind my ear a few minutes earlier. I thought of him breathing on the other side of the wall. This was maybe a year after Chuck died, everything barely scabbed over, that feeling of needing to keep everything close. "I'm glad we have each other, too," I said.

"Good." She patted me on the shin through the blankets, cartoonish. "Just try not to wake me up when you sneak out of my room to go bone."

"Oh, *gross!*" But I was giggling, I remember, and Julia was giggling, too, the sound of her laughter the last thing I remembered hearing before I fell asleep.

"Molly?" Penn's still watching me curiously, like she's pretty sure there's more to the story here. "Hey. You okay?"

I nod resolutely, the first time I've lied to her. I can tell she doesn't buy it one bit. "Just an accident," I tell her brightly, blinking back a stinging in my eyes and my sinuses. "Nobody to blame but myself."

DAY 16

I stop by French Roast the next morning on the way back from my run—awkward or not, I need to talk to somebody about what's going on here, and Imogen's possibly the only girl in all of Star Lake who isn't secretly applauding Julia for dishing out exactly what I deserve. I'm fully intending to throw myself on her mercy, but when I burst through the doors of the coffee shop I find her taking her break at one of the long wooden tables, sitting across from Tess with a Celtic cross spread of tarot cards laid out between them.

My first instinct is to turn around and walk right back out, my skin going hot inside my T-shirt. I haven't seen Tess since the night of the party, when I took off like my hair was engulfed in flames—our shifts hardly ever overlap, they won't until the Lodge opens for real, and the few mornings I've noticed her on the schedule I've hidden out in the office like a political dissident seeking asylum. Beyond the shock of locking eyes with Patrick was the sting of seeing him with his new girlfriend. Tess is living, breathing proof I can't fix what I broke.

"Hi, Molly," Tess calls before I can make a break for it, obviously raised with better manners than I was. She's wearing a big pair of tortoiseshell glasses and picking at a fruit cup, peering down at the cards as Imogen flips them over.

Imogen looks up guiltily as I approach, offering a little wave. *I'm not really doing that anymore*, I think of her saying. What she meant was she wasn't going to do it for me.

"Hi, guys." I offer a watery, pulpy smile and glance at the major arcana cards laid out on the table—justice and judgment, temperance and strength—and wonder what question Tess wanted answered, if there's anything she's unsure of at all. I wonder what things are like between her and Patrick, if he tells her stupid jokes when she's feeling worried. If he talks her back to sleep when she has bad dreams. I feel a fresh, familiar ache behind my rib cage, like re-tearing a muscle that never quite healed right. *He's moved on*, I remind myself silently. Everyone has.

Except for me.

Patrick has a new girlfriend now. Imogen has a new best friend. Bristol was supposed to be this great fresh start, but the reality is I was a ghost there, too. I laid low. I did homework. I kept to myself. I thought of my time at boarding school like a jail sentence, and for the most part it suited me just fine.

More than two weeks at home now, though, and it occurs to me I'm still serving it out.

"I can do yours after this," Imogen offers now, flipping over the Four of Cups and laying it down on the table—an olive branch, maybe, but I'm too exhausted and stung to reach out and take it. I shake my head and hold up my wallet. There's no way I can tell her about Julia, I realize belatedly. I've got nobody to talk to here at all.

"I've gotta run," I tell her, wanting to let the both of us off the hook—I lost her somehow, I was careless, same as I lost everything else I used to have. I don't need the cards to shine a light on things for me. I already know I'm the fool.

DAY 17

The next day Gabe comes by the Lodge with two cups of coffee and the hoodie I left at the party. "Here you go, Cinderella," he announces. Fabian, who darted into Penn's office with the giddy announcement that a *boy* was here to see me, peers at us openly from behind one of the fraying brocade sofas in the lobby.

"Cinderella left her shoe," I inform Gabe, turning Fabian around by the shoulders and sending him off to find his sister with a pat between the skinny wings of his shoulder blades. "Not her grotty track sweatshirt from freshman year."

Gabe grins. "I'm familiar with the fairy tale, thank you."

"Thank *you*," I correct. "For picking it up and everything." I busy myself with the plastic lid on the coffee cup, taking way longer than I need to pull it back. I know in theory there's no reason to feel embarrassed in front of Gabe—if I'm a slut, he's a slut, right?—but all the piss and vinegar that had me agreeing to come to the party to begin with feels like it's been bleached out by everything that's happened in the last few days, like there's no fight left inside me at all. Nobody's putting condoms in Gabe's locker, I don't think.

"Hey, there." As if he can read my thoughts, Gabe takes a step toward me, ducking his face to meet my gaze. "We're on the same team, remember? You and me." He scrubs at his neck, shakes his head a little. "Look, I know you caught the brunt of the bullshit when everything hit the fan, and I should have said something way before now. It's messed up that I didn't. But you and me, this summer and whenever else? We're on the same team."

That makes me smile in spite of myself, a warm, pleased flush. I try to remember the last time I had anybody else on my team, and can't. Track, maybe. Maybe track. "We are, huh?" I tease, lips twisting. "Partners in shame and degradation?"

"Exactly." Gabe laughs low and easy. I can't tell if stuff genuinely rolls off his back like a duck in the lake, or if maybe he's just a born politician, a master of spin and PR. Patrick's never been like that—everything he feels is always written across his face like a sign on the highway, no secrets to suss out there at all. It's one of my favorite things about him, or it was.

"So, hey," Gabe says now, perching comfortably on the edge of the sofa like he hangs out here every day of his life. "In the spirit of being dirty rotten scoundrels, what do you say we get out of here, huh? Go for a drive?"

"Gabe." I shake my head even as I'm still smiling back at him, the crooked grin I'm starting to realize is possibly more than just friendly on his part. Right away I want to say yes just as much as I need to say no. "I'm working."

Gabe raises his eyebrows. "You must get off sometime, right?"

"I—yes." In less than an hour, actually, but it's not that easy. It can't possibly be that easy, and it's not. "Your whole family hates me," I remind him. "It's a disaster wherever we get anywhere within fifty feet of each other. I think it's pretty clear the whole of Star Lake would rather I just stayed in my room and watched documentaries all summer. I mean, there's one about farmers who grow giant pumpkins for cash prizes that I'm really looking forward to, so . . ."

"So." Gabe just looks at me, patient, like someone who's willing to wait me out. The lobby is quiet, sun streaming in through the freshly wiped French doors at the far end of the lobby and a jungle's worth of green plants newly arranged on the mantel of the tall stone fireplace. "So *what*, exactly?"

I huff out a noisy breath instead of answering. *"Why?"*

Gabe laughs. "'Cause I like you. I've always liked you, and now you're a social outcast, so I'm figuring you're free."

I snort. "Rude," I scold, ignoring the compliment. Ignoring the *always*, and everything that might mean. "What happened to being on the same team?"

"I'm a social outcast, too!" Gabe exclaims immediately, which is as absurd as it is weirdly winning. He grins wide and pleased when I crack up. "Come on," he says, like he senses he's got me. "Nobody will see, you can crouch down in the seat until we get to the highway. Wear a disguise."

"Those glasses with the nose attached, maybe," I suggest, shaking my head and smiling. *Screw it*, a tiny voice inside my head is saying—the same voice, just maybe, that told me to go to the party at the lake. Almost everybody in this whole town hates me or is totally indifferent. Everyone, it feels like, except for—*"Gabe."*

"Molly," he says, echoing my tone exactly. "Trust me."

So. I do.

We drive an hour to Martinvale with the windows of the station wagon rolled down to let the wind in; it's bracing, the feeling of old skin sloughing off in the breeze. "So, biology, huh?" I ask him, reaching across the center console and flicking the Notre Dame key ring dangling from the ignition with one of my short, naked fingernails. I expected the ride out to be loaded or awkward. Instead it just feels nice. "What're you gonna be, a mad scientist or something?"

"Uh-huh, exactly." Gabe lets go of the wheel and puts his arms out like Frankenstein's monster, his warm shoulder bumping against mine as he does it. "Sex robots, for the most part. Some secret stuff with lizards." Then, as I'm laughing: "Nah. I'm premed."

"Really?" That surprises me for some reason. I always thought of Julia as the brains of the Donnelly family. Gabe had the personality. Patrick had the soul. "What kind?"

"Cardiologist," he says immediately, then huffs out a wry little breath and shakes his head at the windshield. "I guess it's kind of lame and obvious why, huh? 'Ladies and gentlemen, this kid's dad keeled over from a heart attack, behold as he works out all his issues in the world's most obvious way.'"

I've never heard Gabe talk about his dad before. I don't know why I always thought of Chuck's death as Patrick's loss more than anyone else's—because I felt it from him most, I guess, because Patrick was my favorite Donnelly and so somewhere in the back of my unconscious head I'd always assumed he must be Chuck's, also. That was the great thing about Chuck, though, why six hundred people showed up at his funeral: Everybody he knew thought they were his favorite. That was just the kind of person he was.

"Not the most obvious," I tell Gabe now, tilting my head to look at him in profile. The sun makes dappled patterns on the smooth skin of his cheeks and forehead. His nose is very, very straight. "The *most* obvious would be joining a band."

That makes him laugh. "True," he allows, signaling to pull off the parkway. "Joining a band would be worse."

We get lunch at a drive-through burger joint not far from the exit, wax-paper sacks full of French fries and tall plastic cups of iced tea. I feel weirdly self-conscious as I'm eating, glancing down at the wide white expanse of my thighs sticking out of my shorts. New running routine or not, probably the bacon on my burger is not helping the situation here.

"What's the word?" Gabe asks now, nudging me in the shoulder—it's an old expression of his mom's. I shake my head, crumpling my fry bag up into a little ball.

"Your sister keyed my car," I confess.

Gabe gapes at me. "Wait, *what?*" he demands, blue eyes widening. We've been sitting in the open hatchback of his station wagon, our legs dangling out over the bumper, but all at once he's springing to his feet. "Jesus Christ, Molly. When?"

"At work," I mutter, looking down at my lap again, hiding behind the curtain of my long, wavy hair. I haven't told anyone until right this minute and admitting it to Gabe feels like lancing a blister, a combination of satisfying and completely, abjectly gross. I don't know how I became this person, one of those girls with a lot of drama around her. A person whose romantic garbage literally fills an entire book. Patrick and I would have judged the shit out of me, two years ago. I'm judging the shit out of myself right now.

Gabe doesn't seem to be, though: When I glance out from behind my waterfall of hair his face is painted with anger, but it's definitely not directed at me. "Look," he says, "I'll deal with her, okay? That's, like . . . that is actual bullshit, right there. Julia gets away with murder sometimes. And, like, I've been trying to go easy on her lately because of—" Gabe breaks off, shaking his head. "Whatever. I'll handle her."

"No, no, no," I protest, scrambling out of the hatchback myself. God, that would only make it worse, if Gabe got in the middle. Maybe it's fair and maybe it isn't, but whatever this is between me and Julia—between me and Patrick, between me and Gabe himself—I'm the one that needs to handle it. "It's okay," I lie, wanting it to be for both of our sakes. I reach out and touch his arm below the elbow, warm skin and the rope of muscle underneath. "Seriously, please don't. I'll figure it out."

Gabe rolls his eyes, but he doesn't argue. I like that— that he seems to trust my judgment. That he doesn't try to convince me he knows best. For a moment I follow his gaze out to the tree line; he parked with the back of the wagon to the summer woods, this wide expanse of uninterrupted green. I forgot how much I missed this when I was in Tempe. "Okay," he says, sliding his arm back until our hands catch, squeezing for a moment before he lets go. The gesture sends a clanging all the way up into my elbow, like I banged my funny bone. "But I just—I know your life has basically been one long, uninterrupted shitshow since you got back here. And I know a lot of that is my fault."

I shake my head, ready to protest. "It's not—"

Gabe makes a face. "It kind of is," he says.

For a second I remember the feeling of his warm mouth pressing at mine. I feel safe when I'm with Gabe, I'm realizing slowly, like the station wagon is a getaway car and we're headed for the border by nightfall. It's not exactly an unattractive thing to pretend. "Okay," I admit finally. "It kind of is."

"Same team, remember?" Gabe shrugs, sun catching the lighter streaks in his hair, brown and amber. He sits back down in the trunk of the Volvo, picks some dog hair off the interior, and drops it on the ground. "I won't do anything you don't want me to, it's your rodeo, but . . . same team."

"My rodeo, huh?" After a moment I sit down beside him, stretch my palms out behind me, and turn my head to look at him. "Okay."

"Okay," Gabe echoes. He leans back so his arms are behind him just like mine are. His pinky brushes mine on the floor of the trunk. I glance over my shoulder, look at our hands side by side, my ragged cuticles and the pale fuzz of blondish hair on his wrists. I imagine him grown up and finished with med school, patients lying on the operating table—reaching inside people's rib cages, fixing their broken hearts.

DAY 18

The Lodge opens in a few days, and Penn's dialed up to eleven: This morning she had me and Desi dusting the details of the crown molding with Q-tips, then interrupted us halfway through that to taste-test three different ketchup options in the kitchen. I'm exhausted, a wrung-out kind of limpness in my arms and my shoulders—so tired, in fact, that when Mean Michaela waves to me in the hallway on my way to the time clock, I'm stupid enough to wave back in the moment before she turns her hand and flips me off instead. "Night, bitch," she singsongs cheerfully, the door slamming behind her as she goes.

"Nice," I mutter, rolling my eyes even as I feel the familiar heat of shame flooding my face. All I want to do is go home and crash without speaking to another human person, but when I grab my bag out of my locker and head for the exit, I find Tess already there punching her card.

"Long day?" she asks, looking pretty wiped herself—I can only imagine what pool duties were today, if she had to scrub tile grout with a toothbrush or something. Tess is wearing shorts and a Star Lake Lodge T-shirt with the old logo on it, one she must have found floating around the hotel somewhere. Her hair's in a messy knot on top of her head. She doesn't look like a supermodel or anything, isn't tall or extraordinarily pretty. It makes her a lot harder to hate.

"Long day," I echo, punching my card and slipping it into the appropriate slot. The time clock dates way back to the sixties. I start to wave good-bye, feeling awkward just being around her, but Tess holds up a hand so I'll stay.

"Look, Molly," she says, shrugging her broad athlete's shoulders. She's holding a half-eaten peach in one hand. "I guess I just wanted to say—" She breaks off. "God, this is awkward. This is really awkward, right?"

That makes me smile. "A little," I admit.

"Okay," Tess says. "Well, we're in it now, so I'm gonna push through. I guess I just wanted to say that I know it's weird between us, but, like—we work together, we're gonna see each other a lot now that we're opening, and I just—whatever happened before I moved here, you definitely never did anything to me, you know? And even though—" She stops again, wrinkling her nose up. "I hope you feel the same way about me."

Right away I feel enormously grateful, and also two inches tall. "I thought you *hated* me," I blurt, blinking at her in the bright lights of the staff hallway. "I mean, 'cause of—"

"I read the book," Tess confesses. "And I mean, Patrick told me—"

I cut her off with a nod. "Yeah—"

"But I definitely don't hate you. I was kind of scared of you, to be honest."

"Seriously?" I gape. "*Why*? I have no friends! Have you noticed I have no friends?"

"You have Gabe," Tess points out. Then, like she realizes that's possibly not the best example to be using: "And you're Penn's favorite, clearly. I just, I don't know, you've known those guys forever, you've known Imogen forever—"

"It's not like that." I shake my head. "Whatever it used to be—it's definitely not like that anymore."

"Well, whatever." Tess smiles, then takes the last bite of her peach and tosses the pit into a nearby trash can. "So we're okay? I just didn't want to spend the whole freaking summer doing that *Mean Girls* stuff, that's not really how I roll. We're okay?"

"We're *fine*," I tell her, and my smile then is genuine. Even if Patrick's going to hate me forever, it occurs to me to be glad he's got someone like Tess. "Yeah, we're good."

DAY 19

They're doing a Summer of Spielberg thing at the hundred-year-old theater over in Silverton, and Gabe's grin is bright and crooked in the light from the vintage marquee. "Oh, hey, I brought you something," he says as we're crossing the parking lot, digging into the cargo pocket of his shorts and coming up with one of those plastic glasses sets with the nose attached, complete with a fuzzy synthetic mustache. "To avoid detection."

I laugh out loud as we head into the lobby, grabbing them out of his hands. The very tips of his fingers brush mine. "Oh, you're funny," I tell him. "Nobody will notice me now."

"Nope." Gabe smirks, reaching for his wallet as we step up to the ticket counter. "I got it," he says easily, waving me off when I try to pay.

"You sure?" I ask, tucking my disguise into the collar of my shirt. Until now we've always split dead even when we did anything together, lunch at Bunchie's or the first night we went to Frank's for hot dogs. I'm not totally sure what it means that he's changing the rules. *It's not a date*, I told myself as I got ready tonight, even as I wiped vanilla behind my ears and flicked on mascara.

In any case, Gabe lets me pay for the popcorn, and we settle into the tattered red seats, bits of crimson thread dangling from the edges. The chilly air is heavy with the smell of old butter and salt. The theater's old, and the rows are crammed close together: Gabe's knees bump the back of the seat in front of him hard enough that the girl sitting there whips around and shoots him a dirty look in the half second before she realizes how cute he is, and smiles instead.

Gabe shakes his head sheepishly. "Look at me, I'm like Andre the fucking Giant," he murmurs to me, snorting a little. "Do you know I actually got asked to go stand in the back of a bar in Indiana last winter? It was a *Game of Thrones* watching party; I was blocking everybody's view of the dragons."

That makes me laugh. "Life's hard," I tell him, and he mock-scowls and makes a big show of not knowing what to do with his elbows. It's surprisingly goofy, not a side I've ever really seen out of him before—growing up, I always thought of him as Joe Cool, not somebody who ever felt self-conscious or unsure about anything.

"Is this a date?" I blurt as the lights dim, squinting a little to track his curious, open expression in the fading light. He looks surprised. "I mean, like, right now? You and me?"

Gabe looks surprised. "I don't know, Molly Barlow," he says, shaking his head like he's setting me up for a riddle. "Do you want it to be?"

Do I want it to be?

"I . . ." *don't know, either*, I almost tell him, but just then the lights darken completely, the familiar old score starting up. Gabe reaches for my hand in the dark. Instead of holding it like I'm expecting, he turns it over, though, rubbing the tip of his index finger in patterns over the inside of my wrist, stroking over my pulse point until it feels like every nerve ending in my body is concentrated in that one place, an icy hot sear like the stuff my old track coach used to have us rub on our knees after practice. It's Gabe. It's *Gabe*, and I'm pretty sure it *is* a date—that I *like* that it's a date, the dark private feeling of being here alone with him, even though the theater is more than half-full. It feels illicit, like if anyone found us we'd be hauled off to jail in handcuffs. But it also feels good and easy and right.

Gabe's fingers play over my wrist all through the first third of the movie, drawing idle curlicues there. I wonder if he can feel blood beating against the inside of my skin. I hold my breath, feeling my heart twitch with anticipation at the back of my mouth as he touches me, like one of my mom's crazy fans speeding through her chapters to see what will happen next.

What happens next, as it turns out: nothing.

E.T. and Gertie watch *Sesame Street*. Gabe reaches for the popcorn. I wait for him to take my hand again but he doesn't, just sits back in his seat right through *E.T. phone home* and the bicycle over the moon, arms crossed over his chest like he's been there all night long, like this was never anything but a friendly hangout to begin with.

So. That's confusing.

I could take his hand myself, obviously. I'm not twelve years old or Amish or from the year 1742, and God knows I used to reach for Patrick's whenever I felt like having mine held. I'm not shy. But there's something about Gabe's sudden retreat that throws everything else into sharp relief, the shine wearing off and my foggy head clearing enough so that I can finally see this whole night for what it is—and what it isn't.

I guess I was wrong, then.

I don't know why I feel so disappointed about that.

I pull it together as the lights come back up and people start shuffling out into the narrow aisles, pasting the same "everything's great" smile on my face I've used for everyone but Gabe all summer long. "That was fun," I say brightly, in a tone so fakely jocular I might as well add ". . . bro." Gabe only nods. I pick up my purse and follow him out toward the exit, telling myself there's no reason to feel so let down.

"You okay?" he asks now, and I look up at him. We came out through a side door, just the two of us walking along a narrow strip of sidewalk outside the theater, the lights from the parking lot casting orange pools onto the concrete and everything else shadowy dark. He bumps his arm against mine, gentle. Right away I feel the hair stand up. *"Hm?"*

"Uh-huh." Both of us have stopped walking. I can hear car doors slamming out in the parking lot, the sound of engines rumbling to life. I swallow. "I'm good. I just—"

Gabe interrupts. "Look," he says, "I didn't mean to wig you out earlier, if I did. With, like, the date talk. You were with my brother a long time, I get it. I'm not trying to be a creep."

Wait. "What?" I ask. "No, no, no, you didn't wig me out. I mean"—I shake my head—"I'm the one who brought up the date talk, remember? I thought I wigged *you* out."

"You sure?" Gabe asks, taking a step in my direction slow and easy. Like an instinct I lift my chin. He's not touching me at all, but I can feel him everywhere anyhow, so many atoms vibrating between us that it seems like the air should make a sound.

"Uh-huh," I promise, feeling a smile, feeling something like relief spread itself across my face. "Definitely not wigged."

"Oh, no?" Gabe puts his hands on my cheeks, careful. I can feel the heat of his body bleeding through his shirt and mine. "What about now?"

The smile turns into a grin. "Nope," I say.

"What about now?" he asks again, then kisses me before I can answer.

DAY 20

Kissing Gabe stokes a fire I didn't know I had in me; when I wake up the next morning it feels like everything's spilling open all of a sudden, like maybe this summer holds a sliver of possibility in its pocket after all. I march into French Roast like a general heading to battle, like Gabe stamped a badge of courage on my heart. For the first time in a long time, I feel brave.

"Here's the thing," I tell Imogen, leaning over the counter where she's wiping down the espresso machine, her hair twisted up in a tidy hipster sock bun. The shop is mostly empty, just one guy in big headphones near the door. "I know you're super mad at me, and you have Tess, so you probably don't need me anymore, but, like"—I take a deep breath, and admit it—"I could really use a friend, Imogen."

For a second, Imogen just stares at me, rag in hand, unblinking. Then she laughs out loud.

"*You* need a friend?" she asks, shaking her head like she's been waiting for this moment, like she saw me coming a mile away. "Seriously? What about all last year, Molly? I stuck my neck out the whole entire time everybody was being shitty to you, and you didn't even say good-bye when you left." She drops the rag down on the counter like a red cape at a bullfight, eyes wide. "My mom had skin cancer last fall, did you know that? She had to get a giant chunk of her back carved out, she couldn't walk or move or do anything, and I couldn't even talk to you about how scared I was because you ran away and never returned a single phone call. And now you're back and Patrick's here and, yeah, it's probably weird for you, I get that, but honestly I don't know if I want to stand here at my job and listen to you tell me how *you need a friend*."

For a moment I just stand there, motionless, rooted in place like one of the hundred-year-old pine trees lining the shore of Star Lake. "You're right," I tell her, my cheeks flushed red and the tips of my fingers gone icy; I feel more cowed in this moment than if Julia Donnelly keyed my car every day for the rest of the summer. I feel like the worst friend in the world. "I'm so sorry; you're totally right."

There's a long, loaded beat before Imogen answers: "She's okay now," she says quietly. "My mom." She looks wrung-out, now that she's said it—Imogen has always hated to fight, or people being mean to one another. When we were in third grade some boys pulled the wings off a butterfly at recess, and she was inconsolable all afternoon. "It didn't spread."

We look at each other for another long minute. We breathe. Finally, Imogen shrugs and picks the rag up again, wiping the shiny chrome body of the espresso machine even though it's already gleaming. "I like a boy," is what she says.

I feel a smile spread over my face, slow and uncertain. I know a gift when I see one, and I'm so very thankful for this. "Yeah?" I ask her carefully. "Who's that?"

His name is Jay, Imogen tells me as she finishes cleaning up behind the counter, switching the music on the ancient iPod they use for music in the shop. He's a regular at French Roast; he's nineteen, goes to culinary school in Hyde Park. He's in town to do an externship at the Lodge.

"Oh! I know Jay," I realize, grinning. He's quiet and easygoing, the sous chef who puts coffee in the dining room every morning; I've met him a few times on my various detours through the kitchen on one errand or another for Penn. He helped me find juice for Desi once, when I needed three different kinds because she wouldn't tell me out loud which one she wanted. "Jay's *handsome*."

"He is, right?" Imogen goes pink from the tips of her ears down to the neckline of her flowered sundress. "He's half-black and half-Chinese; his parents met in London." She makes a face. "I mean, he volunteered that information,

I wasn't like, 'Hello, nice to meet you, please tell me about your cultural heritage' or anything."

I laugh. "So you and Handsome Jay are chatty, then, huh?"

"Uh-huh." Imogen nods almost shyly. She reaches into the pastry case and pulls out a chocolate croissant, sticks it on a plate, and hands it over. "Here, try that, we switched bakeries, and they're new. We talk a bit, yeah. And he had a lot of really cool suggestions for my art show—"

"Wait, wait, wait," I interrupt, mouth full of delicious croissant. "What art show is this?"

"I'm doing one here at the end of the summer," Imogen tells me. "They gave it over for a night; we're going to have food and stuff. You should come."

"I will," I promise immediately. "I wouldn't miss it; I'll be here with bells on."

"Okay, relax over there, tiger," Imogen says, but she's smiling. "And, hey, what's going on with you and Gorgeous Gabe?"

I shake my head, breaking off a hunk of pastry and handing it over. "You don't want to know," I warn, then settle in to tell her anyway.

DAY 21

I'm rushing out the door on the first morning the Lodge opens when my phone dings in my back pocket, the alert for a new email. I fish it out, thinking it could be a last-minute missive from Penn, but it's actually a notice from school reminding me that I still haven't picked a major. It's not mandatory but *strongly suggested before class registration*, the dean of students wants me to know. *Selecting a field of study in advance of arrival on campus aids incoming students in course selection and maximizes the efficacy of that student's faculty advisor.*

I grimace, clicking the button to close out and shoving the whole outfit back into my pocket. My entire life feels undeclared. It's hard to imagine I'll ever get out of Star Lake, let alone be able to decide what I want to do with the rest of my existence. I can feel the beginning of a headache pulsing hotly behind my eyes.

Luckily, work is busy enough that I don't have a ton of time to dwell on it. It's strange and weirdly gratifying to see the lobby full of people after two weeks of it feeling like a ghost town: dads in dorky cargo shorts wheeling giant suitcases and potbellied kids floating on brightly colored rafts in the lake. A group of middle-aged ladies from Plattsburgh planned their annual book-club retreat for this weekend, and they camp out on the porch drinking rum runners all afternoon.

I wave at Imogen's Jay as I dart through the kitchen, smile at Tess as I hurry past the pool; Penn's got me running all kinds of tiny, urgent errands: sussing out sugar cubes for a persnickety tea drinker in the dining room and wiping up an unidentified spill on the wide-planked pine floor in the hallway off the lobby. Penn went for a vintage-rustic look in the redesign, the big leather couches coupled with thrifted plaid blankets in all the guest rooms, a giant stuffed moose head holding court on the wall above the reservations desk that all of us have taken to calling George. "He's fake," I assure one stricken-looking elementary schooler, although I have no idea if that's true and in fact suspect it's not. Win some, lose some, I guess. Poor George.

"Nice job today," Penn tells me, a lull just before dinner giving her five minutes to play a quick game of tic-tac-toe with Fabian on the back of some hotel stationery. Desi's sacked out on the floor under her desk, thumb shoved into her mouth. "And since you started, really. Thanks for your help."

"No problem," I say, attempting to swallow down a yawn with only partial success—I feel good, though, like how I used to feel after track practice back at the beginning of high school, like I'd accomplished something worth doing. I think of the email from Boston still sitting in my inbox, the one about picking a major—about figuring out, once and for all, what I want. "Can I ask you something?" I say. "How did you know that coming here and opening this place was what you wanted?"

Penn looks over at me for a moment, like she's surprised that I'm asking. She's wearing a suit today instead of the jeans and T-shirts I'm used to seeing; this morning I grabbed her by the arm on my way through the lobby and yanked off the tag that was still sticking out of her collar. "Well, I managed restaurants for a long time," she says, drawing her *O* on Fabian's paper and rattling off the names of a couple of places I actually recognize, spots my mom and her editor go when she's in New York City. "Before that I used to plan parties for rich people."

"You did?" I ask, picturing it—Penn in a fancy dress and heels and a headset, directing caterers and designing lighting schemes. I nudge Fabian in the shoulder, pointing to a spot on the grid that'll give him a win no matter where his mom goes next. "Did you like it?"

Penn considers that. "I liked being the boss," she tells me. "I liked solving problems. I liked being around other people. Kept me from disappearing into myself too much, I think." She reaches out and sifts her hands through Fabian's silky curls, looking almost dreamy. "I loved the city," she confesses softly.

"Yeah?" I ask, curious. "What made you leave?"

Penn comes back to herself then, smiles as Fabian holds up the notepad, triumphant, three wobbly *X*s all in a row. "Was time for a change," is all she says.

DAY 22

The next day is another long colorful blur, a Grand Opening cookout on the shore of the lake and an old-fashioned pie-eating contest, prep for a huge fireworks display set to start at the end of the night. Gabe sneaks in midafternoon and finds me in the office for a quick, guilty kiss, his warm hands resting on my hipbones and his sly mouth moving against mine. "Missed you," he murmurs when my hands wander up to tangle in his silky hair. I'm surprised by how pleased I am to hear him say the words.

"Missed you back," I tell him, and realize all at once that it's true. We've been texting a bit since our date at the movies, but I think he somehow got I needed time to parse stuff out. It's unexpected, how the sight of him—feel, smell, taste—makes me smile.

Gabe grins against my lips, slow and easy. I push Patrick's bruised face out of my mind.

We make plans to meet up for breakfast in the morning, and I walk him out the side entrance of the Lodge to the parking lot, tugging his belt loop to say good-bye. I'm headed back inside when I run into Tess.

"So that's happening, huh?" she asks, pale eyebrows raised and a dozen different embroidery floss friendship bracelets stacked up one arm—she had a poolside arts-and-crafts thing on the schedule this morning, I remember. She grins at me. Then, off my clearly stricken expression: "Oh, God, sorry, no, I'm not trying to give you a hard time or anything. I like Gabe, I think he's a good guy."

"No," I say immediately, the impulse to lie like a reflex. I remember what I said to Patrick that day in the store, *I know what you think, but there's nothing going on here.* "I mean, he's a good guy, I just—"

"Hey, don't worry about it." Tess holds a freckly hand up, shaking her head. "You know, don't even answer that. It's none of my business, I won't say anything to anybody."

"No, it's fine," I say, exhaling. "Thanks."

Tess shrugs. "No problem," she tells me, reaching up to scrape her hair into a ponytail. "Hey, listen, I don't know if this is hugely weird or whatever, but Imogen and I were talking about it, and we were going to ask you anyway—we're gonna do Crow Bar tomorrow, if you wanna come with."

It's a suicide mission. It's completely absurd. *Why are you even talking to me?* I want to ask her. *Why are you being so nice?* Still: "Sure," I hear myself answer, like this summer's got a swiftly moving current, like somehow I'm getting swept away. "That could be fun."

Tess grins. "Good," she declares, turning around and heading for the lakefront. "And, hey, your Chapstick's totally smeared."

DAY 23

Crow Bar is a squat stucco building near the entrance to the highway, a giant silhouette of the black bird in question leering down from the wooden sign outside. It's after ten when the cab drops us off, the short, stocky bouncer giving us a perfunctory once-over before he waves us inside. The place is a dive right off the highway in Silverton that's notoriously easy to get into even if you don't have an ID, and for good reason: It's dingy enough that no self-respecting adult would ever want to hang out here. It smells dank and beery, with a pool table at one end and a jangling game of Buck Hunter, the crush of bodies and the clang of a dumb Kings of Leon song on the jukebox. I freeze for just one second in the doorway, and Imogen slips her hand into mine and tugs me along through the crowd.

"Shots?" Tess asks, eyes wide and grinning. She's more dressed up than I'm used to seeing her, her red hair loose down her back and a scattering of freckles along her cheek-bones that make her look sort of mischievous. I can see what Patrick likes about her: In the cab over here she offered me both her drugstore-brand lip gloss and some dried mango from her purse, friendly enough to make me wonder if maybe girlfriends aren't totally out of the question for me this summer, even one as improbable as Patrick's. If maybe it's okay to relax.

"Shots," Imogen echoes, and I laugh, digging some cash out of my purse to hand to Tess. I can see Patrick across the bar along with Jake and Annie from the Lodge, their faces lit by the blue-red glow of a neon sign for Pabst. After a moment they catch me looking: Jake waves and Annie tips her beer in not-quite-friendly recognition, but Patrick just stares at me, eyebrows raised, before saying something I can't make out to both of them and disappearing toward the back of the room.

Tess heads over to say hello to them. Imogen weaves her way to the bar. I scan the crowd for another moment, spotting some faces I recognize and more who clearly rec-ognize me—a few girls who used to sit at my lunch table, and Elizabeth Reese in a slinky black top. I stop and blink when my gaze lands on a girl not two feet away from where I'm standing, raven hair and red lips, pale skin like Snow White in the enchanted forest; the Donnellys have always been a ridiculously good-looking family, but Patrick's twin sister is the winner of that genetic lottery, no question.

Julia's dressed in skinny jeans and ballet flats and a long, loose tank top with a bright purple bra underneath, and she's frowning.

I gasp. I can't help it, like seeing a wolf in the middle of a shopping mall or the feeling of tumbling off a cliff right before you fall asleep. Julia was totally straightedge the first two years of high school, didn't drink or smoke at all. Crow Bar is the last place I ever expected to see her.

Looks like the feeling is mutual; her blue eyes widen when she notices me, like maybe she thought her *welcome home fuck you* campaign was enough to keep me in the house for longer than this. Then she sighs. "Bitch," she mutters, just loud enough so I can hear her. She sounds profoundly annoyed, like she's irritated at having to expend the energy it takes to hate me, like it's a game I keep making her play even though she's bored. Julia and I grew up like sisters, shared clothes and dolls and makeup until we were sixteen years old. Now, standing here in the middle of Crow Bar at the beginning of our last summer before college, she tilts her delicate wrist so that the contents of her beer glass tip right down the front of my shirt.

For a second, I only just gape at her, Julia who loves *Full House* reruns, Julia who snorts when she laughs. We've got a little audience by now, the half-dozen people standing in our immediate vicinity, plus Imogen, who's crossed the bar like some long-dormant Spidey-sense was tingling in her brain stem. "Jesus, Julia," Imogen says, grabbing my arm and pulling me back like she thinks maybe Julia's about to do something worse. "What the hell?"

"It's fine," I say, holding up both hands in surrender. I was right; this was a terrible idea. I don't know what I was possibly thinking. I can feel the scorching heat through my whole entire body, the cold shock of the beer where it's soaking through my top. I shake Imogen off. "It's *okay*," I manage, more sharply than I mean to. Then, to the back of her receding figure: "Good to see you, too, Jules."

Julia doesn't stop moving. "Might want to lay off the beers, Molly," she singsongs over her shoulder. "You're looking a little thick."

"Okay," I manage once she's gone, hands shaking. I can see Patrick watching from across the bar. All I want is to shut my eyes and be as far away as humanly possible, but if I can't have that then I want my third-floor bedroom, the big gray blanket and the glow of the computer in my lap. I want to go home. "I've gotta—I mean, this was—I gotta *go*, Imogen."

"What just happened?" That's Tess, coming up behind us and bumping Imogen's hip with hers, three shots of something amber in her hands and some orange slices she stole off the bar for a snack. Her eyes widen when she sees my shirt, alarmed. "Did Julia do that on purpose?" she asks.

Imogen shakes her head. "Don't ask." Then, taking two of the shot glasses out of Tess's hand and handing me one like I never said anything about leaving: "You ready?"

I look at the two of them—improbable teammates after everything that happened, but here they are. Gabe is right; I can't hide forever. I've only got seventy-six days to go. "Ready."

DAY 24

I wake up in the blackest of moods, the pulse of a hangover beating behind my eyes and my mouth tasting cottony and foul—there's no way I'm running, that's for sure. Instead I brush my teeth and throw my tawny, knotty hair up into a ponytail, then shuffle downstairs for coffee. My mom's sitting at the kitchen island, reading the *Times* in her new thick-framed glasses and a striped T-shirt that could as easily have come from my closet as from hers.

"Morning," she says, a pointed glance at the clock on the wall meant to let me know it's well after noon. "How you doing?"

I sniff the milk carton, wrinkle my nose. "Fine," I mumble. My stomach doesn't feel so great.

"Really?" she asks, sitting back in her chair to eye me with the kind of motherly skepticism I'm not used to from her anymore, how she hasn't tried to parent me in more than a year. Emily Green, conveniently, was an orphan. "Because, I have to say, you're not really looking fine." She takes a sip from her steaming mug, swallows. "You want to tell me?"

"Tell you *what*?" I snap irritably. That's what she said the night I blabbed about Gabe sophomore year, I remember all of a sudden, me out of my stupid brain with guilt and panic and her sitting at the desk in her office, *You want to tell me?*

And I did.

I told her everything.

God, any curiosity from her is so gross to me now, the instinct for self-preservation kicking up like a stiff autumn wind across the lake. I feel like she wants to pick the meat off my bones. "What do you have, writer's block or something? Looking for new material? I said I'm okay."

My mother huffs out a noisy sigh. "Okay, Molly," she says. "Have it your way. I know you'd rather not be here this summer, and I've apologized to you. I'm sorry if you feel like I violated your privacy, but I'm still—"

I whirl on her. "If I feel like you violated my *privacy*?" I can't believe her. I honestly cannot believe her. "Who are you? Who *says* that? How can you possibly—"

"I'm a writer, Molly," she interrupts me, like it's a religion or her freaking culture or something, like some kind of messed-up moral relativism will explain this away.

"I take real-life events and I fictionalize them—that's what I do, that's what I've always done. Of course there are going to be—"

"You're my *mom!*" I counter, my voice cracking in a way that betrays all the nasty coldness I've spent the last year and a half cultivating, an ugly break in the shell. I shake my head, slam the coffeepot down on the counter hard enough I'm afraid it might shatter. "Or, like—you were supposed to be. You *chose* me, remember? That's what you always said. But really you just wanted to sell me for parts."

My mom blanches at that, or maybe I just want her to. "Molly—"

"And you're right, that I'd rather not be here. I'd rather not have anything to do with you for the rest of my life, actually. And you know what? *That* you can go ahead and put in your next book. You can tell the whole world, Mom. Have at it."

I leave my empty mug on the counter and stalk up the stairs, scaring the crap out of Vita and sending Oscar scrabbling into the mudroom. The old stairs creak under my weight.

DAY 25

"Hey," Gabe begins, pulling back for a moment and taking a ragged, rattled breath that's kind of weirdly satisfying to me, how I can tell I'm getting to him. The skin of his neck is very, very warm. "Can I float something here without you totally freaking out?"

I nod distractedly, sitting back in the passenger seat of the station wagon and breathing a smidge hard myself. We've been parked in the dark in the lot of the Lodge for almost an hour, alternately making out and talking about nothing in particular—a little kid who streaked naked through the lobby the other day, the fig-and-gorgonzola pizza that was the special at the shop this afternoon. Gabe's warm hands crept slow and steady up the back of my shirt. I can't totally decide if I think it's fun or seedy, fooling around like this in his car underneath a low canopy of pine trees, the radio turned down low, but the reality is I don't want to bring Gabe home to my house and we're certainly not about to go to his, so . . . station wagon it is.

"Sure," I reply now, pushing my hair behind my ears and looking at him curiously. My lips feel swollen and itchy from too much kissing. Gabe's cheeks are flushed pink in a way that makes me grin, like I've accomplished something—it's different, messing around with him, more and less serious both at once. Neither Patrick nor I had done much of anything with anybody when we started dating, and we took things almost achingly slow—each new milestone stretched out and a little scary, the two of us so familiar and everything we did so completely brand-new. With Gabe it's not like that, not really: one, because we've already *been* wherever this is possibly going, and two, because—well, because it's *Gabe*. Things are easy with him. *This* is easy with him. There's nothing to obsess about or overthink. "What's up?"

Gabe wrinkles his nose like he's bracing for something. The pale glow of the parking lot lights catch the side of his face through the window. "Here's the thing," he begins, sounding more careful than normal, more hesitant than I'm used to from him—I think he's a person who gets what he wants, generally, who's comfortable asking for things. "How do you feel about maybe coming to the party?"

Just like that, the full-body buzz I've been working on, the heavy pleasure that's been tumbling through my arms and legs and everywhere, straight-up evaporates. I actually snort. "No *way*," I tell him, shaking my head so hard and resolutely, it just might snap off my neck and go bouncing behind us into the backseat of the wagon. I don't even have to ask which party he means. "*Noooooo* way. Nice try. No. No, a thousand times no."

"I said don't freak out!" Gabe protests, laughing. He reaches for my hand across the gearshift, laces his fingers through mine, and tugs until I'm close enough that he can plant a tiny kiss on the curve of my jawline. He adds a scrape of teeth, just lightly, and I shiver in spite of myself. "Look," he murmurs, his nose brushing the skin back by my ear. "I know it's ridiculous even to ask you—"

"It's a *little* ridiculous, yeah," I agree, pulling back again. The party's the one the Donnellys hold every year to celebrate all three of their summer birthdays, Julia's and Patrick's and Gabe's. It's a giant cookout on the sprawling green expanse of the family farm, complete with a volleyball game and fourteen different kinds of baked goods, Beatles music blasting all night long. Growing up, it was the best day of the summer. Last year was the first I ever missed. "Like, can I come to your joint birthday with your mom who hates me, and your sister who hates me, and your brother who hates me more than anyone and who I used to *date*, and *you* who I'm—"

I break off abruptly, embarrassed all of a sudden, not

knowing how to continue. Not knowing exactly what Gabe and I are. The idea of turning up at the biggest event on the Donnelly calendar with anyone other than Patrick is enough to clam me up completely, enough to have me wondering who in the hell I think I am. Gabe and I kissing in the station wagon is one thing—a selfish, stupid thing, admittedly, but one that's fun and free and easy and ultimately harmless. It's a secret, one that's not really hurting anybody.

The party? That's a different animal altogether.

"Me who you're *what*?" he prods, kind of teasingly. He reaches out with his free hand and draws a circle on my bare, slightly stubbly knee, fingertips creeping higher until he reaches the hem of my shorts. I breathe in. "Me who you're *what, hm*?"

"Shut up," I mutter, feeling my skin go prickly in all the places he's touching, not to mention some he isn't. I wait a minute before I continue, can hear the faint sound of cicadas and the far-off hoot of an owl in the pine trees. "You who I'm screwing around with in the car every night, for starters."

"Oh, is *that* what you've been doing?" Gabe grins at me, near wolfish, but there's something else behind it, something I can't entirely read. "That's what this is, huh?"

"I mean"—I wave my hands a bit, vaguely, feeling awkward in a way I hardly ever do in front of Gabe—"isn't it?"

Gabe shakes his head. "I don't know, Molly Barlow," he

says, eyes steady and even on mine. "I've been waiting for you to offer to make an honest man out of me, but so far, no dice."

"You have, huh?" I ask, and my voice comes out a lot softer than I'm expecting it to. "That what you want?"

"Yeah," he tells me, the quiet pitch of his voice matching mine almost exactly. It sounds like he's been thinking about it, like it's not something that's only just occurring to him in this moment. "It really, really is." He's still got his hand on my knee, and he squeezes once before he says it: "What about you?"

"I don't *know*." I yank a hand through my tangled hair, feeling cornered and exhilarated in equal parts. It's like I've lost all decision-making capability since I came back here, like I can't tell the difference between love and loneliness. I *like* Gabe—I like Gabe *so much*, his smile and his steady heart and how easygoing he is, like he expects the world to be on his side and so it is, simple as that. The days I spend with him feel like gemstones threaded into the long, fraying rope of this summer, valuable and unexpected. "I mean *yes*, but—"

"Yeah?" That makes Gabe smile.

"Maybe!" I throw my hands up, laughing a little, nervous or something else. "Come on, you're *you*, obviously I've thought about it."

Oh, he likes that, too. "I'm me, huh?" he asks, eyebrows up.

"Ugh, don't be gross." I roll my eyes, trying to picture it:

how I'll never be accepted by anyone in his family, how dating Gabe for real would be opening myself up to all kinds of fresh torment, ripping the scabs off injuries that have barely even begun to heal. Not to mention that I'm headed to Boston the first week of September—what happens at the end of the summer, do we just high-five and say it was fun while it lasted? The threat of distance was the thing that undid Patrick and me to begin with—or at least, it was one of the things. There were a lot of them. Still, it's piling stupid on top of stupid to start something with Gabe that's already got an expiration date stamped on the container with indelible ink.

But Patrick never asked me to be his girlfriend like this, I realize suddenly. We always just sort of *were*. No conscious decisions, just the two of us sliding right into it—sliding right into each other—and staying there. Neither one of us knowing how to climb back out.

"What would it look like?" I ask finally, sitting up a little straighter, my spine pressing against the passenger side door of the wagon. "You and me dating, how would it look?"

"What, to other people?" Gabe asks, shaking his head.

I boggle. "To your *family*, to start with."

"They'll get over it." Gabe's voice is urgent. "Or they won't, but they're not over it now, either, are they? Why are you going to let people who are hell-bent on not forgiving you keep you from something that could actually be great?" He stops short then, looking suddenly embarrassed, like it's just occurring to him that maybe he's taken things too far. "Assuming that's all that's holding you back, I mean. Like"—oh my God, he's actually blushing—"assuming you want to, otherwise."

"I *do* want to," I blurt, realizing as I say it that it's true: I want to take a chance with him; I want to try being happy for the rest of this summer. "Screw other people, you're right. I mean, no, you're not right, not totally, I think there's a lot of stuff you're not considering, but—"

"*Molly.*" Gabe laughs and nudges his mouth against mine then, a clumsy bump that's nothing like the smooth moves I'm used to seeing out of him, how sometimes I get the impression he's thinking a half beat ahead. This is spontaneous, a little awkward. Our teeth click. Still, it's maybe my favorite kiss from him all summer; when it's over Gabe smiles and leans his warm forehead against mine.

"I'm still not coming to your freaking party," I mutter stubbornly.

Gabe laughs, low and pleased, against my cheek. He wrestles me into the backseat of the wagon, all our limbs and the smell of his neck and clean T-shirt; out the window I can see the white moon rising, heavy and nearly full.

DAY 26

I startle awake at four-thirty, heart pounding, and throw my messy covers off. The thrill of what's happening with Gabe—and it *is* a thrill, how my body was still humming a full hour after he dropped me off at home, the ghost of his mouth on my stomach and ribs—didn't exactly translate to a full night's sleep. The opposite, in fact. Now, after three Patrick-themed nightmares, I give up and slip into my running shoes in the darkness, my mind churning with memories and regrets.

Eventually, my legs give like hair elastics, sweat dripping down my spine—I'm woozy with heat and dehydration, a sprint like something is chasing me, a dash like my life is in danger. When I quit it's with my hands on my knees and my face red and blotchy, a stitch in my side that feels like someone's grabbed my lungs and twisted, *hard*.

I can't believe there was a time when they actually wanted me to come to Bristol specifically so I could run, but that's what happened: the tan, athletic woman in the stands at my meet against Convent of the Sacred Heart in March of sophomore year, then again at practice the next morning. They called me into Guidance after lunch, sat me down in a plastic-y chair, and handed me a pamphlet.

"Think about it," the recruiter urged me. Her hair was pulled into a neat little ponytail at the crown of her head, athletic sneakers on her feet like possibly she was planning to run on back to Arizona right after this meeting. "It's just something to consider, for next year."

I found Patrick in the parking lot after last period, waiting for me in the driver's seat of the Bronco. There was an old county law on the books that said kids could get their licenses six months ahead of everyone else if their parents needed their help with farm work, and because of the way the Donnellys' house was zoned, all three of them got to drive way before everyone else did. Gabe usually drove us anyway, 'cause he was oldest, but Gabe was getting a ride with his sort-of-girlfriend, Sophie, and Julia had cheer practice until quarter of five. Tuesdays always worked that way, me and Patrick alone for the ride. Tuesdays were my favorite.

He was listening to Mumford with his head tipped back against the worn leather seat when I opened the door, afternoon sun making patterns on his smooth, April-tanned face. He kissed me hello with two hands on my face, familiar and good. "Whatcha got?" he asked when I handed him the pamphlet, curious gray eyes flicking from it to me and back again. His expression clouded over as I explained.

"Wow," he said when I was finished. He handed the pamphlet back to me, glancing briefly over his shoulder and shifting the Bronco into reverse. "I—wow."

"It's weird, right?"

"Uh-huh." Patrick laughed a little. "It's *really* weird."

"It is?" I asked, stung even though I was the one who'd said it first. "Oh."

"No, I don't mean because you're not a fast runner, I just mean—wait," Patrick said, looking at me again before turning out of the student lot. The wrapper from Julia's before-school granola bar crinkled under my feet. "Do you want to go?"

"I don't know." I shrugged, wishing all of a sudden, and weirdly, that I hadn't told him. I'd never felt like that before with Patrick. Every thought I had spilled out more or less constantly whenever he was around, practically since I knew how to talk. It was strange and disorienting, like stepping on a piece of broken curb. "No. I mean, I don't think so. No."

"What is it, like, a Hogwarts place? You live in the woods with a bunch of other girls, who make you do hazing rituals with virgin blood?"

"It's not Hogwarts." That chafed me a little, truthfully. It wasn't like him to be so hugely dismissive—or okay, it *was*, but not when I was the person he was talking to. I was the one he listened to, who spoke his language. "We live in the woods anyway," I pointed out, ignoring the bit about the hazing—and the bit about the virgins—and picking at a loose plastic seam on the interior door of the Bronco. It was rare for me to sit up in the front, since usually Julia called shottie and Patrick and I crowded into the back. "I think this place is in the desert. Whatever, I don't know. You're right; it's dumb. Forget I said anything."

We were stopped at a red light then—Patrick reached across the front seat, poked me gently in the thigh. "Mols," he said, looking at me like I was yanking his chain, like he thought I was trying to shake his hand with a joy buzzer or get him to sit on a whoopee cushion, offering him one of those pieces of gum that turn your teeth black. "Hey, talk to me. Do you want to go?"

"No," I repeated stubbornly. "I don't, I just—I don't like you talking like it's not even a possibility, you know?"

"But it's *not* a possibility," Patrick countered, looking honestly confused. "Right?"

Right?

I'm only just thinking about it, I wanted to tell him. *It's nice that somebody wants me for something. Sometimes I get afraid that you and me are too attached.*

I looked at him across the car for a moment, laced my fingers through his, and squeezed. "Right," I said. The light turned green, and Patrick went.

He turns up at the Lodge late that afternoon just as a blue-black thunderstorm is tumbling through the mountains in our direction, the low rumble of weather and a gust of cool, humid wind through the door. "Hi," I say, blinking, my heart tripping like a reflex for one stupid second before I realize it's not two years ago, when he used to come pick me up at the end of my shift every night. That was then, I remind myself, fingers curling around the edge of the reservation desk anyway, like I'm bracing for something physically painful. This is now. "You here for Tess?"

Patrick nods; he's halfway across the lobby, the desk and two chairs and a leather ottoman between us, but he takes a step back anyway like I'm radioactive, like possibly he could catch what I have. "She texted," he says, hardly any intonation in his voice at all. "She's finishing up."

I nod back slowly. "Okay." The polite thing to do would be to leave him alone, but I find myself staring anyhow, rude like a little kid with no manners. He's shorter than Gabe by a couple of inches, just shy of six feet now maybe. He's got the faintest hint of stubble on his chin. He's not close enough for me to see it right now, but I know he's got an eye freckle, this dark fleck in the gray iris of his left eye; I used to look at him and concentrate on it when we were

120

kissing, like I could see right into his heart that way.

"I heard my brother invited you to the party," Patrick says now. I'm surprised he's saying anything, how he's still keeping a distance wide enough to prevent catching anything communicable. He's wearing a baseball T-shirt with the sleeves pushed halfway to his elbows. I can see the bean-shaped birthmark on his wrist.

"He did," I reply, tucking my hair behind my ears and wondering what else he's heard, what the hell that conversation possibly looked like. "Yeah." I can't imagine Gabe would throw our barely started relationship in Patrick's face—after all, he kept that night in his bedroom a secret for nearly a full year—but not for the first time I ask myself what on earth I think I'm doing, getting mixed up with the Donnellys again at all. "I told him I wouldn't come, if that's what you're worried about."

Patrick shakes his head, just slightly. "I don't care what you do, Mols. I thought I told you that."

I feel my cheeks get hot. "Yup," I agree, picking up the papers I came out here for to begin with, the list of reservations for this weekend coming up. Penn's waiting for me back in the office, Desi cuddled in her lap afraid of the storm. "You did."

I turn to go but look back at the very last second; Patrick's staring right at me, the force of his gaze like a physical thing. Patrick and I never had sex—to this day, Gabe's the only person I've ever done that with, and just the once—but still I know almost every inch of Patrick anyway, the kind of learn-by-doing familiarity you get when you spend every day with somebody for years on end, how stupid he sounded when his voice was changing and how in seventh grade he point-blank asked me if I was wearing a bra.

"I saw what my sister did to you at Crow Bar the other night," he says, still looking. I miss him so stupidly, absurdly much. "You should tell her to go fuck herself."

I cross my arms over my chest, instinctive and embarrassed: *You're looking a little thick*, I remember, my limbs going hot and numb with shame. Of course he would hear that, of course he would. Of course he already thinks I'm gross. "I thought you didn't care what I did," I reply.

Patrick's eyebrows shoot up, like he wasn't expecting an argument from me. I don't think I was expecting it from me, either. For one crazy second I think he's about to smile and I actually hold my breath in anticipation, like waiting for a sneeze or for a butterfly to land on your finger. In the end he just shakes his head.

"I don't," he says, this expression on his face that I can't read exactly. "You wanna come to the party, come to the party."

I blink, unsure if he's serious or if he isn't. "Is that a dare?"

"Call it whatever you want," Patrick tells me, turning and heading for the doorway, for the storm hissing and blowing outside. "I'll see you, Mols. Tell Tess I'm waiting in the car."

DAY 27

Gabe's pretty sweetly happy about it when I text and tell him I'll come to the party after all; he even picks me up at my mom's house so I won't have to turn up by myself like Hester Prynne facing the town scaffold. "Ready to go?" he asks as I buckle myself into the passenger seat of the station wagon. "Loins girded, et cetera?"

"Shut up." I smile even as I clutch my potluck tomato-dip-and-bread-bowl so tightly it's apt to be nothing but sludge and crumbs by the time we get to the farmhouse. I can tell Gabe knows how freaked out I am, and also that he thinks it's kind of unnecessary, but I like that he's humoring me anyway. "I'm cool, okay? This is me being cool."

"Oh, is that what this is?" Gabe grins. "I'll make sure to spread the word."

I glower at him, exaggerated. "Don't you dare."

"I mean, I'm just saying," he continues, in this even teasing voice, "if you're being *cool*. People should know."

"Uh-huh." I nod at the road out the windshield. "Just drive, will you? Before I come to my senses and duck and roll out of your car."

The Donnelly farmhouse is big and white and weathered, three crumbling chimneys and the listing brown barn. I haven't dared come here since I got back at the beginning of the summer, but the familiarity of this place takes my breath away, the tangle of Connie's rosebushes on either side of the porch and the cracked window way in the top right corner of the house where Patrick hit a baseball the autumn we were eleven. I used to curl myself into the crawl space in the stuffy, sloping attic, when all four of us would play hide-and-seek. I'm surprised at the clutch in my chest at the sight of the barn.

My plan is to avoid both Patrick and Julia as much as humanly possible, so of course, they're the first two people I see when we pull up, sitting on the sagging side steps peeling the silky husks off ears of summer corn and tossing them into a brown paper bag at their feet. My heart takes a traitorous leap inside my chest. Everybody uses the side door at the Donnellys', even the mailman. Only strangers ever ring the bell in front.

As Gabe parks the car I spy Tess opening the screen and coming out of the kitchen in a floaty white sundress holding one of Connie's vintage Pyrex bowls, the blue ones with the weird little farm scenes on them. She passes her free hand through Patrick's short dark curls, casual. He turns his head to plant a kiss against her palm.

I flinch once at the sight of them, then a second time at the unfairness of my own reaction. It's like I'm some kind of jealousy demon, like I have any right to be even a tiny bit stung. I'm here with *Gabe*, aren't I? I'm literally about to walk into this party with Patrick's brother. I need to get my head on right.

Gabe doesn't seem to be paying attention, thank God: "Come on," he says now, taking the dip off my lap and opening the driver's door to the heat and hum of the outside, sunlight trickling down through the ancient trees. I can hear the chat and jabber of the party drifting out of the yard. Patrick and Julia look up at the sound of the door slamming shut again, both of them practically double-taking with this vague, offended incredulity—it's like they have just seen a moon landing, think it's a hoax, and are pissed at whoever's trying to get one over on them. It would be comical—Patrick and I would have thought it was comical, watching it happen to somebody else—if it didn't ache so damn bad.

I raise my hand in a wave, sheepish. Tess is the only one who waves back.

"See?" Gabe says grandly, rolling his eyes at his siblings' stony tableau and slipping his hand into mine, squeezing once as we cross the wide green expanse of the yard. "Tell me you're not already having the time of your life."

"Uh-huh," I mutter back. "This is me, being cool."

The backyard is already populated by a cavalcade of aunts and uncles and cousins and family friends, faces familiar to me from more than a decade's worth of these summer parties—graduations and ski trips, the receiving line at Chuck's funeral. Heading toward them feels like being advanced on by an army made up entirely of people who are slightly older than they are in my head. I swallow hard.

"You're okay," Gabe murmurs, head ducked down low so only I can hear him. "Stick with me."

That sounds like the exact opposite of a good plan, actually—for a moment I glance back over my shoulder at Patrick, think wistfully of how good he's always been at ducking a crowd—but it's not like I've got another option, really, so I smile as wide and as humbly as I possibly can. "Hey, guys," Gabe says over and over, weaving through the crush of people, the plates of macaroni salad and the beer bottles sweating wetly in people's hands. The Donnellys' arthritic mutt, Pilot, sniffs around the yard distractedly, and something twangy and festive, some band with *Whiskey* or *Alabama* in the name, pipes through Patrick's big old speakers. "You know Molly, yeah?"

He does it over and over, reintroducing me around with a hand on my back and an easy smile, asking after his cousin Bryan's baseball league and his aunt Noreen's book club. He's hugely, enormously, unremarkably casual about the whole thing.

And—hugely, enormously, unremarkably—so is every-body else.

"See?" Gabe asks once we've done a lap around the perimeter and settled in by one of the food tables, scooping some mayonnaise-y potato salad onto my plate. We've talked to Chuck's old drinking buddies and Gabe's cousin Jenna's new fiancé; I've explained to no fewer than three different aunts that no, I don't know what I want to major in yet. We steered clear of Julia and Elizabeth Reese, now piled in the hammock with their heads tipped close together—they're wearing matching chambray shirts and, thank God, seem more interested in yakking with each other than in tormenting me on this particular day. Meanwhile, Patrick's a ghost. I caught glances of him out of the corner of my eye like possibly he can walk through walls and disappear at will, like he's full of magic tricks, here and gone again.

He and I used to do our own thing at this party—he and I used to do our own thing at every party, truth be told—creeping out into the barn to play Would You Rather or just hang out, legs crossed over each other's and Patrick's hand playing idly in my hair. I remember being here the summer after sophomore year, after I'd slept with Gabe but before he'd left for college; Patrick and I were back together by then, and we spent the whole day camped out on the couch in the barn by ourselves. Usually I would have tried to get him to hang out with everyone else, but that day I was grateful for Patrick's penchant for solitude—after all, it made it easier to avoid his brother.

Gabe's a social animal, though, and I knew coming in that being here with him would mean being *here* with him—digging in and being part of the party, the kind of person who shows up in the forefront of pictures instead of hiding somewhere in the background, cut off, face turned away.

Patrick and Julia aren't the only Donnellys avoiding me—I haven't seen Connie yet, either, only caught a glimpse of her disappearing into the kitchen out of the very corner of my eye. Still, save a couple of admittedly confused looks from Gabe's uncles, for the most part this afternoon isn't exactly the medieval gauntlet I was expecting. "Not that bad, right?" Gabe prods, nudging my shoulder with his solid one. "I told them all you were being cool and to play along."

"Oh, funny guy." I try to roll my eyes at him, but I can't keep the smile off my face. It feels like a victory—a tiny one, maybe, but a real, tangible victory. I reach out and tug the belt loop of his shorts.

"Angel Gabriel!" That's a shout from the driveway—here's Ryan and a bunch of Gabe's other friends from the lake party, a whole tribe with cases of beer and soda in hand.

"You have got to get them to stop calling you that," I tell Gabe as we head over to meet them. That girl Kelsey is here, with the painful-looking earrings and a platinum-blond pixie cut, plus gladiator sandals that lace all the way up to her knees. There's a long-haired kid whose name I think might be Scott or Steve, maybe, a couple other people I don't know, all of them in sunglasses and smiles, like there's no place besides Gabe's family party they'd ever want to be.

Kelsey hugs me like we're the oldest of friends when she spots me, then immediately launches into a long and complicated story about the designer of this artisan turquoise jewelry she just ordered for the shop. The big group of us decamp to a cluster of lawn chairs near the vegetable garden, where we drink hard lemonade and eat chips for a good portion of the afternoon. I feel protected and included, surrounded by the crowd of them. With Gabe's friends, I realize, I feel safe.

The weird, sweet truth, though, is that nobody at this party seems particularly interested in me one way or the other. Nobody trips me and snickers; nobody blows a gum bubble into my hair. Around four, Kelsey gets up to track down some more pasta salad, and thanks to her—and also, okay, thanks to the margarita one of the boozy Ciavolella aunts poured me—I'm relaxed enough to risk a solo trip to pee. I'm just coming out of the tiny powder room underneath the stairs when I hear Connie around the corner in the living room: "Come outside and help me with the ice cream, will you, birthday girl?" she's saying, familiar voice echoing off the high ceiling and shiny wide-plank floors. We used to love to slide around in there in our socks, all four of us. Then: "And maybe wipe the look off your face like you smell something bad, just for the company?"

"I *do* smell something bad, thanks," Julia retorts immediately. "And her name is Molly—"

"Enough," Connie interrupts, even as I feel myself blanch so hard I worry I've actually made a sound: It's like a trapdoor has opened up underneath me. This used to happen a lot, before I left for Bristol, overhearing people talking about me whether they knew I was listening or not. I ought to be more used to it by now. The familiar wave of shame is physical as dizziness. "Can we not do this now, please?" Connie continues. "Just as long as the girl is, you know, in this house?" I wince at that, *the girl*—at the idea that that's who I am to Connie now, after all the times she hugged me hello and put me to bed and generally mommed me. I used to be pretty sure she loved me like one of her own three kids. "There's no point in getting yourself all worked up about it now, Jules, letting it ruin the day."

Julia's not convinced. "I *am* worked up about it," she counters. I can picture her so clearly, her J.Crew clothes and her swan limbs, long and graceful. Julia's a warrior, she always has been. I used to tell her that if I ever had to bury a body or wage a ground campaign in Tasmania, she was the one I would call. "I think it's tacky. It's tacky and gross of Gabe to bring her here to begin with, and it's *doubly* gross of her to come when Patrick—"

"Patrick's here with Tess," Connie points out.

"Mom, that nice girl is a giant rebound, and everybody here knows it, so—"

"Can you give it a rest, Julia?" Connie sounds exasperated now, like there's no way this is the first time they're having this conversation—I remember, bizarrely, the summer we were eight and Julia decided she didn't ever want to wear shoes, how adamant she was no matter how anybody argued with her. "Come on, we're going to have cake. It's your birthday, we're all together, let's not—"

"It's not my birthday today," Julia points out.

Connie sighs. "Liz, help me out with her, will you? Explain to her that Molly doesn't matter?"

There's a high, affable laugh— Elizabeth Reese, too, then, all three of them, shooting the breeze about me and my *tacky, gross* behavior—but all I can hear over and over are those last three words:

Molly doesn't matter.

I can taste the metallic ticking of my heart at the back of my mouth. I know they're not even wrong, that's the worst part—it was *absurd* of me to come here, it was way out of line.

"Ugh, whatever, don't bring Lizzie into it," Julia's saying now, disgust dripping from her voice like gasoline. "She isn't worth it, blah blah, even if she is a filthy—"

"Are you guys serious right now?" an angry voice interrupts her—*Gabe's* angry voice. I shrink farther back into the half darkness of the bathroom—heart pounding with even more force than it was a moment ago, if that's possible, humiliated at the thought of him hearing what they said. "Sitting in here shit talking like a bunch of stray freaking cats?"

Julia snorts. "Like a bunch of *wha*—"

"I expect it from you, Jules, but, like—what the hell, Ma? Like, who even are you right now?"

There's a beat before Connie answers, the silence hanging pregnant in the air. "Gabriel . . ."

"Molly was our *family*. Molly was here when Dad died. And I don't—not to put too fine a point on it, but it takes two people to do what we did, okay? And Patrick's my brother. I just, I've had it with this shit. I really have."

"Easy, tiger," Julia is saying, voice hard and brittle. Connie doesn't say anything at all—or maybe she does and I just don't hear it, how the back of my wrist is pressed hard to my mouth so I don't sob outright and give myself away.

I slip out of the bathroom as I hear him stalking down the hallway, put a finger to my lips at the sight of his surprised, baffled face. I yank him around the corner into the kitchen, press him against the wall and plant a kiss against his startled mouth. "Thank you," I keep it together enough to say.

Gabe just shakes his head and laces all ten of his fingers through mine, squeezes. "Come on," he says, and nips at my bottom lip, friendly. "There's a party outside, did you hear?"

Things start to wind down around midnight, citronella candles burning low and the after-dinner Stevie Wonder replaced with Ray LaMontagne crooning quietly about Hannah and Jolene. Tess waved good-bye a little while ago, her hair like a beacon in the blue-purple night. It's chilly away from the fire pit, goose bumps rising on my arms and legs.

I find Gabe stretched out in a lawn chair, alone for maybe the first time all night, a mostly done bottle of Ommegang dangling from his fingers. I raise my eyebrows. The Donnellys were never strict, as parents go, and once Chuck died Connie basically gave up on discipline altogether— even if he'd lived, though, I think they still would have been *do-it-in-the-house-if-you're-going-to-do-it* kind of parents. But as he sits up, I can tell Gabe's drunker than is really toward at a family affair. "Hi," I tell him, perching at the edge of the lawn chair, down by his tan ankles. "I should probably think about an alternate route home, huh?"

Gabe furrows his brow in mock consternation, then grins. "I . . . definitely shouldn't drive, yeah," he says cheerfully, reaching for my hand and tugging until I scoot closer on the chair, the heat of his body bleeding through his T-shirt and mine. "I'll find somebody to take you, though."

"I could take your car," I suggest. "I could drive it back tomorrow before work, or—"

Gabe shakes his head. "I gotta open the shop tomorrow,"

he tells me, then, like he's just realizing: "Ugh, I gotta open the *shop* tomorrow, I'm stupid, I'm gonna hurt. Anyway. Let me see if—"

"I can take her."

I startle, head whipping around in the darkness: There's Patrick, hands in his pockets and the same hard, unfamiliar stare I've gotten used to lately, like we never slept side by side in the hayloft in summer or told each other our ugliest fears. He scratches at a mosquito bite on his elbow, idle.

I feel myself go pale, sitting there on the lounge chair. I've left him alone all day on purpose, wanted to give him as much space as I could—or, at least as much space as I could after showing up at his party. "Patrick." I swallow. "You don't have to."

But Patrick's already turned toward the driveway, car keys jingling like bells in his hand. "You coming?" he calls over his shoulder.

All I can do is nod.

DAY 28

According to the clock on the dashboard, it's twelve-thirty A.M. by the time I climb into the passenger seat of the Bronco across from Patrick, fussing with the tricky seat belt until I finally hear the buckle snick into place, just like I have a million times before. This is the car I think of when I think of the Donnellys—the one Connie used to haul us all around in, the one we crowded into every morning for the sleepy drive to school. We used to climb up onto the roof and look for comets.

"Thanks for taking me," I say now, swallowing down the strange thickness of memories in my throat as Patrick pulls out of the driveway. "You really didn't have to do that."

Patrick keeps his eyes on the road, his face cast reddish in the dashboard light. He's got the faintest batch of freckles across his nose. "I know," is all he says.

We ride in silence the whole way to my mom's house, no radio and the woods pressing in on either side of the road, close and haunted. The headlights carve broad white slices through the dark. There's not another car on the road, just me and Patrick; I open my mouth and close it again, helpless. What can I possibly say to him? What could I possibly tell him that would matter?

After what feels like a living eternity Patrick turns up my mom's winding driveway, the Bronco coasting to a stop on the side of the house. "Okay," he says, shrugging a little, hands resting loosely on the steering wheel. It's the first time he's opened his mouth since we left the farm. "See you, I guess."

"Uh-huh." I nod mechanically like a robot or a marionette. "Okay. Thank you. Seriously. I—seriously, yeah. Thank you."

"No problem," Patrick mutters. He barely waits until I'm out of the car before peeling back down the driveway, which is why I'm so wholly surprised when he slams on the brakes again before he's even halfway to the road.

"Fuck it," he says, getting out and slamming the door of the Bronco behind him, closing the distance between us in what feels like three big steps. "I just. Fuck it. I hate this."

"Patrick." My heart is pounding wetly in my throat, fast and manic. I didn't even make it up the walk. "What the hell?"

Patrick shakes his head. "I *hate* this," he repeats when

he's reached me—when he's close enough so I can smell him, overwarm and familiar. "Jesus *Christ*, Mols, how can you not hate this? Just being in the same car with you makes me want to scrape my own skin off. I fucking hate this. I do."

I stare at him, stunned, unsure if this outburst is global or specific, if I should apologize or yell back or kiss him hard and honest right here where we're standing.

If he'd even let me. What it would mean if he did. What it means that part of me might want to, even as I can feel myself falling into Gabe.

"I hate it, too," I venture finally, ten years of history pressing at the insides of my rib cage, like time itself is expanding in there. I wish for the hundred thousandth time that I knew how to make this right. "I'm so sorry, I—"

"I don't want to hear you're sorry, Mols." God, he sounds so, so tired. He sounds so much older than we actually are. "I want it to stop feeling like this." Patrick shakes his head. "I want . . . I want . . ." He breaks off. "Forget it," he says, like he's suddenly remembered himself, like a sleepwalker coming back from a dream. "This was stupid, I don't know. I wanted to make sure you got home; you're home. Like I said, I'll see you."

"Wait," I say too loudly, my voice ringing out in the quiet yard. "Just. Wait."

I sit down on the ground where I'm standing, night-damp grass whispering cool against my legs. Then I turn my back. "Come on," I say, facing away from him just like we used to when we were kids and needed to talk about something important or embarrassing. "Sit for a sec."

"Are you serious right now?" he asks me instead. "I—no, Molly."

Even though I can't see him I can picture the look on his face exactly, the barely contained annoyance, like I'm embarrassing us both. For once, I don't care. I tip my chin backward until just the top of his head comes into view behind me, that curly hair. "Just humor me for a second, okay?" I ask. "You can go back to hating me right after, I promise. Just humor me for one second."

Patrick looks at me for a long minute, upside down and scowling. Finally, he sighs. "I don't hate you," he mutters, and sits down on my mother's front lawn with his broad, warm back pressed to mine.

I breathe in. "No?" I ask when he's settled on the ground behind me, the first physical contact we've had in over a year. I can feel each individual pleat of his spine. We're hardly even touching—it's nothing to write dumb romance novels about, certainly—but it's like my body is full of sparks anyway, like I have no skin and I can feel him in my organs and my bones. I try to hold very, very still. "You don't?"

"*No,*" Patrick says, then, all in a rush: "I don't like you with my brother," he tells me, so fast I know that's what he was trying to get out a minute ago. The back-to-back on the ground trick still works. "I just—I think about you with him, and I don't—I don't like it."

I feel the blood moving through my veins, a low frantic swish. *What does that mean?* I want to ask. "Well, I don't like you with Tess," I say instead, addressing the trees at the far end of the property. Patrick's hand is planted on the grass not far from mine. "As long as we're airing our grievances."

"I don't know if you get to have an opinion about me and Tess," Patrick says immediately. He moves his hand away from me then, sitting up a little bit straighter. A breath of cool air slices between his back and mine.

"We were broken *up*," I blurt, turning around and losing the physical contact entirely. "Come on, Patrick. Before anything ever happened with him, you *broke up with me*, remember?"

I'm surprised at myself for saying it—I never even think about it that way, because it feels like making excuses. It's true, at the basest of levels: Patrick wasn't my boyfriend when I slept with his brother at the end of my sophomore year. We'd been fighting for months, ever since I'd first floated the idea of going to Bristol, when we finally hit a wall and he told me to get out. But technicalities have never, ever mattered when it came to the two of us.

"Are you really going to try to argue that with me right now?" Patrick demands, still facing away from me. "We were together our whole lives and he's my *brother*, and you're telling me it doesn't matter cause we broke up five minutes before?"

"That's not—" God, it feels like he knows how to twist everything, to make it seem like I'm trying to wriggle out of what I did. "I'm not saying—"

"You kept that secret from me for a *year*," Patrick says, and he sounds so hurt it's heartbreaking. "A whole year. If your mom hadn't written that freaking book, would you ever have told me? Before we got married or whatever? Before we had kids?"

"Patrick," I say, and I know that I've lost this one. He's right—the secret was almost worse than the act, how every single day we were together after that was a lie of the most epic proportions, a million small untruths hardening like a crust on top of the big one. I faked the flu at Christmas junior year just to avoid seeing Gabe while he was home from Notre Dame, I remember suddenly. Patrick brought me soup and *Home Alone* on DVD.

Now I turn around again, settle my shoulders against his one more time. "I'm so sorry."

"It's fine. I mean, it's not." Patrick exhales, waits a minute. Leans back, so I can feel him breathe. "We're even, then, is that what you're saying?"

It takes me a minute to realize he's looped back around, that he's talking about me and Gabe versus him and Tess. I shake my head though he can't see me—he can feel it, probably, and that's enough. "I don't know that I'd call us even, exactly."

"No," Patrick says, and I don't know if I'm imagining him pressing back a little bit harder against me, like he's letting me know he's still there. "I guess not."

We sit there for a long time, both of us breathing. I can hear crickets calling in the trees. A dog barks far away, and Oscar answers. My stomach makes a sound, and Patrick snorts.

"Shut up," I say automatically, sending my elbow back into his rib cage. Patrick grabs it for a second before letting me go. "What do we do now?" I ask him quietly.

"I don't know," Patrick tells me. For somebody who thought this was a stupid experiment he hasn't made any move to turn around, I notice: I wonder if he's afraid of it like I am, like seeing his face again will break whatever spell we're under, the night and the privacy and the feeling of being home. "I have no idea."

"We could try being friends," I venture finally, feeling like I'm edging dangerously close to a precipice, like I've got more to lose than I did twenty minutes ago. If he shuts me down again that'll be the end of that. "I mean, I have no idea if we can actually do it, but . . . we could try."

Now Patrick does turn to look at me; I turn, too, when I feel him moving, his gray eyes locked on mine. "You want to be friends?" he asks, the barest hint of a smile I can't read pulling at the edges of his mouth. "Seriously?"

"If you'll have me." I shrug. "I don't know."

"Yeah." Patrick shakes his head as he climbs to his feet, like that's typical. "You never did." Then, before I can contradict him: "Let's be friends, Mols, sure. Let's try it." He heads back across the lawn toward the Bronco. "Can't be any worse than what we are now."

DAY 29

I take a different route than usual on my run, closer to the highway, past some weird commercial remnants of Star Lake's failed 1980s redevelopment—a McDonald's, a family-owned water park called Splash Time that looked like a lawsuit waiting to happen even when I was five, and a Super 8 with a scrubby lawn housing a broken fountain and a flimsy sign stuck into the grass reading BUILDING FOR SALE BY OWNER. I'm so distracted thinking about Patrick—have been thinking about him for more than twenty-four solid hours by now, the moment in front of my house and everything it might or might not mean—that it doesn't really register until I pass it again on my way back, pushing hard through the last couple of miles.

BUILDING FOR SALE.

Huh. I wonder if the contents are for sale, too.

Probably the smart thing to do would be to go home and call them like a grown-up, but the truth is I'm excited now, this little lick of adrenaline flicking its way through my veins. I cross the mostly empty parking lot and the drab, faded lobby to where a sleepy-looking clerk is slouched greasily behind the desk. "Can I help you?" he drones, blinking twice.

I take a deep breath. "Hi," I say, sticking my hand out in what I hope is an authoritative manner, pasting a let's-make-a-deal smile on my red, sweaty face. "I'm Molly Barlow, from the Star Lake Lodge. I was hoping to talk to somebody about purchasing your TVs."

"Oh, you're clever," Penn says, grinning across her desk at me when I report my early morning success story—forty late-model flat screens available for a fraction of what I've been able to negotiate anywhere else, provided we can haul them away by next weekend. Turns out the owner is about to foreclose. It feels kind of bad, making bank of somebody else's bad fortune—but not bad enough that I don't grin back when she continues, "You're *good*."

I'm embarrassed all of a sudden, not used to the praise. "It wasn't that big of a deal, really."

"Don't do that," Penn advises, shaking her head at me. "Don't downplay what you did over there. You saw an opportunity, you took the initiative, and you got it done. I'm impressed with you, kiddo. You should be impressed with yourself, too."

"I—" I shake my head, blushing. "Okay. Thank you."

"You earned it." Penn looks at me from over her coffee cup, curious. "Hey, Molly, what are you studying in the fall, huh?" she asks. "Is that a thing I know about you?"

I shake my head. "It's not a thing I know about me, even." I shrug. "I don't really know what I want to do."

Penn nods like that's not at all unusual, which I appreciate. It feels like everybody else I know is a hundred percent sure of where they're headed—Imogen off to art school, Gabe headed back to his org chem classes. Pretty much every girl in my graduating class at Bristol was enrolled in specialized programs in things like engineering and political communications and English lit. A lot of times it feels like I'm the only one still lost. "They've got a business program at BU, don't they?" she asks.

"Oh." I nod back, unsure where she's headed. People always ask me if I want to be a writer like my mom. "They do, I think, yeah."

Penn nods. "You should think about it," she advises. "You're good at it, what you do here. You should know that about yourself. You're doing a really good job at this."

I grin at that, wide and happy. It's been a long time since I felt good at much of anything. "You're doing a really good job at this, too," I tell Penn finally, head out to the lobby to see what else needs to get done.

DAY 30

My mom's in New York for a meeting with her editor and a stop at *Good Morning America* to hawk the *Driftwood* paperback, so Gabe brings over a pizza from the shop and we put an Indiana Jones marathon on cable. I haven't seen him since the other night at the Donnelly party. We haven't been alone in nearly a week.

"You sure you wanna watch this?" he asks me, settling back into the man-eating leather couch and grinning around his slice of pepperoni. We kissed for half an hour in my kitchen when he got here, my hands fisted in his wavy, tangly hair and the capable press of his warm mouth on mine. Gabe really, *really* knows how to kiss. He ducked his head to get to my collarbone and sternum, and I tried to push Patrick out of my mind as best I could, *I don't like you with my brother.* I keep remembering the other night on my lawn. "There's not, like, a documentary about juicing or the soil content of West Africa you were hoping to catch instead?"

"Already seen both of those, thanks," I tell him cheerfully. I dressed up a bit before he came over, skinny jeans and a scoop-neck tank top, two thin gold bracelets on my wrist. With Patrick, I only ever wore my usual ripped denim and flannels, but there's something about hanging out with Gabe that makes me feel like I should dress the part. It's kind of nice, making the effort. "There's a thing about killer whales at SeaWorld I've been meaning to get to, though."

"Dork." Gabe swings his free arm around my shoulders and pulls me close in the half dark, just one Tiffany table lamp casting a warm glow across the room. Then, turning to face me: "So, hey, how'd it go with my brother the other night?" he asks, frowning just a little. "In the car, I mean. I'm sorry; I totally threw you under the bus there, huh? I didn't realize how smashed I was till I was really smashed."

"No, no," I protest, "it was fine." I pause, feeling careful and not totally sure why. "We had kind of a good talk, actually."

"Oh, yeah?" Gabe grins, fingers tracing the strap of my tank top over and over. "I knew he'd mellow out eventually."

"I—yeah." I don't know if I'd describe what happened the other night as Patrick mellowing out, but I'm not sure exactly how to explain that to Gabe—or if I even want to. "Yeah," I finish lamely.

Gabe doesn't seem to notice my hesitation, thank goodness; instead he kisses me again, licks his way into my mouth until I'm gasping. I've never kissed a guy and had it be like this. His hand is warm and heavy on my waist—I've been nervous about letting him see any part of me that isn't normally covered by my clothes, how soft and doughy my body still feels in spite of all the running I've been doing, but when he tugs my shirt up it's so slow and easy and I'm so distracted that I almost don't even notice until it's already happened. His fingertips set off tiny firecrackers all across my skin. "Jesus," I mutter against his lips, breathing hard enough that I'm almost embarrassed, my chest moving with the quickness of it.

"That okay?" Gabe asks.

I nod, liking that he's asking. I smell salt and his old woodsy soap. Over his shoulder Indy's outrunning the boulder, the swell of the old familiar music: "This is the good part," I murmur quietly, then close my eyes so he'll kiss me again.

DAY 31

Connie's outside the pizza place turning the flowers in their pots when I show up the following afternoon, the sun yellow and beating on my back. "Hi, Molly," she says when she sees me, looking surprised: For the most part, I've steered clear of the shop all summer. The butterflies in my chest thrum their papery wings.

"Hi, Con," I say.

"Hi, Molly," she says again, expression neutral as the paint on the walls in a hospital. "Gabe's not here."

I nod, trying to mirror the bland look on her face. Of course I already know the Donnelly boys work opposite shifts now, that they spend as little time together as humanly possible. That they hardly even speak, and it's my fault. "I just came for some pizza."

A slice of sausage and pepper is my cover, maybe, but I

find the brother I'm looking for in his sauce-speckled apron behind the counter, scattering cheese on a wheel of raw dough. Patrick likes assembling pies, or at the very least he used to. He used to say it made him feel calm. "Hey," I say softly, not wanting to startle him; the shop's pretty empty at this hour, just the jabber of a little kid playing Ms. Pac-Man in the corner and the sibilant hum of the lite music station over the loudspeaker. Then, stupidly and a beat too late: "Buddy."

Patrick rolls his eyes at me. "Hey, pal," he says, the corners of his mouth twitching: It's not a smile, not really, but it's as close as I've gotten with him since I've been back. He looks even more like his dad than he used to. I grin like a reflex. "How's it going?"

"Oh, you know." I shrug, hands in my pockets. "The usual. Kicking ass, fiending pizza."

"Uh-huh." Patrick smirks. He used to tease me for this exact thing when we were together, how when I get nervous sometimes I'll just get cornier and cornier until someone finally stops me. He looks at me. He waits.

I make a face: He's not going to make it easy, then, this *being friends* thing. I guess it's not his job to make it easy. I try again. "You're coming to Falling Star, yeah?" I ask. It starts in a few days, the Catskills' exquisitely lame take on Burning Man: a bunch of teenagers camping in the mountains, all the weed you could possibly smoke and somebody's brother's fratty band playing the same three O.A.R. songs over and over. We went two summers ago, though, a whole bunch of us, just for the day—it was after me and Gabe but before the book came out, and I remember feeling happy, just for the space of one sunny afternoon. "You and Tess, I mean?"

Patrick nods, finishing up with the cheese and sliding the pie into the oven. He's a little shorter than his brother, and ropier. He leans the paddle against the wall. "Looks that way, yeah. She wants to check it out."

"Okay, well. Me too. So"—I shrug awkwardly—"I guess I'll see you there, then."

This time Patrick really does smile—at how hard I'm floundering, probably, but I'll take what I can get.

DAY 32

"Hey," Tess says the next morning at work, finding me in the hallway outside the dining room as I'm readjusting the old black-and-white photos of Star Lake that Fabian for some reason loves to reach up and tilt askew. "This is probably a stupid question, but . . . what do people *wear* at Falling Star?"

I smile. "Like, do you need to pack bell-bottoms and macramé?" I ask her, standing back a bit to see if the frame is level. "Nah, you're probably good. Unless you wanna join the love-in; then there's a special dress code."

"For the orgy, right." Tess laughs. "I was thinking more, like, just shorts and stuff, right? I mean, it's just camping; I don't need a dress or anything?"

"I mean, I definitely will not be wearing a dress," I assure her. "If you ask Imogen I dress kind of like a dude, though, so . . . she might be a better person to ask."

"Shut up, you always look cool. Okay," she says, before I can react to the compliment. "Thanks, Molly." She starts to go, then turns around at the last second, pivoting on the hardwood in her lifeguard flip-flops. "Listen," she says, "it doesn't have to be, like, weird or anything, does it?" She gestures vaguely, as if the *it* in question is possibly the whole world. "Like, all of us going, I mean?"

"No, not at all," I assure her, though I can't actually imagine how it could possibly be anything *but* that. I wonder if Patrick told her about us on the lawn the other night. I wonder if it's weird that I didn't tell Gabe. "Of course not."

"Okay, good." Tess nods. "I'm sorry we didn't get to hang out more at the party," she says then. "I know Julia hasn't exactly rolled out the welcome wagon." She looks hesitant, like she's not sure if she's crossing a line here, but before I can say anything she presses on. "Anyway, I'm glad you're going."

I look at Tess's freckly face, open and expectant; it's impossible to hate this girl, truly. God help me, I want to be her friend. "I'm glad you're going, too."

DAY 33

Handsome Jay isn't coming up to Falling Star until tomorrow, so Gabe and Imogen and I all carpool into the mountains, a winding drive that takes just over an hour and a half. I'm worried the trip is going to be hugely awkward—I'm worried this whole weekend is going to be hugely awkward, truthfully, that the whole thing is going to feel like some extended blast-from-the-past double-date nightmare with everyone I know there to witness the carnage—but Gabe and Imogen are both talkers, and she's hardly even settled herself into the backseat of the station wagon before they're engaged in a cheerful debate about the new Kanye West album. After that they move on to the lech-y driver's ed teacher at the high school and a gross new sandwich place near French Roast that Gabe keeps calling "Baloney Heaven"; I let out a breath and lean my head back against the seat, happy to listen to them talk.

"So, Handsome Jay is working today?" I ask Imogen, turning around to glance at her in the backseat. She's wearing a vintage-looking scarf as if she's Elizabeth Taylor in some old movie, dark sunglasses obscuring half her face. She's too glam for camping, but she's always loved doing it, ever since we were little kids tucked into a fort on her living room rug. She was the one who got us started coming to Falling Star to begin with.

"Uh-huh," she says now, sighing dramatically, then, peering at me over the tops of her lenses: "Don't you *make* the schedule at that place, P.S.?"

"Not the kitchen one!" I defend myself. "Just the front desk and stuff."

"Sure, sure," Imogen says, smirking. She leans forward a bit, nods at the bag of Red Vines I've got in the console. "Pass those back, would you?"

"*Mm-hmm.* How's that going, anyway?" I ask, once she's pulled a handful of licorice from the package, snapping the end off one of the strips with her molars. "You and Handsome Jay."

"It's going *goooooood,*" Imogen says, laughing a little. "He took me to Sage the other night, actually."

"Fancy!" I crow. Sage is the only white-tablecloth place in Star Lake other than the dining room of the Lodge. My mom used to take me on my birthday, just the two of us, but going with a guy is an entirely different thing.

"Right?" Imogen says. "I know it's totally just a fling,

we're both out of here at the end of the summer, but, like—I *like* him." She glances at Gabe, wrinkles her nose a little. "Sorry," she says, "is this enormously boring to you?"

"No, no." Gabe shakes his head, sincere. "Floor's all yours."

Imogen grins. "Well, in *that* case," she says, and dives in. I reach over and squeeze Gabe's knee, dumbly proud of how easy things seem between them.

It's almost . . . normal.

Imogen's chatting happily about Jay's family, his dad who likes to paint. Suddenly, I remember running into her before homeroom the morning after I slept with Gabe—how I hadn't talked to Patrick or my mom or anyone else yet, how I'd been walking around in a soup-thick fog all morning and the sight of her smiling at me across the hallway, her flowered dress and her cork-heeled shoes, was enough to have me swallowing back tears. "Morning, sunshine," Imogen said brightly. She never carried a backpack. She didn't think it was ladylike. "What's up?"

Don't be nice to me, I wanted to tell her. *Don't be nice to me, I'm awful, I don't deserve it, I did the worst thing I could possibly do.* For one moment I wanted to tell Imogen everything, to pour it all out regardless of the mess it would make, to stand back and stare at the horribleness of it like the world's ugliest piece of art.

Then I realized I never wanted to tell anyone ever.

"Nothing," I called back, shaking my head resolutely. "Morning."

Now we stop for gas at a grimy station off the side of the highway, cars rushing by packed with suitcases and camping gear. It's high summer, vacation time. It's hot. "Can I tell you something?" Imogen asks me, both of us waiting in line for the questionable bathroom. "You seem, like, really happy."

"I do?" I blink at that, surprised—it's the first time anyone's described me that way since I got back here. It's the first time anyone's described me that way in more than a year. Hearing it feels oddly incorrect, like someone pronouncing your name wrong.

Imogen laughs. "Yeah," she says. "You do. That so hard to believe?"

"I—no, actually. I guess not." I glance at Gabe, who's pumping gas across the blacktop. He catches me looking and grins. I think of his goofy stories, the interested way he chats with every last person in town; I think of how he knows my ugly parts and likes me anyway, how he's not perpetually disappointed by the person I turned out to be. I'm still nervous about this weekend—ugh, actually just thinking about meeting up with Patrick and Tess makes my stomach flip unpleasantly—but out here in the middle of nowhere with Gabe and Imogen, I'm really glad I said I'd come.

The gas pump shuts off with a noisy *thunk*. "I am happy," I tell Imogen, tipping my face up toward the sunshine.

DAY 34

Falling Star's in full swing by the following afternoon, the whole campsite crowded with people. The air is thick with the smell of weed and sunscreen and grill smoke, girls in bikinis lounging on the rocks and the constant clang of a dreadlocked white boy strumming away on a guitar. Imogen and I made totally undrinkable coffee over the campfire this morning, then gave up, got in Gabe's station wagon, and drove twenty minutes to the nearest town. I brought a cup back for him, waving it under his nose where he was still sleeping inside the tent we're sharing. "You're my fucking hero," he told me, and I laughed.

Now we're clustered around a couple of the picnic tables eating chips and playing poker with handfuls of crumpled one-dollar bills—me and Gabe and Imogen, Kelsey and Steve, who wandered over from their campsite down the way, and Handsome Jay, who drove up after his breakfast shift at the Lodge this morning. Even Patrick and Tess are playing, Tess's red hair braided into a heavy-looking skein hanging over one shoulder. She looks like something out of an Anthropologie catalog, rustic and effortless. I pick at my cuticles and sip at my water bottle, trying not to notice Patrick's hand on her knee. They showed up last night, the two of them ambling over to the campfire. Tess hugged me hello while Patrick hung back in the shadows: "Hey," I said to him, making a point of it. After all, we said we'd try and be friends, didn't we?

Patrick just looked at me, even. "Hey, yourself," he said, so quietly no one but me could hear.

Now Gabe lays down three tens, which is a winner, all of us grumbling good-naturedly as we toss our cards onto the rough wooden table. "Thank you, thank you," he says grandly, reaching for the pot with silly, exaggerated movements.

"Oh, no, wait, hold up, though," Imogen says, pointing, just before Jay reaches out to clear the deck. "Patrick's got a full house, right?"

Patrick looks up at that, then down at the table, surprised—he's been playing with half a mind, no question, lost in Patrickland while the rest of us hang out here on Earth. Then he smiles. "Oh, hey, no shit, yeah I do." He reaches for the cash, but his brother stops him.

"Wait a second," Gabe says, shaking his head a little.

"Isn't that how we play, though: You don't notice, you don't take the pot?"

Patrick makes a face like, *nice try*. "I don't think so, dude."

Gabe frowns. "I'm just saying, you're hardly even playing, you needed somebody else to tell you that you even won—"

"Yeah, okay, but I did win," Patrick says, the faintest hint of an edge creeping into his voice, the kind you wouldn't even notice if you hadn't known him pretty much forever. I've known him pretty much forever, though. I shift my weight, not liking the trajectory here.

So has Gabe: "Dude, it's, like, twenty bucks we're talking about," he says now, shaking his head like Patrick's being stupid.

"Dude, it's, like, my twenty bucks."

Shit. Patrick mimics his tone *exactly*, which I know from when we were kids is one of the fastest ways to get under Gabe's skin. Sure enough: "Why are you being such a dick about this?" Gabe asks, eyes narrowing.

"Why am *I* being a dick?" he asks, sounding pissed about a whole lot more than twenty bucks in George Washingtons. I wince. "*You didn't win*, bro. I know it contradicts your whole entire understanding of the universe, but—"

"It contradicts my understanding of the universe to be a little bitch about everything, yes," Gabe interrupts.

"You wanna talk about who's being a little b—"

"I left my sunglasses in the car," I announce suddenly, standing up so fast I almost turn over the table. "I'm going to go get 'em."

"Molly," Gabe starts, sounding more irritated than I'm used to. "You don't have to——"

"No, no, I'll be right back." It's bailing, I know it is, just like I always do, but sitting there listening to them argue feels like trying to hold still while centipedes crawl all over my naked body. I can't do it; I don't have the stomach. I gotta, gotta go.

"You want company?" Imogen asks me.

"Nope, I'm good."

I take off at a pretty quick clip, but the raised voices have already caught Julia's attention; I pass by right as she's getting up off the old Donnelly camp blanket, where she's been reading magazines with Elizabeth Reese. "Did you just start *another* fight between my brothers?" she demands, shaking her head like she honestly can't believe me. "Seriously?"

"I—no," I defend myself. "Jesus, Julia. They're into it over a stupid game, I don't know."

"Uh-huh," she says, brushing by me. "Sure they are."

On my way to the lot I see Jake and Annie from the Lodge, who've got a complicated setup involving a generator—Jake's an Eagle Scout, I remember vaguely. He works behind the reception desk, so I see him more than I see Annie, who's a lifeguard. "Hey, Molly," Jake calls. "You want a beer?"

For a second I almost accept, but as soon as the words are out of his mouth Annie's shooting him a look that could peel the sap right off a pine tree, so I shake my head awkwardly. *I swear I'm not after your boyfriend*, I want to say.

Instead I get my sunglasses out of the station wagon and sit on the bumper for a minute, trying to take deep breaths and calm down a little. In my logical brain I know this one wasn't really my fault, not entirely—Patrick and Gabe were never super-close, even before everything happened. When we were kids it was fine, regular brother stuff, but once Chuck died it was like they swerved sharply in opposite directions or something, like they were never quite traveling in the same car after that. Gabe's personality, his gregariousness, got bigger and more exaggerated, like if he was surrounded by his friends 24/7 then it meant he never had to be alone. Meanwhile, Patrick did exactly the opposite: He didn't want anything to do with anybody who hadn't known Chuck well enough to have a nickname, didn't want to go out or hang out or do much at all besides sit in the barn or his bedroom with me, the two of us wrapped up in our own private Idaho. Julia would drop in and watch movies with us sometimes, but for the most part it felt like other people just didn't understand what was happening: "His *dad* died," I protested when Imogen complained about how often I'd blown her off lately.

"Yeah, a year ago," she countered.

I didn't know how to reply to that. I'd always known how Patrick's aloofness sometimes played to the outside world. It didn't look that way to me, though—after all, Patrick was my person, my other half. I never felt stuck or cut off or like there was other stuff I'd rather be doing, never felt like there was anyplace else I'd rather be.

At least, not until the moment it did.

It was a few weeks after my meeting with the Bristol recruiter in the guidance office, April of sophomore year—I'd gotten another email from her a couple of days before: *Just wanted to say again how nice it was speaking with you.* I'd written back, asking a few more questions. I hadn't brought it up with Patrick again, but the idea was still itching at me like the tag at the neck of a cheap cotton T-shirt, like walking around with a tiny shard of glass in my shoe. It was weird, feeling like I had something to say that he didn't want to hear about. That had never happened to me before.

I tried to push it out of my mind, though, which felt easier now as Patrick kissed a trail down the side of my neck, both of us sprawled on the couch in the family room at the Donnellys', killing time before that night's baseball game at school. We were the only two people in the house. His warm fingers traced the pattern of my rib cage, trailed down over my still-flat stomach, fussed tentatively with the button on my jeans. I breathed in. In spite of how long we'd been dating we'd never gone much further than this, and every inch of new skin he touched felt scary-amazing, icy hot. "What do you think?" he muttered into my ear, so quiet. "You wanna go upstairs?"

I did, truly—I wanted him to keep doing exactly what he was doing, wanted his familiar face and body and the rumpled T-shirt sheets on his bed. "Yeah," I said. "Yeah, I do, let me just." I took a deep breath, my head swimming. Were we really about to do what I thought we were maybe, possibly, probably about to do? "Let me just pee first, okay?"

Patrick laughed. "Sure." He stood up off the couch, adjusted himself a little. Took my hand and pulled me to my feet. "You got Chapstick?"

"Ha, why, too much kissing?" I grinned. "In my backpack, yeah."

"Smartass."

"You love me," I called over my shoulder, confident in the fact that he did, that he always would; when I got back a minute later, though, his darkened face threw me into sudden doubt. "What's this?" he asked me, holding up a sheet of printer paper.

Shit. It was my email exchange with the recruiter, the paper he'd clearly found in my backpack—I'd printed it out at school earlier, intending to show it to my mom that weekend.

I took a deep breath. "Patrick—"

"Are you going?" he asked, zero to totally pissed in 3.5 seconds. "To Arizona?"

"No!" I said, wanting to calm him down as fast as possible—wanting to get back to how everything had felt a minute ago, safe and exciting both. "Probably not, I mean, I just wanted—"

"*Probably* not?"

"I don't know!" I said. "I was going to talk to you about it, I *wanted* to talk to you about it, I just—"

"Thought you'd lie to me about it for a week instead?"

"Hey, kids," Gabe said just then, pausing in the doorway to the family room, rapping twice on the frame like he knew he was interrupting something but wanted to give us a heads-up that he was there. "You almost ready to go?"

"Oh, crap, what time is it?" I looked up at Gabe, then at the clock on the cable box, blushing at the idea he'd heard us fighting. He was supposed to give us a ride to the baseball game. I'd totally lost track of time. "We gotta go, huh?"

"Got some time," Gabe assured me. He was a senior that year, would be graduating in a month. "Game's not till seven."

I looked from him to Patrick's stony expression, back again. "I know, but I told Imogen we'd go early." Sports weren't a huge deal at our school, but our baseball team was in the playoffs and it was a Friday game, a night one that we'd been talking about all week. Julia was cheering, and Annie had made a bunch of banners with the art club; we had plans to go for pancakes at the diner afterward. It felt like a long time since I'd hung out with everyone, a weird ache I'd started to notice, like my friends felt far even though they were right where they'd always been. Like some secret part of me was already getting ready to leave. I took a deep breath, looked back at Patrick, putting my hand on his wrist like a peace offering. Tried to ask him telepathically: *Please, please can we just table this for now?* "Come on," I said, out loud. "Let's get ready."

"What if we skipped it?" Patrick said, standing frozen in place with his arms crossed. It was still cool out and he was wearing this lightweight hoodie I loved, gray and hundred-wash soft.

"Skipped it?" I repeated. "Why would we skip it?"

"I don't know." Patrick glanced at his brother, shook his head. "You don't think it sounds lame?"

"Not really," I said, "no. I kind of wanna go, actually."

"I . . . kind of really wanna stay here."

"Whoa, dissent in the ranks," Gabe teased from the doorway. "All right, you guys figure it out. I'm gonna change my shirt. Train leaves the station in five minutes."

I perched on the arm of the couch to face him. "I'm sorry, okay? I'm not going anywhere, I promise. I was being dumb, I should have told you I was thinking about it. But I'm not even thinking about it anymore."

I thought that would fix things, that we'd get back to having a fun, normal night, but Patrick sighed. "I think it's lame," he said, ignoring what I'd said about Bristol, like we'd moved onto a different conversation entirely. "I just think it's so boring and fake, to go hang out with a bunch of people I don't even like and cheer for a baseball team I literally could not care less about. I don't feel like going."

"They're our *friends*," I countered. "Since when do you not like our friends?"

"I like our friends fine," Patrick said, shaking his head. "I don't know." He sat back down then and picked the remote up off the couch, flicking through the channels. "Look, that show about the pit bulls and the criminals is coming on. How can you possibly say no to a show about pit bulls and criminals?"

"Paaatrick," I said, laughing a little uneasily—he was kidding but also not, I could tell, wanted me to ditch our friends and the baseball game and stay here.

To ditch *Bristol* and stay here, too.

God, it felt so suffocating all of a sudden, the idea of spending the rest of the night watching whatever five-year-old episode of *How I Met Your Mother* came on next, the air inside the house close and stale. We'd spent any number of Fridays like that, just the two of us, and it had never, ever bothered me, but all of a sudden it made me want to scream.

Gabe turned up in the doorway again then, jacket on and car keys rattling inside his hand. "You guys figure your shit out?" He looked back and forth between us, undoubtedly the twin faces of two people who had emphatically *not*. He made a face like, *definitely not getting in the middle of that*. "I can just take you over, Molly, if my brother's being a pain in the ass about it."

"Screw you," Patrick muttered.

"No," I said, "he's not—"

"Just go," Patrick said to me harshly. "Seriously, you wanna go with Gabe, go with Gabe. I'm not your warden."

"I—" I put one foot back down on the floor, uncertain. We were supposed to meet Imogen in ten. "Come on, Patrick, don't—"

"Jesus Christ, Molly, can you not make a federal fucking case out of it?" Patrick huffed out an irritated breath. "I'll see you tomorrow."

That made me mad, that he'd talk to me that way in front of his brother. That he'd talk to me that way at *all*. I felt my cheeks heat up, embarrassed and pissed. This was me and *Patrick*, was the thing here—we were a unit, a package deal, us on one side of the road and everybody else on the other. We never, ever fought in public.

Except that apparently now we did.

Well, if he was going to be that way, I wasn't going to sit here and ruin my night trying to talk him out of it. "Fine," I said, grabbing my backpack off the floor and swinging it over my shoulder. I looked at Gabe, smiled a little. "Ready to go?"

Things seem to have calmed down by the time I get back to the campsite. Patrick and Tess are gone, and Jake and Annie have wandered over, the cards forgotten in the center of the picnic table; Gabe pulls away from the herd when he spots me. "Hey, you," he says, slinging a warm, heavy arm around my shoulders. "Get your sunglasses?"

"Uh-huh." It's surprising and a little weird to me, how he seems happy to brush off the scene I walked out on. "Everything okay?"

"What? With my brother?" Gabe shrugs a bit. "Yeah, it was fine. You know how he is; he was just being an asshole."

That stops me. It was a small, stupid thing, maybe, but Patrick *did* have the winning cards. I remember Patrick complaining about Gabe what feels like forever ago, the two of us stretched out barefoot in the barn: "Everybody thinks he's this great sport about shit, but he's a great sport about shit because he always gets his way." *Is that what just happened here?* I wonder.

I don't say any of that out loud, though, just hum non-committally and reach up to lace my fingers through his. "We're gonna play Frisbee for a bit," Gabe tells me. "You want in?"

I shake my head, suddenly exhausted—the heat, maybe, or just the slightly overwhelming feeling of being with every-one again, the same as we used to and completely different all at once. "I might just nap," I tell him, then immediately feel guilty about it—after all, isn't this exactly what I used to do when I was with Patrick, duck out and away from the group? *We came here to hang out with our friends*, I remember telling him the last time we were here together. *Shouldn't we, you know, hang out with our friends?* "I mean, unless you want me to? I can rally."

Gabe doesn't seem bothered, though: "Nah, take a

rest," he says, planting a casual kiss on my forehead. "We're gonna do the campfire thing again later anyway, will probably be another late night."

"Okay," I tell him, tipping my face up so his next kiss lands on my mouth instead of on my forehead. "Just for a little bit."

I borrow a big flowered sheet from Imogen and sack out in the sunshine, never mind that it's the middle of the baking day. It takes me a long time to get comfortable. I can't stop thinking about the night of the baseball game a hundred years ago, the weird backward feeling of leaving Patrick in the family room and walking out the back door of the farmhouse with Gabe. *Jailbreak*, I thought, then immediately hated myself for it.

It was early spring still, the air getting chilly as the sun disappeared behind the mountains, all blue and purple twilight. "You can turn that off," Gabe said when the radio in the Bronco started up along with the ignition, one of those alt-country stations that played a lot of Carrie Underwood. "I think Julia was listening to it."

"A likely story," I teased, then right away felt awkward about it. I tucked my hands between my thighs, looked out the window. I tried to remember the last time I'd been on my own with Gabe, and couldn't. I thought of Patrick by himself back at the farmhouse. Maybe this had been a mistake.

Gabe glanced over at me as we turned out onto the parkway, curious. "You okay over there?" he asked.

"He's mad at me," I blurted before I even knew I was going to do it, then shook my head. God, what was my malfunction tonight? "I'm sorry. I mean, yeah, I'm fine."

Gabe laughed a little at that, but not meanly. "Okay," he said, then: "What's he mad about?" he asked.

"I talked to a recruiter a few weeks ago," I confessed, pulling one knee up on the bench seat. "About going and running track for this boarding school in Arizona."

"Boarding school?" Gabe asked, sounding surprised—but not appalled like Patrick had. "Yeah?"

"Do you think that's totally stupid?"

"No, not at all," Gabe said, no hesitation. He had one casual hand hooked over the steering wheel, his face open and honest in the fading light. "I think it could be awesome, actually."

"I think it could be awesome, too!" I told him, almost embarrassed by how dumbly enthusiastic I sounded. "But, duh, it would mean being not here, and . . . I don't know." I shrugged and glanced out the window again, the moon beginning to rise. "Patrick . . . does not think it's a good idea."

"Yeah," Gabe said. "I can see him thinking that. Do *you* think it's a good idea?"

I considered that for a moment—how I felt when I was running, how my head got quiet and my body was strong. I wondered how it might feel to run for a school that took that seriously. And even though I didn't want to, even though I knew I was just pissed at Patrick and would probably see things totally differently in twenty minutes, I thought of that word *jailbreak* again. "I . . . think I might, yeah."

"Well," Gabe said, just as quiet. "That's something to think about, then, isn't it?"

"Yeah," I replied. "I guess it is."

We rode the rest of the way in an oddly comfortable silence, both of us breathing in the purple darkness. I'd never changed the country station, and neither did Gabe. When we pulled up to school, I was almost sorry to be getting out of the car.

"I can give you a ride home, too, if you need one," Gabe said before we split up at the gate to the baseball field, as if he'd read my thoughts somehow. Already his friends had spotted him and were hooting his name. "Just come find me later on."

"I can probably go with Imogen," I told him. "Thanks, though."

"Yeah," he said. "No problem." He waved, and we headed off in opposite directions, but not five seconds later: "Hey, listen, Molly—"

"*Hm?*" I turned back around, surprised and curious. "What's up?"

Gabe shook his head. "Never mind. Just, congrats on getting recruited, is all I was going to say."

That made me smile—nobody had congratulated me yet, I realized. Patrick certainly hadn't. "Thanks," I said, smiling one more time before I went to go find Imogen in the stands.

It's hotter than I realize, and when I wake up on Imogen's flowered sheet sometime later the first thing I register is the red roasting sensation all up and down the skin of my arms and legs, on the tops of my feet and the bridge of my nose around my sunglasses.

The second thing I register is Patrick.

"Mols," he says, looming above me, so his face is all in shadow, nudging my hip with his ankle until I startle. I sit up fast and disoriented. Everything stings.

"Did you just wake me up?" I ask stupidly. I've been avoiding him on purpose since we got here, trying to give him and Tess their space. Not that they need my help, really—after they got here they spent most of last night sitting on a huge rock near the water, heads tipped close together, telling secrets I couldn't even begin to guess. I'd taken the beers Gabe offered and sat with everyone else around the fire. Tried not to feel jealous about that. "Where is everybody?"

"You're frying," Patrick tells me now, not particularly friendly. "Come on, you gotta put sunblock on, get in the shade or something."

"Oh," I say, disoriented, that underwater nap feeling where you're groggier after than you ever were before. I'm eye level with his knees, ripped denim he's had for as long as

I can remember and a swatch of tan skin showing through. It occurs to me to wonder how long he's been standing there, and what went through his mind while he did. *I'm sorry about earlier*, I want to tell him. *Gabe was being a jerk, and I'm sorry*. "Okay."

"Here," Patrick says, thrusting a bottle of Coppertone in my general direction, the callused pads of his fingers brushing mine. By the time I get it together enough to look up and say thanks, he's already gone.

There's a concert that night, the clang of drums and guitars echoing through the mountains like a call-and-response from some other lifetime; Gabe pulls me away from the crowd to make out for a while in the darkness, his palms scraping pleasantly across my stinging, sunburned face. "You're fun," he mutters, biting my bottom lip a little.

"You're funner," I tell him, and grin.

I'm coming back from the bathroom when I run into Tess standing by herself near where our tents are, arms around herself and looking confused. "Where'd everybody go?" she asks when she sees me. She smells like booze and bug spray. "I lost everybody."

"They're still back over by the field," I tell her. Then, looking a little more closely: "You okay?"

Tess shakes her head. "I'm fucked up," she says bluntly. "*Ohh*, Molly, I am fucked up."

"You are, huh?" I'm a little buzzed myself, to be honest,

the few beers I had singing through my blood and brain and bones. "Hit it hard?"

"Yeah," Tess says vaguely. "Too hard. I don't really feel so good."

"Okay," I tell her, frowning a bit, taking her arm and leading her over to a picnic table. "You're okay. Just sit for a second, I'll grab you some water."

"No, don't leave," Tess says immediately. "I just—please don't."

I blink, surprised and a little alarmed. "Okay. It's okay." New plan, then. "I'm not going anywhere." I'm squinting through the darkness to see if I spy anybody from our group when all of a sudden Tess is up off the bench.

"Nope," she says. "*Nope*, nope, I'm gonna—"

From the green, panicky look on her face it's pretty clear what she's going to do, even when she doesn't finish the statement—I don't see a garbage can anywhere nearby, so I take her by the shoulders and steer her toward a clearing that's not too close to anybody's tent. "Right there," I instruct, basically forcing her to bend down, arranging her limbs like she's a doll. "You're okay."

I keep saying it over and over while she's sick—*you're okay*—rubbing her back a little and making sure the thick rope of her ginger braid doesn't swing into any oncoming grossness. It feels like it goes on a long time. I actually *really* hate the sound of throw-up—like, it pretty reliably makes me gag—but it's not like I'm going to wander away and leave her, so I look around at the trees and try not to listen too closely.

"Oh my God," Tess says when she's finished, standing upright and wiping the back of her hand across her mouth, eyes red-rimmed and face puffy. She looks about ten years old. "I'm sorry. I'm so sorry. Don't tell Patrick, okay? Please don't tell Patrick."

"Patrick wouldn't care," I assure her, peeling a loose strand of hair off her forehead, although I actually get her impulse to want to hide it from him. I know from experience he's not the easiest person to admit a screwup to. "He'd just want to make sure you're okay. But no, of course I won't. You wanna go lie down?"

"I need water," Tess says, so I nod and lead her by the hand back to where our stuff is, digging around until I find my big plastic Nalgene bottle. "Drink it slow," I tell her, not wanting her to get sick again. Tess nods obediently and glugs it down, then pretty much crawls into her tent before passing out fully clothed on top of Patrick's sleeping bag. I refill the water bottle and stick it in there beside her for later. Her hangover is going to hurt.

I head back across the field to find Gabe, but Patrick's the first Donnelly I come upon, sitting by the low-burning embers of the campfire and staring into the flames like he's trying to solve a mystery, the light flickering over his serious face. His dad used to build us fires just like this one in the backyard of the farmhouse, tell us long, involved stories before we fell asleep. We'd pass out side by side in our sleeping bags. We sat side by side at Chuck's wake.

I don't know if he sees me or just senses me lurking, but after a moment Patrick turns and raises his hand to wave. I stand there for a minute, looking at him and remembering, wondering what would happen if I walked over and sat down beside him.

Wondering what would happen if I leaned in and kissed him good night.

God. What is my *malfunction*? I just held his girlfriend's hair back while she puked, for Pete's sake. I shake my head once to clear it, embarrassed. I raise one cautious hand and wave back.

DAY 35

Tess takes it easy the next day, predictably, mostly prone in a nest of sleeping bags with a Stephen King book and a bag of pretzels, which is the closest thing to saltines that anybody brought. The rest of us hike until our blisters are bleeding, till it feels like the mountains are having their way with all of us: Patrick has a run-in with some poison sumac. Imogen gets stung by a wasp. My sunburn chafes against my clothes until I'm swearing to anyone who'll listen that I'm done with outdoor activities forever. "I mean it," I tell Imogen, hobbling along back down the mountain, hair falling out of its messy bun. "As soon as we get home I'm going to set up shop in a hermetically sealed bubble and never come out again."

"Sounds like a great plan!" Julia calls brightly, coming up behind us. Imogen and I look at each other wide-eyed for a moment before bursting into wild, slaphappy giggles.

"That Julia," I gasp, practically doubled over with laughter. It's been a long time since Imogen and I cracked up like this, since before I left, definitely. I don't know if the two of us are just exhausted or what, but it almost makes the burn worth it. "You can always count on her."

Tess has perked up enough by the time we get back that she helps Patrick grill burgers and hot dogs over the camp-fire, lining the buns up along the table in neat, symmetrical rows. "Feel better?" I ask when I come over to grab a pair for me and Gabe, along with one of the knock-you-naked brownies Imogen made. Tess nods quickly, tilting her head to accept a kiss on the cheek from Patrick that might or might not be for my benefit, it's impossible to tell.

"Good," I say brightly, paper plate in each hand, feeling my face do a weird thing and willing it not to. *You're welcome*, I think nastily. "I'm glad."

I tell myself there's nothing to feel strange about all of a sudden, that I'm cranky and uncomfortable because of my sunburn and sleeping on the ground for a third night in a row. But later on I'm coming back from the campground bathroom holding my toothbrush in one hand and rub-bing my opposite arm with the other—it's chilly this high in the mountains, goose bumps blooming up and down my limbs—when I spy Patrick holding the flap of the tent open for Tess so she can climb on in ahead of him. I can't hear what he says to her, but I hear her full-bodied laugh in response, muffled as Patrick zips the door shut. It's the same tent Chuck set up for us behind the farmhouse summer after summer when we were kids. Inside, I know it smells like mothballs and dirt.

I breathe in sharply, hit all at once with this weird, strong instinct to scream out *Stop*, like seeing someone about to step in front of an oncoming car or put their hand down on a hot burner. Like I'm trying to stave off something awful and disastrous—only I'm the one about to get hurt.

God. I actually shake my head as I turn purposefully back toward the tent I'm sharing with Gabe. I don't know how to make myself quit feeling like this. Of *course* I knew the two of them were sharing a tent, of *course* the various implications of that fact had occurred to me—and, I guess, so had the fact that those various implications were irrelevant as long as Tess was puking her guts out.

Gabe reaches for me almost as soon as I'm inside, one hand in mine and tugging me down onto the soft pile of our sleeping bags, rucking my practical tank top up over my head. "This is some sunburn, Molly Barlow," he murmurs, looking at me in the dim moonlight shining in through the vent in the ceiling. He presses his mouth against a red place on my shoulder, another one near my hip where yesterday's shirt rode up as I slept. "That hurt?"

Tess is thinner than me, I think meanly. *She's probably better-looking with her clothes off than I am, she's probably—*

Stop it.

"Doesn't hurt," I promise, closing my eyes and sinking

into it a little, Gabe's hands and his mouth and the now-familiar hum he cranks up in my body. Patrick and I were babies when we started dating, young enough that it didn't feel like we were in a hurry to do anything, both of us probably shyer than we'd admit even to each other. But we're older now, we're at the point where it's definitely not inconceivable for him and Tess to have moved way faster, for him to be pulling off her T-shirt right now, tugging at the elastic on her underwear and—

"I can't," I blurt suddenly, sitting up with such force I pretty much shove Gabe right off me, bolt upright in my half-unzipped sleeping bag with my face flushed sweaty and red. I completely don't know how to follow it up, how to explain to him that it's Patrick and Tess one tent over and the two of us in here, and that everything feels connected, too close, terrible, and right this second all I want is for no one to ever touch me again. We've done it already, haven't we? Maybe it shouldn't be so big of a deal, but it just, it *is*, I don't—"I'm sorry," I try, "I just—"

"Hey, easy," Gabe says, sitting up and scrubbing his hair out of his face. "You're okay; we don't have to do anything. Easy, hey." He reaches out and laces his fingers through mine, squeezing. "You wanna go for a walk?"

I smile at that, embarrassed and grateful, reaching for my shirt and fussing with the hem for a moment. "Are you, like, perfect or something?" I ask him, shaking my head before pulling the shirt over it. "Is that your superpower?"

"Nah," Gabe says seriously. "My superpower is X-ray vision."

I snort. "Oh my God, I take it back."

Gabe grins. "Come on," he says, standing up and pulling me to my feet along with him. "Let's go see some fucking stars."

I grab some snacks and supplies, and we pick our way across the campground, past parties still going strong and intense late-night conversations happening around dying fires. I shiver as the night air hits my sunburned skin. Gabe's hand is warm around mine, though, and by the time we reach the clearing where the concert was last night I've pushed Patrick and Tess and whatever they might or might not be doing resolutely out of my mind. This is what's happening, me and Gabe and these fucking stars above us. This is right where I'm supposed to be.

We find a patch of grass mostly clear of garbage and spread the blanket on the damp ground, leaning back to look up at the sky. We're far enough from any real civilization that the moon looks like a spotlight—there's Orion, one of the Dippers, Cassiopeia in her upside-down chair. "This is the part where we talk about what specks we are compared to the universe," I inform Gabe wryly, but the truth is I'm really, really glad we came out here to look. "Here," I say, pulling a couple of beers out of my backpack. "To being specks."

Gabe grins at that, surprised. "Look at you, Girl Scout,"

he says, twisting the caps off both of them and handing one back to me. "I love you, you know that? You're something else."

I blink at him for a moment, Gabe blinking back at me. Then both of us start to laugh. "You know what I mean," he says, and I *do*, I think, sitting out here with the bowl-shaped sky above us. I kiss him hard to show I understand.

DAY 36

Back at home there's another email from the dean in my inbox: *Dear Incoming Student, please, for the love of all things holy, hurry up and figure out your life.*

Or something like that, at least.

I make a snack of apple and peanut butter, shoot Gabe a text to let him know what a good time I had.

You're okay, too, for a speck, he texts me back, and I giggle. With Gabe I never feel like a walking, talking letdown. With Gabe I just feel like me.

So why can't I stop thinking about his brother?

I finish my apple and take Oscar out into the yard for a while, pushing the image of Patrick and Tess disappearing into the tent out of my mind and telling myself I'm being melancholy and dumb. I make a list of projects to tackle when I head back to work in the morning. Finally, I dig my phone out of my pocket.

How's the rash? I text Patrick, just teasing.

He doesn't text back.

DAY 37

He does the next morning, though: *itchy*, he reports, just the one word and no punctuation. A couple of minutes later, though: *how's the burn?*

I grin down at my phone, feeling silly and glad. *Burn-y*, I reply.

DAY 38

My mom's got an aloe plant, he texts while I'm filing invoices in Penn's office. *Could come by and get some if you still look like a lobster.*

I don't, not really; the worst of the burn's faded, is beginning to peel away like so many layers of snakeskin, like I'm becoming something entirely new. All I can do is deal with the grossness and wait for whatever's underneath.

Still: *will do*, I text him back, no hesitation. *When's good?*

DAY 39

I don't know what it means that Patrick tells me to come over at a time I know Gabe's working at the pizza shop— just that he doesn't want anything to do with his brother, maybe, or possibly nothing at all.

"Hey," he says, letting me in the feeble side door—it felt strange to knock on the frame and then wait for him, how I used to barge right in and sneak bites of whatever Chuck was making in the kitchen, usually something with lentils or whole-wheat flour. Patrick's barefoot in his shredded old jeans. His hair's grown out a little since he's been back in Star Lake and he looks a bit more like I remember, some of those sharp edges filed off. "Come on in."

"Sure," I say, stepping past him into the dark, empty house, the familiar smells of dust and wood and sunlight. "Hey." Pilot hauls himself up off the floor and comes across the room to wag his hello. It makes me feel sort of disproportionately happy that he remembers me somewhere at the back of his loyal canine brain, like maybe in some alternate universe I'm still part of this family after all. "Hey, Pilot. Hey, boy."

"His hips are going," Patrick says quietly, reaching down to scratch behind Pilot's affable, furry ears. "He's ten; he can't really do stairs anymore. My mom rigged up a little step-stool thing so he can get up on the couch."

I look down at Pilot, who's panting cheerfully. His muzzle's gone a silvery-gray. I remember when the Donnellys brought him back from the ASPCA, wriggly and wormy— Patrick and I rolled around in the yard with him anyway, muddy and covered in grass stains. Julia didn't want anything to do with any of us. Gabe was off with his friends, I think. "Shoot, I didn't know."

Patrick shrugs. "Yeah, I can see how that's the kind of thing my brother wouldn't have told you," he says, giving Pilot a final rub and heading for the kitchen door.

That stings. "Patrick—" I start.

"Aloe's in the sunroom," he interrupts me. "Come on."

"Sure." I follow him through the hallway, past the creaky staircase and into the bright, airy sunroom that Connie's filled with fiddle-leaf fig and cacti, an enormous and vaguely terrifying spider plant that's been holding court next to the picture window since I was a little girl. There's a bright patterned rug spread over the floor, oranges and reds. Patrick picks a pair of scissors out of a jar on the bookshelf—one is encouraged to prune, if one is going to spend time in here—and snips a couple lengths of aloe off the plant.

"Thanks," I tell Patrick quietly—our fingers brush as he hands me the aloe, this stupid useless shiver I feel all over my body. Way before anything romantic ever happened between us Patrick and I were always touching-friends, his arm slung around my shoulders or our palms pressed together to see whose hand was bigger. It used to make me feel reassured, when I bothered to think about it at all, a way of orienting myself in space, like running your hand along the wall in a dark room. Now even this much contact feels foreign and strange.

For Patrick, too, apparently: "I'll get you a baggie," he says, clearing his throat and heading back toward the kitchen, leaving me alone in the sunlight and green.

DAY 40

Imogen invites me over to have my cards read, which is how I know I'm really forgiven; I head over after work with two slices of the Lodge's midnight chocolate cake and a CD of a singer-songwriter Penn turned me on to, this new chick from Brooklyn who plays the slide guitar. The night's summer-cool, the sky over the lake a toasted rose gold. It rained this afternoon, quick and violent, and the road is still shiny and wet.

I haven't been to Imogen's house much since I got back here, a cottage off a side road not far from the high school, full of crystals and an altar to the Goddess set up in the front room. It smells like vanilla and patchouli oil, familiar. "Well, hey, Molly," her mother says when she answers the door in a pair of flowy pants she's had as long as I've known her; her hair's different, though, pure white and cropped short around her face. I remember what Imogen told me about the cancer, and I squeeze her long and tight to say hello.

I grab two forks from the kitchen and head up the back staircase to Imogen's room, where she's putting the finishing touches on a huge brush script painting she's working on, twenty-four by forty-eight inches that just says *EASY DOES IT*. "Not bad advice," I say.

"I like to think so." Imogen grins, dunking her paintbrush into a mason jar full of water and motioning toward the bed. There's a picture of her and Tess in their graduation gowns tucked into the mirror. Her RISD sweatshirt's slung over the chair. "You ready? *Ooh*, you brought cake, huh?"

"As per the agreement," I tell her, passing a fork over and settling myself down on the ancient quilt. She hands me the cards to shuffle; after a moment, I hand them back. "Ready," I say, taking a breath.

Imogen nods. "Think of your question," she instructs me, just like always. When we were in middle school I remember wanting to know if Patrick *liked*-liked me. After Gabe I remember silently begging the cards to tell me what to do. Tonight I'm not even sure what I'm after exactly, but before I can articulate it even to myself Imogen sets the cards down on the bed.

"You hurt me," she says, and I snap to attention, like hearing my name called in class. "When you peaced out like that." Imogen glances down at the deck in front of her.

She's wearing purple mascara, and her lashes cast shadows across the apples of her cheeks. "You were my best friend, Molly. You always had Patrick. But I only ever had you."

I open my mouth to tell her I'm sorry, to start apologizing and never ever stop, but Imogen looks up and shakes her head before I can get there: "Think of your question," she says again, more softly. She takes a breath and flips the first card.

DAY 41

"You know what tomorrow is, right?" Gabe asks me. We're perched at the counter at the shop eating messy slices of pizza and drinking fountain Cokes, orange grease pooling in the ridges of the cheap paper plates. I forgot how much I loved Donnelly pizza until this summer: It's like I'm craving it all of a sudden, like there's some secret ingredient my system's been lacking.

I squint at him. He's got a stringy bit of cheese stuck to his bottom lip, and I reach up to peel it away. "The day after today?"

"*Yeeeeessss,*" Gabe says. "That's very astute of you, thanks for that. It's also first day of Knights of Columbus."

"Is it really?" The Knights of Columbus carnival is the dorkiest of all summer traditions, a handful of slightly sketchy rides folded out of trucks at the park downtown, vendors hawking sausage and peppers and sugary fried dough. It's put on to take advantage of the tourists, but we all used to love it anyway, would go four times in a week if we could find someone to take us, all blinking neon lights and beepy music like Las Vegas in the middle of Star Lake. The summer after fourth grade Patrick rode the swings six consecutive times over Chuck's patient warnings and then threw up hot dog all over himself—and me. It occurs to me that I ought to remind him of that, that he actually barfed on me once and our relationship previously survived.

Gabe's still looking at me expectantly, his eyes blue blue blue in the overhead lights of the shop: There are a couple of high school kids parked in the red plastic booths, a family splitting an extra cheese pie and a pitcher of grape soda. I blink, and the memory of Patrick recedes like a cloud of semolina flour, disappearing into the air. "I'd love to," I tell Gabe, stealing the crust of his pizza off his plate and finishing it in two big bites. "I can't wait."

DAY 42

We hit Knights of Columbus with a crowd of Gabe's friends, a noisy herd ambling down the midway in the pink-purple twilight. My boots kick up tiny clouds of dust under my feet. The whole Falling Star crew has turned up, too: Tess and Patrick, Imogen and Annie and Handsome Jay; my spine rattles in time with the chorus of mechanical beeping coming from the long row of games, the periodic *Hey!* as the water-gun booth broadcasts "Rock and Roll Part 2" over and over. I'm taking my change from the cotton candy vendor when Tess touches my arm, urgent. "Can I talk to you for a sec?" she asks.

"Sure thing," I tell her, forehead wrinkling, wondering immediately what Patrick's told her—not that there's anything *to* tell, but still. I rip off a wad of spun sugar and stuff it into my mouth as I follow her around the corner beside a giant whirring generator. "What's up?"

"I never really said thank you," she tells me, tipping her head close even though there's nobody but me around to hear her. She's wearing clean white shorts and a plaid button-down, a smudge of lip gloss the only makeup she's wearing as far as I can tell. Her eyelashes are pretty and pale. "After the other night."

"For what?" I ask, swallowing my cotton candy and staring at her blankly. "Oh, for the water and stuff? Don't even worry about it. Seriously, it could have been any of us. We were all pretty banged up."

Tess shakes her head. "That wouldn't happen to you."

That surprises me. "I like how you think I'm this person who has my shit together," I say, laughing a little, waving my cotton candy in her direction until she nods and pulls some off. "It's very charming."

"I don't know." Tess smiles back. "Sometimes it just feels like—"

"Hey, ladies!" That's Patrick from a distance, motioning to where the rest of our group has already receded down the midway, bound for the hulking cluster of rides. "You wanna join us over here or not so much?"

"We're talking about our periods," Tess informs him loudly, which makes me laugh. "Anyway. Thanks," she adds quietly.

"Don't mention it," I tell her. "Really."

We rejoin the group and head for the Scrambler, which Annie swears beheaded somebody at a carnival outside

Scranton. I spy Julia and Elizabeth Reese waiting in line for the giant slide. I turn to point them out to Gabe, find Patrick at my side instead, and startle; Tess is chatting animatedly with Imogen, nobody paying attention to us at all.

"How you feeling?" Patrick asks, quiet enough so only I can hear him. He's wearing jeans so holey they're basically shorts and a faded ringer T-shirt, hands shoved into his pockets. "The sunburn, I mean."

I blink. "Better now," I tell him, surprised not just that he's walking beside me but that he's actually speaking to me in public—Patrick, for one, definitely doesn't share his girlfriend's opinion that I'm somebody who knows what she's doing in this life. "Really wasn't so bad after all."

He and Tess break off to ride the Scrambler with Jay and Imogen. "There you are," Gabe says when I catch up to him, swinging a sturdy arm around my shoulders. He keeps it there as we walk, easy and casual in a starchy button-down with the sleeves rolled to his elbows, like he really is the mayor on his night off; his buddy Steve chats to me about Boston, if I'm planning to root for the Red Sox once I move.

"The Sox are filthy," Kelsey puts in, sniffing like they've done something to personally offend her. "Don't do it."

I win a bright orange monkey at the water-gun game,

which I pass off to Gabe with great fanfare amidst groans and catcalls from his buddies; he stamps a kiss against my temple, pulls me into line for the Ferris wheel just as the sun slips below the horizon line. Paused at the top I can see the winking lights of town in the distance, the dark spine of the mountains, and the first few pinprick stars.

"I used to think about bringing you up here," Gabe tells me now, an arm around my shoulders and his face half shadow, half brilliant light. "When I was, like, thirteen or fourteen or whatever."

"What? You did not." I actually scoff, the bark of my laugh good-natured and incredulous.

Gabe laughs back, but he nods as he's doing it. "I did."

"Yeah, okay." I shake my head. Gabe's spent his life as the host of a party Star Lake's most wanted, a million different people all around him all the time. The idea that he was harboring secret Ferris wheel fantasies—that he was harboring any fantasies at *all*, that there was anything he wanted that he didn't already have and, more than that, that that something was *me*—is hugely surprising. "No, you didn't."

"I *did*. You just didn't notice because you were running all over the place playing Peter Pan and Tiger Lily with my brother, but I used to think about it a lot."

"We weren't playing Peter Pan and Tiger Lily," I pro-test automatically, although the truth is that probably we were—Patrick and I pretended until we were way, way too old. I shake my head anyhow. "If you were fourteen, I was twelve."

"Uh-huh." Gabe grins. "Missing the point there a little bit, Molly Barlow."

I shake my head again, ducking it down close so he'll kiss me. "I'm not," I promise seriously. "I'm not."

"Uh-huh." Gabe smirks and obliges, his mouth warm and friendly and wet. Him feeling something for me when we were younger, him having this whole other side I never guessed—I wonder how my life would have been different if I'd known and understood that before this summer. I wonder about the things it might have changed. For so long I belonged to Patrick, the two of us so close we weren't even two distinct people, like conjoined twins or one of those mutant double crackers you get sometimes if the Nabisco machinery slips up and doesn't separate them correctly. It was good until it wasn't, it worked until it broke, but sitting here at the top of the Ferris wheel with the whole world spread out in front of me, all I can wonder is what would have happened if I'd spent all of high school—all my *life*— with Gabe instead. What if I'd gone to lake parties and hung out at Crow Bar instead of hiding out in the Donnellys' barn with Patrick, the two of us casting idle judgment and breathing each other's air? Would I have left so much horrifying wreckage? Would I have had more than just a tiny handful of friends? It feels good, being here in this rickety little car with him, Steve and Kelsey directly behind us and a crowd of friendly faces on the ground. It feels easy and healthy and *right*.

So I kiss Gabe again, sinking into it as the motor jolts back to life, a rapid creak and the swooping feeling as we sink down toward Earth.

DAY 43

Patrick comes by the Lodge to pick Tess up in the middle of the afternoon, and this time he doesn't bolt the second he gets a fleeting look at my face. "Want me to get her?" I ask. She's teaching an old-lady water aerobics class this afternoon, I know—she and I ran out to French Roast on our break this morning, and she told me how much she was dreading it. But Patrick shakes his head.

"I'm early," he says, sitting down beside me on one of the porch rockers. I brought the schedule out here to fuss with, everybody's PTO requests stacked up on the rough-hewn coffee table beside me. I made some watery iced coffee, cubes melting faster than I can drink it down. "How's your day?"

"Oh, you know." I wave the papers at him, surprised and pleased. "Trying not to piss anybody off too much."

Patrick's eyebrows twitch, but he lets that one go. "Could always settle employee disputes via mud wrestling," he suggests, stretching his long legs out in front of him.

"A dance-off," I counter.

"Rock Paper Scissors," Patrick says, then: "Or just flip a fucking coin like Emily Green."

That stops me, the reference to *Driftwood* and its dumb heroine's decision-making strategy of choice, how in the book she keeps an Indian Head penny tucked in her shoe for whenever things got real sticky—or so I've heard. "You *read* it?" I ask, surprised.

Patrick shrugs, looking away from me. "I read parts," he mutters.

We're quiet for a minute, both of us breathing the piney, dirt-smelling air. "Penn thinks I should be a business major," I say finally, more to make noise than anything else.

"Yeah?" Patrick leans forward and considers that for a minute, all bunchy shoulders, his elbows on both denim-covered knees. "Remember when you made Julia and me start an iced-tea stand because you said the lemonade market was flooded? Or that time you had us make mac and cheese for my mom and dad and then told them they had to pay for it?"

I snort. "I was seven, thank you."

Patrick smirks. "I'm just saying, that's a head for business right there."

"Shut up."

"Or that track team fund-raising thing you did sopho-more year," he points out, more serious this time. "The run-ning in heels thing."

"You thought that was the stupidest fund-raiser ever," I protest, remembering—we needed new uniforms, so we had the guys and girls race to raise money. "You told me so every day."

"I mean, yeah, but it worked," Patrick says. For a second he looks sort of sorry, like maybe he regrets how he blew it off back then. "That was real. You're good at organizing and planning stuff; your boss is right."

"Yeah?" I ask. I've had the idea in my head on and off ever since Penn mentioned it, but something about Patrick—who knows me better than anyone, or who at least used to—saying it's a good idea, that makes it feel like an actual possibility. *Molly Barlow*, I imagine myself saying the next time someone asks, *business major*.

Patrick nods. "Yeah," he says. "I think so."

We're quiet again, the late-afternoon lull of the Lodge all around us, that pre-dinner pause. Across the parking lot a boy and a girl shuffle along the blacktop in their bathing suits and flip-flops, both of them holding bright plastic pool rafts. All of a sudden my chest aches so hard I can barely breathe.

"Could we ever hang out?" I blurt before I can rethink it or get too embarrassed or cowed. "Like, on purpose? Not just when we run into each other or whatever?"

For a moment, Patrick doesn't answer, and it's like I can't backpedal fast enough. "I mean, I get that that's probably colossally weird," I say. "On top of which you're probably busy with Tess and the shop and stuff, I just . . ." I trail off, a little helpless. "I don't know."

For a minute, Patrick just looks at me, wordless. I feel like he can see the tissue underneath my skin. "I don't know, either," he says finally. "But, yeah, let's try."

DAY 44

Sasha at the front desk has her break at three-thirty, so I offer to cover, straightening my ponytail and my Star Lake Lodge name tag both. I check in a family with three triplet girls, all blond and bespectacled, and a pair of paramedics from the Berkshires who wanted to try a different mountain range for variety's sake. Their two redheaded toddlers climb on the leather couches, all dimpled arms and legs.

The couple who comes in behind them is older, a guy in khaki shirts and a sun-leathered woman in a brightly colored parrot T-shirt, a plastic tote bag with hula girls, and lime-green flip flops on her feet. "Welcome to the Lodge," I say as she hands over her credit card.

The woman ducks her yellow-gray head forward conspiratorially, like we're old friends. "Maybe you can tell me," she says, voice lowered, just-between-us-girls. "Does Diana Barlow really live in this town?"

Well.

"She does," I confirm, trying to keep my face neutral. I fish their keys out of the cubby behind the desk. "You a fan?"

"Oh, the biggest," the woman assures me. "Mostly her early stuff, but have you read *Driftwood*? I cried for two days. And you know it's about the daughter." When I turn back around she's leaning almost all the way over the desk as if she thinks my mother is possibly crouched back here, hiding. She shakes her head. "It's heartbreaking stuff."

"Terrible," I agree, my whole body heating up like a torch held to copper, like if you looked at me from above I might seem to glow. This is the worst part, I remind myself, working to keep my face impassive. Except for all the other worst parts. "So sad."

The woman takes her room keys and her bloated-looking husband and heads upstairs, finally, leaving me alone in the lobby with no one to blame but myself. I hold one palm to my flaming cheek, unpin my name tag with the other. *Molly*, it reads in big block letters, innocuous, anonymous enough that the woman with the parrot shirt probably didn't even think to look.

That's when I turn and see Tess.

"Don't," I say, holding my hand up. She's hovering in

the doorway that leads to the office in her flip-flops. I have no idea how long she's been there, but from the look on her face I can tell it's been long enough. "It's fine."

"I wasn't going to say a word," Tess says, and something in her voice telegraphs she's serious, that she probably would have brought that particular exchange to her grave. She nods at Sasha, who's crossing the lobby to reclaim her post. "Was gonna take my break, though. You wanna come for a walk?"

I open my mouth to refuse her, then close it again. "I—sure."

We wander out onto the back porch, down the crooked wooden steps to the pool level. It's overcast today, just a couple of little kids gallantly dog-paddling their way across the shallow end, teeth chattering and lips tinted purple. "We used to be just like that," Tess says, gesturing with her chin. "Me and my brother. We'd have swum in February, if we could."

That makes me smile. She's never mentioned her brother before. "Is he older or younger?"

"Older," Tess tells me. "He's at NYU, so I'll get to see him a little bit in the fall. I'm going to Barnard, so it's pretty close."

"That's cool." We slip our shoes off and sit down on the concrete edge of the pool, dangle our feet into the chilly water.

"Uh-huh," Tess says, reaching down to skim a leaf

off the surface of the pool. "I had to promise my mom I wouldn't stop shaving my armpits once I got there, but I don't know, their econ program seems interesting enough. We'll see, I guess."

I think of my email from the dean about declaring a major, still flagged in my inbox and awaiting a response. "How is that a thing you knew you wanted to do?"

Tess shrugs. "I'm good at math," she says. "I've always been good at math; I've been doing my parents' bills since I was eleven. And I like international stuff—like, how what happens in one country money-wise affects what happens in another country." She grins. "I get that that's, like, really boring to most people, don't worry."

"No, it's not at all. I'm super impressed." I shake my head a bit and pick at a place where the caulk is peeling on the side of the pool, making a mental note to tell the maintenance guys about it. Tess leans back on her palms, turning her face up like she's trying to wring sunshine out of the clouds. "Do you think you and Patrick will stay together?" I ask, then immediately feel awkward about it—feeling like a creep and not even knowing why I'm asking, exactly. "Sorry." I look down at my feet. "That's totally weird and over the line."

Tess shakes her head. "No, it's fine; I'd be curious, too. I think so, yeah. We've talked about it a little. He's not sure where he'll be, but it's not so far from there to here." She wrinkles her nose a bit. "Did you guys used to talk about going to college together?" she asks me. "As long as we're, you know, being over the line?"

That makes me smile—it *is* weird, no question, but in some strange kind of way I appreciate it. "Yeah," I tell her, "we did."

Tess nods at that, seemingly unbothered. "Sun's coming out, " is all she says.

DAY 45

My first act with Patrick as People Who Are Trying to Hang Out is to meet for the world's most awkward run around the lake, a couple of boats bobbing along in the current and a woodpecker knocking around in the trees. On one hand, we don't actually have to talk very much, so that's helpful. On the other, while the running itself isn't the painfest it was when I first got back from Bristol, trying to keep pace with him makes me realize how easy I've been taking it.

"You good?" Patrick asks, not looking at me.

"I'm good," I say, eyes straight ahead.

It didn't used to be this uncomfortable—nothing about being with Patrick used to be uncomfortable, but running around in particular was part of our everyday: racing to the tree line at the edge of the farm and back, suicides up and down the bleachers at the high school on weekends.

Sometimes Patrick won, and sometimes I did. As far as I know neither one of us ever threw a race.

Now I ignore the burn in my leg muscles and keep going. I feel hyperconscious of how soft and out of shape I probably still look in my leggings and tank top, like there's a layer of pudding under my clothes. I wonder if he's been running every day since he got back, too, both of us orbiting circles around each other all over town. The idea makes me lonely and sad. Then again, he's got Tess, doesn't he? Tess, who I drove home from work last night; Tess, who put her flip-flops up on my dashboard and sang along in the world's most off-key, unselfconscious voice to the Miley Cyrus song on the radio.

Tess, who I definitely didn't tell about this little outing.

"Way to be," Patrick says when we're finished, throwing me a high five to say good-bye like he's congratulating me on something, even though it doesn't feel like we've accomplished anything at all. "We should do it again."

I shake my head in wonder as I watch him jog away from me, back in the direction of the farmhouse. The sun feels prickly and hot at the back of my neck.

DAY 46

"You should pay them," I argue after dinner the next evening, sprawled on the grass in my mom's damp backyard. A couple of fireflies flicker lazily in the pine trees. "They're doing a job, they should get paid."

"They're college athletes!" Gabe says stubbornly. "You get a scholarship, that's the compensation. If you don't go to class and *use* it, that's—"

"You can't go to class and use it!" I fire back. I like this, arguing with him good-naturedly. Patrick and I agreed on everything . . . until the moment we emphatically didn't. "You've got practice, like, eighty hours a week; the coaches actually *tell* you not to study and focus on your games."

Gabe makes a face. "I get paid eight bucks an hour to swipe cards at the student center at school," he tells me, warm ankle nudging against mine. "You want to pay them eight bucks an hour?"

"Maybe!" I say, laughing. "Better than not getting paid at all."

"Uh-huh." Gabe grins at that, ducking his face close to mine in the darkness. "This is a stupid argument," he decides, bumping our noses together. "Let's make out instead."

"You wish," I tell him, climbing up onto my knees so I can reach over him and grab the bag of gummy worms he brought me—the movement ignites a searing ache in both thighs, though, and I groan a little bit.

"Easy, tiger," Gabe says, reaching for the bag himself and handing it over. "Been running a lot, huh?"

"I—yeah." *With your brother*, I almost tell him—*could* tell him, could just slip it in right now and it wouldn't have to be weird, it could be normal, like I have nothing to hide there at all.

I *don't* have anything to hide.

Do I?

"Could rub," Gabe offers now, pulling my calves into his lap and squeezing. I smirk at him in the blue twilight and keep quiet, tilt my head back and enjoy the view.

DAY 47

I'm supposed to go shopping for dorm stuff with Imogen in the morning—she has a very specific type of shower caddy in mind—but Patrick texts me to run again, so I ask her if we can reschedule for the afternoon and lace up my ancient sneakers even though the sky above the lake is purple-gray and heavy-looking, threatening a biblical kind of rain. Sure enough, we're only a quarter mile in when it starts to pour.

I'm ready to turn back, but Patrick raises his eyebrows like a challenge: "Wanna keep going?" he asks, and I nod.

The rain falls cold and fast and steady. We run. Water soaks my tank top, trickles into my socks; it flicks off my eyelashes and skids in rivulets down my spine. Suddenly, I'm taken down in a giant mud-slick, legs sliding right out from underneath me as I land on my ass and *hard*. For a second, I just sit there, shocked.

"You okay?" Patrick calls, stopping two strides ahead and tracking back to stand beside me, New Balances making deep prints in the muck. He reaches out to pull me to my feet.

"I—" I stare at his hand like it's a foreign object, something from another planet entirely. The night on my front lawn not withstanding, he's barely touched me at all since I've been back.

"I got it," I tell him, conducting a quick inventory of my arms and legs and deciding it's just my pride that's broken. He's seen me wipe out a million times before, but this feels different. "I'm fine. I'm just slow and fat now, these things happen."

"You're what?" Patrick's eyes are the same color as the heavy gray sky. "Are you crazy?"

"Oh God, please don't." I scramble to my feet and slip again like something out of effing Laurel and Hardy, the black-and-white movies Chuck used to lose his shit laughing over when we were little kids. I'm about to do something and I honestly don't know if it's going to be laugh or cry. God, I am so, so tired. "I wasn't fishing. I don't need you to, like, give me a sad compliment or whatever. I'm just saying, I'm sitting in this mud puddle because I'm fat and slow now. In case it's somehow escaped your attention."

Patrick shakes his head, annoyed. "You're sitting in the mud puddle because you won't take my hand, Mols."

"I mean, fine," I say, susceptible to logic and willing to concede that particular point, if not the larger one. "But—"

"And, like, clearly you're beautiful, so I don't know what the hell you're—"

"*Patrick.*" I blurt his name before I can stop myself, stupid and unthinking—he shuts up right away, and it feels like a lighter that's almost out of juice catching just for a second, that spark that's there and gone.

"Take my damn hand, will you?" Patrick asks quietly. "Please."

I take it.

"Thanks," I tell him, shocked and hopeful. Patrick nods and doesn't say a thing. It's still pouring as we take off again, a cautious jog that builds to something faster: just me and him and the sound of the rain in the treetops, running through the end of the world.

DAY 48

Gabe's still in the shower when I come by to pick him up for dinner and Julia's prowling around the downstairs of the house like a hungry tiger at the Catskill Game Farm, so I creep outside to the back of the farmhouse and sit in a lawn chair to wait. Connie's roses are lush and sprawling in the summer heat, their heavy heads fat and drooping like Penn's sleepy kids at the end of the day. The vegetable garden is bright with still-green tomatoes, slowly ripening summer squash.

I squint at the barn at the far edge of the property, its peeling paint and crooked doorways. The roof seems like it's close to caving in. I wonder if I'll ever be able to look at the sloping roof and not remember the first time Patrick kissed me, bundled up in heavy-duty sleeping bags in the loft that's never been used for anything but storage and sleepovers. It was fall, too cold to be camping, but that was right after Chuck died and nobody was keeping much of an eye on Patrick to begin with: Gabe ran all over Star Lake with every girl in the sophomore class, it seemed like, and Julia had one disciplinary notice sent home after another. Patrick was quiet, though, flying under the radar.

Patrick had me.

It was October, the smell of things decaying, being absorbed back into the earth. The wind snuck underneath the floorboards, through the hairline seams in the walls—we weren't talking, both of us paging through Chuck's old *National Geographic*s like a couple of nerds, but we were pressed together without even meaning to be, the instinct to get close to wherever it's warm. I could feel his ribs move in and out as he breathed.

"Listen to this," I said distractedly, the bag of Red Vines crinkling as I rolled over to face him—it was an article about a tortoise called Lonesome George, the very last one of his species. When I looked up at Patrick, Patrick was already looking at me.

Emily Green would have been surprised by what happened next, probably. She would have been prettily baffled, would have never seen this coming, but the truth is of course I had: for weeks and months and maybe years, like if you'd put your ear to the ground on the day that Patrick and I met you would have been able to hear this heading toward us, a rumble from miles and miles away. I'd listened. I'd been paying attention. And when his mouth pressed against mine I wasn't shocked.

It wasn't a long kiss; it wasn't a make-out; just barely a press like, *there you are*. *There you are*, I thought, looking at him in the glow of the cage light hanging on the wall, the camping lantern that had been his dad's along with the magazines.

There you are.

"Hey," Gabe says now, side door clattering shut behind him as he crosses the patio in shorts and a button-down. He smells like soap and water, clean and new, and just like that all my memories of Patrick evaporate like steam off a damp hot sidewalk. That was then, I remind myself. This is now. "Sorry about that. I just had the craziest phone call."

"Dial a date?" I ask cheerfully.

"Oh, you're a comedian." Gabe offers one big hand to pull me to my feet. "No, so Notre Dame does this program with a bunch of different hospitals, right? Like a semester abroad, I guess, but for premed people and you change bedpans or whatever instead of drinking your face off in Prague. Anyway, I applied in the spring and they wait-listed me, but I guess some kid just dropped out, and there's a spot open at MGH."

I blink at him as I reach for the handle on the passenger side of Volvo, baked warm by an afternoon in the sun. "MGH?" I ask, trying to suss out the acronym. "Is that . . . ?"

"Massachusetts General Hospital, yeah," Gabe says, raising his eyebrows across the roof. "In Boston."

"Really?" I ask, taken aback—but not, I realize, necessarily in a bad way. "You could be in Boston in the fall?"

"Oh, you're freaking out now," Gabe says, laughing as he turns the key in the ignition. "You're all, *shit*, I was planning to use this kid for his body all summer and then never talk to him again, what the hell am I gonna do now?"

That makes me laugh, too. "I would love to have you changing bedpans in my new home city. Boston bedpans, I hear, are the best in the land."

"That's what you hear, huh?" Gabe's still grinning. "It's not definite or anything yet. I gotta drive up there in a couple of days, have the interview. I guess it's between me and one other guy."

I nod and let myself picture it for a minute—Gabe and me walking through Boston Common, hanging out and listening to the buskers at Faneuil Hall. It's not what I'd pictured when I sent in my acceptance last April. But I like the way it feels. "You'll get it," I decide, smiling out the windshield. "You'll see."

DAY 49

There are two texts on my phone when I wake up the following morning, two chimes in a row dragging me out of restless sleep. One's from Gabe, who decided at the last minute to make an actual trip of it and is going to take a few days to visit school friends on his way back from his interview: *I'll miss you, Molly Barlow. Will tell Boston you say hi.*

The second text is from Patrick: *run tomorrow?*

I stare at the screen for a moment, the messages stacked one on top of the other like some cruel joke at the hands of the universe.

Then I turn it off and go back to sleep.

DAY 50

I meet up with Patrick again the following morning; it's easier to keep up with him than it was last time, the rhythmic thud of rubber on earth and the breath steady in and out of my lungs. We're halfway around the lake when Patrick stops cold.

"I was trying not to lose you," he says suddenly, and from the tone in his voice I know he's been thinking about it for longer than since we started this run. "That's why I was such a dick about Bristol. I was trying not to lose you." He shakes his head. Then, before I can rub two wits together: "But I lost you anyway."

"You didn't," I blurt, fast and immediate like I think I'm on *Family Feud*. I'm breathing hard, from the run or from something else. "You didn't lose me, I'm right here, I—"

"Mols." Patrick screws up his face a bit, like, *It's me, please cut the crap*. "You moved all the way across the country to get away, you know? And now you date my damn brother." He scrubs a hand through his curly hair. "That's a thing I knew, too, not for nothing. That he liked you. He liked you for a long time."

I blink. I think of what Gabe said at Knights of Columbus, that he'd thought about me on the Ferris wheel. "You did?"

Patrick shrugs his broad shoulders, rolls his storm-gray eyes. "Everybody knew," he says.

"I didn't."

"Yeah." He glances out at the lake, back at me, out at the lake again. "I know. And I didn't want you to find out."

"Why?"

Patrick lets out a breath. "Trying to stave off the inevitable, I guess. I don't know." He sounds annoyed that I'm making him talk about it, like he's not the one who brought it up to begin with. "But Gabe's Gabe."

"What does that mean, 'Gabe's Gabe'?" I ask, although I already kind of know what Patrick's getting at. Probably if I was smart I wouldn't push.

"Molly—" Patrick breaks off, irritated. It's humid today, and his tan skin is damp with perspiration. He's standing so close I can feel the heat. "I don't know. Forget it. Can we just go?"

Did you think I wouldn't want you if I knew I could have your brother? I want to ask him. *Did you worry I was settling for second best?* "Talk to me," I prod him. "Whatever else happened, you used to be able to talk to me."

"I used to be able to do a lot of things," Patrick snaps, a flash of temper. "Can you leave it?"

"No!" I exclaim. It feels like we're tossing a ball back and forth, like Hot Potato, like neither one of us wants to be the one left holding it when it explodes. I bailed on coffee with Imogen to come here. I still haven't told Gabe what's going on. "Tell me." Then, when he doesn't answer: *"Patrick."*

"Mols." Patrick's eyes are darker than I've ever seen them, that fleck in the iris like the North Star. "Let it go, okay?"

Things get weirdly quiet then, the trees and the lake and how empty it is out here, no tourists or anyone to see. Patrick's face is tipped down close to mine. He wants to kiss me, I can tell he does, both of us standing here practically panting. He wants to kiss me so, so bad.

I know because I want to kiss him, too.

"We should go," Patrick says, shaking his head and turning away from me. He takes off so fast I lose my breath.

DAY 51

Tess calls early the next morning—an actual phone call, not just a text, so I fish my phone out of my pocket with the tips of two wet fingers: One of the dishwashers at the Lodge broke overnight and flooded half the kitchen, so it's kind of an all-hands-on-deck situation. "Hey," I tell her, wedging the skinny phone uncomfortably between my ear and my shoulder and dunking some coffee cups in the first basin of the three-bay sink. A wet towel squelches under my feet. "Are you here?"

"No," Tess tells me. "I'm supposed to be on at noon, but I don't think I can come."

"Okay," I say slowly. Something in her voice doesn't sound right. I glance across the kitchen at Jay, who's working on some scrambled eggs for the breakfast buffet. "You sick?"

"Patrick broke up with me."

I freeze where I'm standing, two hands in the sudsy water like I'm aiming to start the second flood of the day, enough water to sweep the whole Lodge out into the lake. A low, nauseated chill swoops through my gut, my brain pinging out in a hundred different directions.

Patrick broke up with her.

"Oh my God," I manage finally, the first coherent thought I manage to put together being that I need to act normal here, and the second being that there's no reason for me to feel one way or another, beyond the fact that Patrick and Tess are my friends. I'm not allowed to be invested. I'm *definitely* not allowed to be so immediately, physically *relieved*. "Are you okay?"

"I—yeah. No. I don't—" Tess breaks off. "I'm sorry, it's totally weird that I'm calling you, I just figured maybe you could tell Penn for me." Another pause. "I mean, that's not even totally true, I just kind of wanted to talk to you about it, you know? Since you—" She stops again. "Sorry."

"Since I'm also somebody who's been dumped by Patrick Donnelly?" I supply, hoping if I can kid around about it Tess won't guess at the taste of my heart pulsing at the back of my mouth, thick and coppery. I think of yesterday on the trail with Patrick, the weird, charged, electrical moment that passed between us.

Tess is laughing a little, this phlegmy, snotty sound like she's been crying. "Yeah," she admits. "I guess that's why."

The urge to hang up and call Patrick feels like trying to hold back a cough: to hear his side of the story and make sure everything's okay with him. I try to think quickly. "You want me to call Imogen? We'll do a girls' night tomorrow? We'll go to Crow Bar or something. I'll try really hard not to get anything thrown on me this time."

"Yeah?" Tess says, sounding hopeful. "You want to? I mean, you don't have plans with Gabe or something?"

The sound of Gabe's name is startling: For a second I forgot he existed entirely, let alone that we're together. God, what's *wrong* with me? My heart is rattling away inside my chest like a shopping cart with a bum wheel. "No," I tell Tess, trying to keep my voice even. "No, he's in Boston for an interview. We'll go just the three of us; it'll be fun."

"Okay," Tess says, sounding a little less wobbly than she did at the start of this conversation. I feel wobbly in the freaking extreme. "Crow Bar, then. Nineish?"

I promise her I'll be there and plunge two more glasses into the soapy water. I leave my phone in the freezer for the rest of the day.

DAY 52

I don't think I've ever done a proper girls' night, but Imogen's an old pro, the smell of steam and burning as she flatirons my hair and a bottle of Apple Pucker she pulled from her purse like Mary Poppins, witchy green and syrupy like melted-down lollipops. Her mom's away at a women's retreat in Hudson. Nobody dresses up to go to Crow Bar, but Imogen insists we should anyway, pulling dress upon lacy dress from the depths of her walk-in closet while Tess and I watch from the bed, calling out our myriad opinions like something out of a chick flick montage. It feels like the kind of pregame Emily Green would have with her girl-friends, not me with my cat-lady tendencies and long queue full of documentaries about baseball and the history of salt. It's nice.

"Okay," Imogen says, shimmying into a black halter that

makes her look even more like a pinup girl than normal. I've got a stretchy skirt and a silky tank top, the closest I've gotten to a dress since seventh grade—I wasn't exactly in a position to go to prom. "Thoughts?"

"Do it," Tess says cheerfully. She's all smiles and spice tonight, brassy, but her alabaster face was a little puffy when she got here, her already short fingernails bitten down to painful-looking stubs. She still hasn't said what the fight was about, if there even was a fight to begin with. I haven't asked. "Your ass looks great in it. And I wanna go out."

"Well, you best chug that delicious beverage, then," I tell her, nodding at her mostly full juice glass of Apple Pucker with a grimace. I like sweet things, but three sips of this stuff and my teeth feel like they're wearing sweaters. "Bottoms up. Go on, it's right up your alley, it's made of produce and everything."

"Basically a health food." Tess nods resolutely. "To getting dumped by Patrick Donnelly," she says, holding it up for a toast.

"To getting dumped by Patrick Donnelly," I echo, clinking. My laugh sounds strange and hollow, though: The truth is I feel dishonest, this pestering nag at the back of my brain like I'm telling whopper after whopper just by showing up here and being with them. I haven't heard from Patrick since our run the other morning, but suddenly he's closer than he's been in a year and a half.

Tess downs her schnapps and makes a truly hilarious

gross-out face, like she just took a swig of human vomit chased with kerosene. "Let's do this," she orders as she hops off Imogen's bed, teetering a little as she lands. She yanks at the short hem of her emerald-green dress, frowning. "I always feel like a drag queen in heels," she mutters.

"You realize we're gonna look like hookers at Crow Bar," I point out, then: "Drag queen hookers," we say at the same time.

"Oh, you're very funny," Imogen says, rolling her eyes at both of us. "Shut up for a second; I'll call a cab."

At Crow Bar we order shots of fireball whiskey and drop them in glasses of hard cider, a trick Gabe taught me that tastes like apple pie: "Apples are the theme of the night," Imogen observes. "Abraham Lincoln would be so pleased." Then, off our blank stares: "You know, cause of the apple tree?" she asks, looking back and forth between us. "He couldn't cut it down? Or he cut it down and couldn't lie about it?"

"It was a cherry tree," I say at the same time Tess points out, "It was George Washington."

All three of us find this hysterical, for some reason, clustered around a table in the far back near the jukebox, doubled over giggling. "Are we dancing?" Tess asks when the music changes over to the Whitney Houston we plugged in with our fistfuls of quarters. "I'm pretty sure I was promised dancing in my time of need."

"Oh, we're dancing." Imogen grabs me by my wrist and pulls me into the crowd.

I laugh as I thread through the crush along with them, shaking my hair and letting Tess twirl me around, Imogen singing along like we're still in her room and not technically underage in a bar full of people. I feel like I'm having two separate nights, though, like I'm only half-present: The urge to check in with Patrick is constant and physical, like an itch on the bottom of your foot when you can't take your shoes off, or a tickle at the back of your throat.

We head to the bathroom after another round, snaking through the crowd one after another. "How you doing?" Imogen asks Tess, bumping their shoulders together as we wait in the long line. It smells like a sewer. "You hanging in?"

Tess sighs. "Yeah, I'm fine," she says. "I just feel so *stupid*." She leans across the puddle-filled counter and peers at herself in the cloudy mirror, wiping away the mascara that's migrated down underneath her lash line. "At least I didn't sleep with him, I guess."

"You didn't?" I blurt immediately, then cringe. God, how desperate do I sound right now? How gross is it that I care so much if they did or they didn't? Patrick and I never had sex—in a lot of ways our relationship reset when we broke up and got back together, and we were only just headed in that direction again when the article came out at the end of junior year. I was terrified I'd give myself away somehow, that if we did it he'd be able to tell I'd done it before. To his credit, Patrick never pushed. "I mean, not that it's any of my business, sorry."

"Uh-uh." Tess seems unbothered, both by my question and by the fact that we're having this conversation in full earshot of, like, six other women. Possibly she's a little drunk. "I mean, I would have, honestly, but, like . . . He didn't want to. Which, what eighteen-year-old boy in the universe doesn't want to have sex? I'm a pretty girl! I should have known something was weird."

"Maybe his penis is broken," Imogen volunteers helpfully. "Or, like, got accidentally lasered off in a childhood accident."

Tess cracks up. "Laser dick," she says over the sound of a toilet flushing, then heads for the open stall. "That's definitely what the problem was."

Imogen and Tess head to the bar, and I weave my way back to our table in the corner and people-watch for a while. I glance at the beer clock on the far wall. I'm digging through my purse for some Chapstick when I feel the buzz of my phone against the back of my hand, the screen lighting up with Patrick's name.

Hey, is all his text message says.

Shit. I look around like I'm expecting to get caught with contraband. I can see Tess and Imogen leaning over the bar, laughing about something. It's the closest I've come in a year to having friends.

Hey yourself, I key in, chewing my lip like I'm aiming to amputate it. Then: *you okay?*

I'm not expecting to hear back right away, that's for certain. I remember how long it took him to respond after the camping trip, how far we are from the perpetual back-and-forth of a few years ago, our lives one long conversation. It's entirely possible he won't text me back at all. Which is why I'm so surprised when my bag buzzes again less than ten seconds later:

fine, Patrick says, just the one short syllable. Then, a few beats after that: *you doing anything right now?*

I take a deep breath, watching Tess and Imogen make their way back through the crowd in my direction, both of them giggling. Imogen waves like we haven't seen each other in years.

I glance down at my phone again, back up at the two of them.

no, I key in quickly. *What's up?*

DAY 53

"I thought you said you weren't doing anything," Patrick says when I show up at his side door after midnight; I had a cab drop me off at the end of the driveway, told Imogen and Tess I had cramps. There's an empty spot in the muddy driveway where Gabe's Volvo usually sits, tire tracks from where he pulled out to head to Boston. I take a breath and look away, ask myself for the forty-fifth time in the last forty-five minutes what exactly I think I'm doing. "That outfit doesn't look like nothing."

"Well," I tell him, tugging self-consciously at Imogen's clingy black skirt, which is way tighter on me than it would be on her. I shrug inside my slinky gray tank top. "I'm a liar."

"That's a fact," Patrick says, but there's no real heat behind it. Then, a moment later, and so quietly I almost don't even hear: "You look nice."

"Yeah?" That surprises me, how he's got these compliments for me all of a sudden, pulling them out of his back pocket like shiny new coins. When I look up his gaze is dark, almost hungry. Something liquid, an egg maybe, feels like it's cracking open inside my chest. I swallow. "You do, too," I say finally.

Patrick makes a face. "Good try," he says, snorting a little. We're still standing in the Donnellys' doorway, half in the house and half out of it. Everything about us feels like an in-between. *I shouldn't have come here*, I want to tell him, or maybe: *I'm so glad you texted me tonight.*

"Why'd you break up with Tess?" is what comes out.

Patrick shakes his head, this face like that's the obvious question and an impossible one, like if I have to ask there's no way for me to possibly ever know. "Don't," is all he says.

"Why not?" I can feel the night pressing in behind me, hear the faint buzz of mosquitoes and the far-off hoot of an owl. "I was just with her, she's—"

"You were *with* her?" Patrick asks, eyes widening. *"Why?"*

"Because we're friends!" I retort, crossing my arms over my chest. "I know you hate me and everything, but I'm still allowed to have friends." Not that I deserve them, a sharp voice in my head reminds me. Look where I am right now.

"You know I—" Patrick looks at me like I'm deranged. "Is that what you think? You think I *hate* you? Why the hell am I calling you to come over in the middle of the night, why am I breaking up with my fucking *girlfriend* if I hate you, Mols?"

I start, an electrical shock jolting through me. Did he just say—? "Because—" I break off, try again. Suddenly, his face is so, so close. "Because—"

That's when Patrick kisses me.

It's clumsy at first, his face butting at mine so hard and unexpected he almost knocks me backward. I taste blood and can't tell if it's his or it's mine. It used to be that Patrick was kind of shy when he kissed me, all bashful and hesitant like he was scared he was going to break me if pushed even a hair too hard.

This . . . does not feel like that.

This feels like a fire in the forest, like one of those carnival rides where the floor drops out and centrifugal force is the only thing keeping you stuck to the wall. Patrick's hands are everywhere at once. I wind my arms around his neck to keep steady, heart slamming with a shocking violence against my rib cage and his sharp teeth biting at the edges of my tongue. His smell is the only thing that's the same. I fist my hands in his shirt and lean into him, standing on my tiptoes to get as close up into his space as I can manage. I'd climb inside him if I could, set up house in there, walk around for the rest of the summer. Walk around for the rest of my life.

And then I remember Gabe.

"Stop," I say before I realize I'm going to do it, heart pounding in a different way altogether, pulling back all at once. "I just," I say, holding my hands up in a panicky flutter. "I can't. Patrick. I can't. Not when—I can't do this again, please."

Patrick looks completely baffled for a moment. Then his eyes narrow. "Because of my *brother*?" he demands, backing off fast enough that it feels like he's shot me, a ricochet and shatter in my bones. I flinch. "Are you serious right now?"

"Patrick, please," I start, but I can feel him receding, feel that I've ruined this all over again, the whole world immolating in front of my eyes. The panic is hot and awful and immediate. I grab his arm before he can turn away.

"Wait," I demand, bossy and urgent. I press my traitorous mouth to his one more time. Patrick makes a sound, a hum or a growl. Kisses back until I can't imagine anything but this.

DAY 54

I wake up before sunrise with a slamming headache, a feeling like my heart's been juiced:

What did I do what did I do what did I do?

DAY 55

I stand in the shower for an hour and fifteen minutes, the water as hot as I can possibly stand it. I want to burn off the top layer of my skin.

DAY 56

Elizabeth and Michaela both burst into giggles when I pass
them in the employee hallway on my way into work the next
morning, so I guess I shouldn't be surprised when I get to
my locker and find a Post-it with a drawing of a stick-figure
girl I'm assuming is me giving blow jobs to a gaggle of stick-
figure guys. Right away, I feel that tightness in my face.

It's the same garden-variety nastiness they've been
flinging my way all summer, I remind myself—there's no
way they could possibly know what happened with me and
Patrick—but still I bolt upstairs and hide in the office for
as long as my shift lasts, realphabetizing the files in Penn's
cabinets and watching *The Blue Planet* on the computer.
Every time I hear someone coming down the hallway, I
flinch.

DAY 57

I'm worried I'm going to run into Patrick if I go my usual route down by the lakefront, so instead I do a couple of laps around the track at the high school, everything closed up tight and empty for the summer like something out of the zombie apocalypse. It's strange to be back here, this place I didn't graduate from, where everything finished up without me while I hid out on the other side of the country.

Still, the track is warm and solid under my feet, and my legs feel strong and easy: My mind rests calm and quiet and blank. I'm jogging back up through the parking lot when I stop so fast I almost trip.

There's Julia, parked in the Donnelly Bronco, her raven hair up in a knot on top of her head: She's got her hands on either side of Elizabeth Reese's pretty, angular face, their mouths pressed together like there's literally nobody else in the world.

I stare for a minute. I blink. It feels like the twist at the end of one of my mom's books or that movie where it turns out the guy was dead the whole time, a million throwaway half clues clicking together all at once: how Julia and Elizabeth are always together, just like Patrick and I used to be. How surprised Gabe looked at the beginning of the summer when I asked him if he and Elizabeth were dating. It occurs to me, not for the first time, that you can never really know what anybody's got hidden in the back of her secret heart.

I mean to escape before anyone sees me: I wonder who, if anyone, knows. I want to slip away and leave her to it, to whatever she's figuring out or already understands, but I'm too slow and too stupid just like always, and a second later she pulls back and blinks alert.

Fuck. I see Julia's mouth move more than I hear it; there's my answer, then, about who knows or might not. I feel myself blush, caught staring like a creep. I want to promise her I won't tell anyone—that I understand things being private, and I'm not the kind of girl who would blab. I never get the chance, though, because Julia's throwing the truck into drive and peeling off toward the exit, her cold gaze locked on mine.

DAY 58

The doorbell rings twice and insistent as I'm changing the water in Oscar's doggie bowl. I'm thinking it's Alex coming to let me know he's here to fix the loose shutter my mom's been complaining about, but there's Julia standing on the other side of the screen door, tank top and a floaty scarf and dark hair in a complicated set of braids pinned on top of her head, like Heidi.

I stand there. I gape at her. She's got her jaw set, hands clenched into tight little fists at her sides: She might as well have them raised like an old-fashioned boxer—*Put 'em up*.

"I'm not going to say anything," I tell her, not bothering to open the door and let her in here. The last thing in the world I have the energy for is a fight. "If that's why you came."

"I—" For a second Julia looks totally confused, like she showed up to a war with tanks and cannons and found me watching soap operas and filing my nails. "You're not?"

"*No,*" I say immediately, feeling a surge of irritation—like that was ever even a question. She *knows* me. She knows I'm not the kind of person who'd go yelling all over creation about something that's none of my business to begin with, especially something as loaded as this is. "I'm not."

Julia blinks, still with that startled expression on her face like I've thrown her off entirely. She thinks so little of me. "Okay," she says after a moment. "Thank you. Elizabeth told me about the Post-it the other day; she says she's sorry." Then: "Nobody else knows about us except Gabe."

She stays still on the porch for a moment, looking at me through the old screen door. I remember how much pleasure she's taken in ripping me to ribbons for the better part of the last year and a half. I remember Chuck strapping her into a life jacket on the *Sally Forth.* "You know your mom wouldn't care, right?" I say, not entirely sure why I'm sticking my nose in. Maybe because her family was my family, once upon a time. "I mean. Not that I'm a person you want to take advice from, probably. But she'd be happy that you were happy, that's all. Patrick, too."

Julia crosses her arms, shifts her weight a bit. Her nail polish is a screaming neon red. "I know that," she says, sounding a little defensive. "Of course Patrick wouldn't care that me and Elizabeth are—whatever. He just doesn't *like* her. He thinks she's vapid, and that I'm vapid for hanging out with her, and I just—you know how Patrick is."

That surprises me—I *do*; of course I do. I know how talking to Patrick requires a certain kind of courage, how it can make you feel stubborn and shy. That's what got me where I am in the first place after all. It was so much easier to tell a secret to Gabe.

I want to explain that to Julia all of a sudden, want to tell her how everything happened to begin with, but I know it's a lost cause before I even open my mouth. "Yeah" is all I tell her. "I know how Patrick is." Then, as a kind of offering: "Elizabeth's pretty."

"Oh, God, *enough*." Julia rolls her eyes at me, shaking her head. "We're not friends anymore, okay? You don't have to, like, try and bond with me over liking girls. I came here to make sure your freaking mom wasn't going to write a book about the lesbian down the road, that's all. We good?"

Julia Donnelly, ladies and gentlemen. I don't know why I expected anything else.

"Yeah," I promise, shaking my head a little. It's all I can do not to grin. "We're good."

DAY 59

I've been pretty much entirely off the grid since Crow Bar—since *Patrick*—hiding in the office at work to avoid running into Tess, and coming straight home at night to work my way through documentaries about girl boxers and the Louisiana Purchase. *how're your lady parts???* Imogen inquires on a group message, and Tess chimes in with an emoji face that's got two *X*s for eyes: *Did you die of cramps?*

The fact that I've got friends who care enough to check in on my imaginary period makes me hate myself even more than I already do, both for the lie and for what happened after I told it. Julia's right: I don't deserve anything good.

I'm alive, I text them back, the only truth I seem to be able to manage, then turn my phone off and hide from the world for one more day.

DAY 60

Gabe stopped off to see some school friends in Rhode Island on the way back from Boston; he gets back in the morning and texts to say he's going to come meet me at work at the end of the day. I spend my entire shift dreading it, guilt and shame eating at my insides like somehow I swallowed a mouthful of the chlorine we use at the pool. Thoughts tumble around in my brain, wild and overheated like clothes in a dryer—by the time I punch my time card and pull my purse out of my locker, I feel like I'm legit about to be sick.

Then, though—

Then I see Gabe.

He's standing outside in the parking lot, all tan summer skin and a soft blue T-shirt, car keys dangling lazily from one hand. "Hey, Molly Barlow," he says, grinning across the blacktop slow and easy.

I launch myself right into his arms.

It's *insane*, the effect Gabe has on me—like a storm at sea clearing, like a hurricane calming down. The churning in my stomach disappears the moment he catches me and all of a sudden everything seems so enormously obvious. He seems so enormously *right*. There's nothing tortured or painful about being with him. Everything about him is easy and good.

"Hey, you," Gabe says, laughing, lifting me off my feet a little. His arms feel like a life preserver, feel safe. "Missed me, huh?"

"Yeah." I clamp my hands over his ears and stamp a kiss on his mouth, decisive. "How'd it go?"

"It went okay, I think," Gabe says, setting me down gently and lacing his fingers through mine. "Actually, I think it went really, really well."

"It did?" That makes me smile. "Think you're gonna get it?"

Gabe shrugs, grinning mischievously. "We'll see."

"We will," I agree. I can picture it now, just like I could before he left but somehow forgot while he was away from me—the two of us sitting in coffee shops or huddled in dark Harvard bars, riding the T over the Charles River with the city lights winking in the distance. What was I trying to do with Patrick the other night, prove that I didn't deserve this?

I tilt my face up to Gabe's, his hair gleaming golden in the late afternoon sunlight. "I'm really glad you're back."

DAY 61

The florist we use for the lobby screws up and sends two dozen extra gladiolas, which are Connie's favorite, so I bundle them up in paper towels and bring them by the Donnellys' after work. I've been thinking about her, about all of them, the secrets they keep from one another. They used to feel like such a solid unit of measure, the ideal family. They used to make me feel so safe.

"My God, Molly," Connie says when she answers the door in her mom jeans and her work shirt, the baffled smile turning her face young and pretty. "What are these for?"

I shrug, feeling shy and awkward—I purposely picked a time I was pretty sure none of her offspring would be around, but I feel caught out and exposed anyway, like possibly this was a giant overstep. Back when *Driftwood* first came out and everything unspooled around me like somebody dropping a ball of yarn, I used to imagine Connie calling or coming to my house to take me out for coffee and waffles with whipped cream, to dispense some kind of sage motherly advice. She didn't, of course—close as we were I was never actually a blood daughter, and it was her real kids that I'd screwed with. I don't even know my own mom's favorite flower, I realize now.

"Oh, Molly," Connie says, sounding pleased and resigned in equal measure. The flowers are a bright, screaming pink. "You shouldn't have."

"I know," I say quietly, and we both know I'm not talking about the flowers. I think of the tourist from the Lodge: *It's heartbreaking stuff.* "But I did."

"You did, didn't you?" Connie agrees, looking at me with something like kindness. "Thank you."

I'm about to say good-bye and go when Julia appears in the doorway behind her in denim shorts and a plaid button-down, wearing her glasses, which she never does outside the house. "Who is it?" she asks. Then she sees me. "Oh. Hi."

"I was just going," I assure her, taking a step back on the crumbling stoop. "I just—" I motion to the flowers. "Have a good night."

Julia nods but doesn't make any move out of the doorway, looking at me for a long moment like she's considering something. I brace myself, a thousand unpleasant possibilities cycling through my brain.

"You should stay for dinner," she announces.

For a moment I just blink at her, baffled. I hallucinated, I must have. "I *should*?"

"Sure," she says, turning around and heading toward the kitchen, the long sharp column of her spine. "The boys'll be home soon; we're having tacos. Right, Mom?"

Connie glances from Julia to me and back again, uncertain—wondering, probably, if this is some kind of elaborate plan Julia's got to murder me and hide the body in the barn under some old camping gear. "Right," she says eventually, stepping back with her armful of flowers. "Come on in, Molly."

Which is how I wind up eating tacos at the long farm table in the Donnellys' dining room like somehow I'm thirteen again, only this time it's Gabe sitting beside me on the bench. He grinned a surprised, tickled grin when he came in through the back door and found me chopping onions with his sister, *Rubber Soul* on Connie's bulky, old iPod docked on the counter. "Sneak attack, huh?" he asked, yanking me back against him by my belt loops and kissing the base of my neck when nobody was looking. "Glad you're here."

Patrick ambled in a few minutes later, Julia setting the table and Gabe gone into his bedroom to change. Patrick stopped for a moment in the doorway and stared at me like possibly he'd never laid eyes on me before, like I was strange and potentially dangerous. I hadn't seen him since our messy, confusing middle-of-the-night kiss in the doorway.

"Hey," I said, eyes on his, steady.

"Hey," Patrick said to me, then turned around and walked away.

"Any word from Mass General?" Connie asks Gabe now, spooning some black beans into her taco. All the Donnellys fix them the same way, with a soft shell wrapped around the hard one to keep the whole affair from falling apart once you bite into it. It's an old trick of Chuck's he taught us all when we were small.

Gabe shakes his head and swallows. "Not yet," he says. "They said it could be a couple weeks; I think the other kid was interviewing after me."

My eyes cut across the table at Patrick, the sleeves of his hoodie shoved to his elbows and his freckly forearms, his serious face. He's looking at his taco, not at me. He must know what it'll mean, if Gabe spends this fall in Boston.

Right now he seems totally unbothered, though; when he lifts his head and gazes around the table his eyes are clear. "Boston seems like your kind of place," he tells his brother blandly, then reaches for a serving spoon and refills his plate.

DAY 62

Penn wants me to train a couple of new front desk girls on the database software, so I'm clicking around in her office while she looks over my shoulder periodically, making sure there's nothing I don't understand well enough to explain. "Do we send thank-you cards?" I ask, scrolling through the records and snapping off the end of my Red Vine. Desi is perched quietly on my knee, her dark head bent over a *Little Mermaid* coloring page. "Or, like, could we? At the end of the summer, maybe, a postcard thanking people for staying and inviting them to come back—or, like, a coupon or a discount code or something for in the fall when it's slow?"

Penn's eyebrows shoot up, a grin spreading over her smooth brown face. "Look at you with your thinking cap on," she says, nodding. "Wanna cost it out?"

"Sure," I say, smiling back at her enthusiasm, shifting

Desi to my opposite knee. She's been sticking pretty close lately, hooking her small fingers in my back pocket as I walk the hallways in the morning and buckling herself into the backseat of my car when Penn sends me into town to run errands. I like her spry, quiet company. I like the skinny-but-solid weight of her little-kid body in my lap. "I'll get it to you tomorrow."

"Sounds good. You're feeling better, then?" she asks, leaning against the edge of the desk and studying me. "That didn't get past me, all that weirdness with you last week."

"I—I'm sorry," I say, embarrassed. "It was personal stuff; I was trying to keep it separate. Were there things that didn't get done?"

Penn shakes her head. "You were fine. You just seemed a bit off, was all. Like you didn't want to be spending a whole lot of time outside this office." She cocks her head to the side, eyes narrowing. "Those two girls who work in the dining room, Michaela and what's her face, the other one. They giving you a hard time?"

I shake my head. Actually, the truth is that since Elizabeth's little drawing they've pretty much laid off lately, leaving me mostly to my own devices with only the occasional nasty look to deflect. There's no way I can tell Penn that I actually spent all of last week dodging *Tess*. "It's fine," I promise. "It's all resolved now."

"Okay." Penn nods, brushing her hands off like they might have some dirt on them, case closed, then. "Good.

You wanna go run by the kitchen, make sure the guys all got their breaks?"

"Sure thing. What do you say, Des?" I ask her, easing her off my lap and onto the carpet. "You wanna go for a walk?" Desi hops up piggyback, and we head out into the lobby. When we round the corner there's Tess in her red lifeguard bathing suit and a pair of mesh shorts, whistle hooked on a long nylon cord she's spinning around two fingers. "Oh, hey, there you are," she says, "I was looking for you this morning. Hi, Desi." She grins at the forty pounds of kid peering over my shoulder curiously. Then, to me: "I have to tell you something, and I feel stupid about it. Or, like, I'm actually really happy about it? But I feel stupid. "

"Okay . . ." I say uncertainly, boosting Des up a bit higher on my shoulders. She's slipping. "What's up?"

"Patrick and I kind of got back together last night."

"Ow!" I flinch as Desi catches a hunk of my hair in the elastic of her shiny plastic bracelet, yanking hard. "Easy, kid." I set her down while we get untangled, eyes watering at the sting in my scalp, though in truth I'm grateful for the distraction and the half beat it gives me to rearrange my face into something more appropriate than my gut reaction.

Back together.

Patrick and Tess.

"Sorry," I say, standing upright again; Desi scampers across the lobby after Virgo, the Lodge's cranky orange cat. Tess is looking at me expectantly. "That's . . . great!"

I manage. I think of how strange it seemed that Patrick was so unbothered about Gabe going to Boston—about Gabe and *me*—at dinner last night. I guess it wasn't actually strange at all.

"I feel like the Girl Who Cried Breakup," Tess explains, shaking her head a little. "Or a traitor to the sisterhood or something."

"What sisterhood is that?" I ask, trying to sound jokey and cool about it. "The International League of Patrick's Ex-Girlfriends?"

"Exactly." Tess smiles. "I made him suffer, for what it's worth. But he showed up and said all this amazing stuff about, like, the future, and I just . . . I don't know. It felt good, you know? It felt right."

I twist my face into a smile I hope looks genuine. Because this is a good thing, isn't it? What happened with me and Patrick while he and Tess were broken up was an aberration, the worst kind of self-sabotage, and I want to put it behind me forever. Here's solid, unequivocal proof that Patrick does, too. I made my choice, and so did Patrick. "I do."

DAY 63

It's Imogen's birthday, so we wolf down a truckload of pizza at Donnellys' and then head for the woods beside the lake, a cooler of watery Bud Light hidden under a blanket in Gabe's station wagon and Tess's iPod sitting in a red plastic Solo cup to amplify the sound. Handsome Jay made cupcakes, which strikes me as incredibly freaking dear.

It's a pretty big crowd, us and Jake and Annie and a bunch of Imogen's French Roast girlfriends; Julia and Elizabeth were hanging out at the pizza place and deigned to tag along for the ride. "I like those jeans," Julia tells me, popping the top off her bottle and nodding at my holey Levi's. Then, off what must be my vaguely stunned expression: "No, Molly, I'm not hitting on you. You can relax."

"That's not what—" I begin, shaking my head quickly. Julia only smirks.

I'm headed to the cooler for a beer of my own when Patrick grabs my arm like it's an emergency. "What?" I demand with alarm. He doesn't answer, just yanks me back behind a giant oak where no one can see us, dark enough that I can barely see *him*.

"What the hell are you doing?" I open my mouth to say but never get the words out because right away he's kissing me hard just like the other night on his doorstep, hot and messy, his tongue sliding into my mouth. He tastes like beer and like Patrick. His hands burn like brands through my shirt.

I should push him away. Oh my God, I *need* to push him away, Tess and Gabe are twenty feet from where we're standing, on top of which it's wrong, it's *terrible*, but it's like I'm outside my body watching myself do this horrible fucking thing and I can't stop, the bark of the oak tree scraping roughly at the skin of my back and the sting as Patrick bites down on my bottom lip. In some enormously messed-up way, the pain almost feels good.

Not almost. It *does* feel good.

Patrick doesn't say anything, just keeps on kissing me, nudging his knee between my thighs and rocking a little, all this heat bleeding through his clothes and mine. He reaches up and cups the back of my skull so it doesn't hit the tree trunk, surprisingly gentle, then tilts my head back and sucks my neck so hard I'm almost sure he's going to leave a mark. It feels like there's a series of bombs going off one after another inside my body, like somehow he improvised a chain of explosions along my spine when I wasn't paying attention.

I don't know how long it goes on for—it feels like hours, like time's bent backward on itself, but in reality it's probably less than a minute or two before Patrick pulls away from me fast and all at once, leaves me gasping. "We gotta get back," he says quietly, reaching up and wiping his hand across his mouth. "You ready?"

"I—" I'm breathing so hard I don't know if I can stand fully upright. I have no idea what just happened here—what I just *let* happen here. "Seriously?"

Patrick looks at me for a moment, unreadable. "Come on," is all he says, tipping his head in the direction of the party. I can hear the high, tickled trill of Imogen's laugh. I close my eyes and count to ten, try to collect myself. When I open them again Patrick's gone.

DAY 64

The house is quiet when I come downstairs for a snack, but there's my mom, watching *Tootsie* on the couch with our old blue quilt piled over her, a bowl of garlic-Parmesan popcorn in a ceramic bowl in her lap. I haven't thought about that popcorn in a full year, but my mouth waters at the smell of it—it's a Diana Barlow specialty, one of my favorite foods from when I was little. She used to let me eat it for dinner sometimes, for a treat.

I stall out in the doorway for a minute, watching as Dustin Hoffman wobbles around on-screen in a pair of high heels, not wanting to talk to her but not really wanting to go back upstairs, either. I don't even think she's noticed me standing there until she holds the bowl out in my direction.

"You want to come and have some popcorn?" she asks

me, sharp eyes still trained on the TV. "Or you want to just stand there and lurk?"

I open my mouth to tell her I was planning on lurking, then shut it again just as fast. Suddenly, I am so, so tired. My mouth feels like it's burning from the kiss Patrick branded there. My chest aches like my legs after yesterday's run.

"Popcorn could be good," I admit finally, shuffling into the living room, the knotty floors creaking noisily under my feet. My mom nods her curly blond head without comment. I perch on the edge of the slouchy leather couch, trying without a ton of success not to get swallowed by the cushions. When she offers me the blanket, I take that, too. The TV chatters quietly. I breathe.

DAY 65

"—and she realizes, as the door locks behind her, that *she just left a bag of poop on the kitchen counter.*"

Imogen, Gabe, and I stare at Jay for a moment before bursting into laughter so loud and so horrified that people clear across Bunchie's turn to look at us. "That's an urban legend!" I protest through my giggles, half-afraid I'm going to snort my milk shake right out my nose. "That's an urban legend, uh-uh, I'm Googling it. No way."

"Go ahead and Google it," Jay says magnanimously, picking the last couple of fries off his plate and nodding. "It happened to my cousin's friend."

"Uh-huh." I reach over, snag one of Imogen's pickles. "I . . . think you are full of garbage, but that's also pretty much the best story I've ever heard, so . . ."

Gabe slings his arm over the back of the booth, the

inside of his elbow brushing my hair. "Molly's a skeptic," he says.

"I am a skeptic!" I agree, but in truth at the moment I'm a happy one—if you'd told me at the start of the summer if I could have something like this, a normal night out with my boyfriend and my friends, I would have asked you what exactly you were smoking and where I could get some, too.

Or, okay—not normal, exactly. I try to ignore the sick pit in my stomach every time I remember what happened with Patrick the other night. I think of the slickness of Patrick's warm skin under my fingertips. I think of the clutch of my legs around his waist. I feel like a horror show, I feel like exactly the kind of nightmare Julia thinks I am—tearing through the Donnellys again and again like some kind of natural disaster, a tornado that changed course halfway through and came back for more.

But other than that? Totally normal.

We're debating whether or not to get a round of potato skins for dessert when the door to Bunchie's opens and Patrick and Tess walk in. I feel a quick, violent sandstorm kick up inside my chest—Imogen asked earlier if it was cool to text Tess and tell her where we were and I made a big show of acting cool about it, but after what happened between Patrick and me the other night I told myself there was no way he'd have the balls to tag along.

I must look visibly rattled, because Imogen glances at me quizzically for one sharp second before she recovers, rearranging her features into a wide, friendly smile. "Hi, kids!" she calls gaily. "You just missed Jay's great story about a girl taking a crap on her one-night stand's kitchen counter. Here, come sit."

"She didn't take the crap *on* the counter," Jay protests as we all shift around to make room. Tess slides into the booth next to Imogen, leaving Patrick no place to sit except next to me—once he's there I'm literally sandwiched in between him and his brother, one warm Donnelly on either side of me and quarters so tight I can hardly move my arms. My whole body goes rigid, some small furry animal that senses a predator. Patrick doesn't look at me once. I try not to think of his mouth on mine, the rough scrape of tree bark against my naked back. When I reach for my water glass, I'm so flustered I knock a dirty fork right into his lap.

"Sorry," I mutter as Patrick hands it back to me wordlessly.

"You okay?" Gabe murmurs in my ear. He's got one warm hand on my knee, reassuring. I nod.

We order the potato skins; Tess tells a story about her new roommate from Barnard, who she just friended on Facebook today. Patrick's arm is hot and solid against mine. I think of spring of sophomore year again, the end of May and our third argument in as many days—about stupid, inane stuff, whether or not to go to the underclassman formal or what music to listen to while we studied for chem. This time it had started over plans for the weekend and boomeranged right back to Bristol, just like it had every other afternoon this week. I kept waiting for things to right themselves between us, for this bizarre alternate universe where Patrick and I couldn't be in the same room without arguing to go back to normal.

Also, I was waiting to stop feeling like Arizona might be a really good idea for next fall.

Neither of those things had happened yet.

"Okay." I took a deep breath and I got up off the bed where I was sitting, pacing past the desk and dresser and back again. I knew every last corner of this room: the warped closet door that never quite closed correctly, the stain on the rug from where we'd ground in Play-Doh by mistake when we were seven. It might as well have been my own. I carved a hand through my hair, frustrated. "You don't think we're—" I struggled for a minute, trying to think of how to say it without pissing him off, without making myself more foreign to him than I already seemed to be right now. "You don't think we sometimes, like . . . spend all this time together at the expense of other stuff in our lives?"

Patrick blinked at me. "What?" he asked, shaking his head faintly. "Like, what are you even saying?"

"I'm just asking!" God, he was irritating me so much lately, moody and intractable in a way he'd never been before—or, if he had, in a way that had never, ever been directed at me. I didn't know which one of us was changing. It scared me to think maybe both of us were. "Can we just—"

"Molly, if you want to go to Arizona to run, you should go to Arizona to run." Patrick's voice was flat and careless. "I didn't realize I was holding you back *quite* so hard."

"You're not holding me back!" I burst out. "I'm asking you a question; I'm trying to have a conversation with you. I thought that's what we do: We have conversations. We've been having one long conversation our whole lives and now—"

"Now you're bored, and you want to go have other ones. I get it, kid. I do."

"Can you not finish my sentences, please?"

"Why, is that holding you back, too?"

"Okay, stop it. Just—stop, for a second." I sat down on the floor, back against the doorframe where Chuck had measured how tall we were the whole time we were growing up, pencil lines and his neat, blocky handwriting: *Julia. Patrick. Molly. Gabe.* This was my family, I thought, looking across the room at Patrick's hardened, hurt expression. This would always be my home.

"We wouldn't have to break up," I told him softly, gazing at him across the bedroom. "If I went. That's not what it would mean. We could visit, we could—"

"Yeah." That was the wrong thing for me to say, clearly—I actually watched him shut down then, the angry set of his jaw. "Whatever. Okay. You can leave now, Mols. We're getting nowhere. I'll see you, really."

"Patrick." My eyes widened—I couldn't believe he was

267

doing this again. It was like he was determined to get rid of me any way he could. "Why are you doing this? Can you stop, like, *actively pushing me away*—"

"I'm not pushing, Mols!" His voice cracked then, hoarse and aching. "You want to run so bad? Go run. Seriously. Don't come back."

I blinked. "What does that—?"

"It means this isn't working," Patrick said coldly. "It means we should just be done."

I stared at him for a moment like he was suddenly speaking Mandarin, like he was someone from clear on the other side of the vast, breathing world. "Are you breaking up with me right now?"

"Yeah, Mols," he said, and he sounded like a stranger. "I am."

A burst of laughter rips me out of the memory, spooking me so hard I startle a second time, though at least I don't send any more silverware flying. Gabe's still got his palm on my knee. He squeezes a bit, then slides his hand farther over, fingertips picking at the seam on the inner thigh of my jeans.

That's when Patrick nudges his leg against mine.

I can't tell if he's doing it on purpose at first, just the barest hint of pressure, heat seeping through his layer of denim and mine. I try to concentrate on what Imogen's asking, about who's around to help stretch canvas for her art show, but I feel like I'm listening from the bottom of the lake. My breath comes fast and ragged all of a sudden, and I concentrate on slowing it down so nobody will hear.

The worst part is I can feel myself responding in other ways also, the low swoop of want in my stomach and the skin all over my body tightening up—and I don't even know *who* I'm responding *to*. What is up with me, how *messed up* am I, that I think it might be both of them?

Gabe's fingers play idly along my inseam, oblivious. Patrick pushes a little bit harder now, the muscle of his thigh insistent enough that there's no way it's not intentional. I feel like I'm on fire, engulfed in hideous flame while everyone else sits around and eats French fries. I feel horrified by my body and my heart.

"I gotta pee," I announce, popping up in the booth and cutting Imogen off mid-sentence, scrambling out of the booth and leaving both Donnelly boys behind.

DAY 66

Gabe asks me over for dinner again the next evening—
lasagna this time, a big pan of it baking in the oven, and
Julia and me putting a salad together side by side at the
kitchen counter, lettuce and tomatoes still gritty with the
dirt from Connie's garden.

"Know what I was thinking about?" Julia asks, rinsing
the lettuce under the faucet and tossing it into the spin-
ner. She's wearing a few of Elizabeth's bangles, I notice, the
jingling sound as she moves. "Remember the Year of the
Zucchini?"

"Oh God, I thought we agreed never to speak of that
again." I snort, knife clicking against the cutting board.
The summer we were eleven Connie accidentally grew a
giant bumper crop of the stuff, more than any sane person
would ever want to eat in a lifetime. She put it in literally

everything—normal stuff like soup and bread, but also chocolate chip cookies and once, hauntingly, this gross ice cream she tried to sneak past everyone, like somehow we wouldn't notice. Finally, Chuck rounded up everything that was left and drove Patrick and Julia and I all out to dump the whole lot of it in the lake. "They used to serve it as a side dish at my boarding school all the time and I'd have to, like, avert my eyes when I passed by."

"Did you like it?" Julia asks me, tossing some grated carrot into the salad bowl and raising her eyebrows. "Boarding school, I mean?"

I still can't believe she's talking to me like this, almost exactly like we used to. How many hours did we spend in this kitchen, back before I set the whole world on fire? "Look, Jules," I tell her finally, opening the fridge just like I have a hundred times before, pulling the bottle of salad dressing off the door. "I'm not going to tell anybody about you and Elizabeth, okay? I meant that, I swear."

"Okay . . ." Julia looks at me mildly. "So?"

"So you don't have to be nice to me, okay? If that's why you are. I mean, if you could not key my car again that'd be awesome, but . . . I don't—" I break off, a year's worth of loneliness and humiliation cresting like a wave inside my chest. "I don't know what you're doing."

Julia shrugs then, hopping up on the counter, picking a chunk of tomato out of the bowl. "I don't know what I'm doing, either, honestly," she confesses. "I mean, yeah,

271

part of it's about Elizabeth, I guess. Look. What you did to my family makes me want to rip your face off, Molly. And I'm the one that brought you into it to begin with, and it's like——" She stops, focusing on the middle distance for a second. I wonder if she's remembering like I am, the equal parts Barbie and freeze tag that made up our days together when she and I were little, before Patrick and I became such an exclusive twosome. Then she shakes her head. "Anyway, it's also pretty obvious that Gabe's, like, on his butt for you." Then, a moment later: "I'm sorry about your car."

I huff a quiet laugh at that, shaking my head—it's a thing, it doesn't matter. I'm so tired of being at war. "So what does that mean?" I ask, setting the bottles down on the butcher block, careful. "We're, like—friends again, or something?"

Julia considers me across the kitchen, snaps a bit of carrot between her incisors. "Not a chance," she tells me flatly, and grins.

Patrick doesn't turn up in time for dinner, and I'm grateful—the last thing I want is to sit across from him at the table, pretending there's nothing there. I've been trying to forget what happened on Imogen's birthday. I've been trying not to think about Patrick at all. I should have stopped him—obviously, I should have stopped him, right? What does it say about me that I didn't? I glance at Julia, who's reaching for seconds, think of her pink-highlighter scrawl:

dirty slut

Gabe hands me a hunk of garlic bread. Connie takes a sip of her wine.

It's late when I kiss Gabe good night and head out to the driveway where my car's parked, the constant trilling of crickets and the soggy earth sucking at my feet. I'm digging through my purse for my keys when I notice a light on in the barn at the back of the property, the telltale yellow glow of a camping lantern.

I mean to get into my car and drive off in the darkness.

I take a breath and cross the yard instead.

Sure enough, there's Patrick hanging out on the ratty couch Connie always swore she was going to toss but never did after Chuck died, a mildewy plaid number we used to like to jump on when we were little kids. He's wearing jeans and a hoodie—it's chilly back here, damp air and the smell of wet leaves, the hard-packed dirt floor. He looks up when he hears me, expectant. He's got a fat paperback in one hand.

It's true that I was glad he wasn't at the table for dinner.

But part of me was a little disappointed, too.

"When did you get home?" I ask him now, hovering in the doorway. The night wind blows gently, goose bumps blooming on my arms and legs, all my nerve endings coming online at once. I keep my distance on purpose, crossing my arms like a shield.

Patrick shrugs. "A little while ago."

"Didn't want to come inside?"

"Not particularly," he says.

"Okay." I exhale. I don't know what I'm trying to get from him, exactly—we said we'd be friends, sure, but obviously that's not happening anytime soon. I have no idea what we actually are.

"What are you reading?" I try, motioning to the book he's got his index finger tucked in, marking his place. Patrick holds it up—it's Stephen King, I see from my post by the doorway. *The Stand*. "What's it about?" I ask.

"The end of the world," Patrick says.

My lips twist. "Fitting."

"Uh-huh." Patrick shifts then, feet on the floor to make room for me beside him on the ratty plaid sofa. Against my better judgment, I cross the barn and perch on the arm of it, feet in my boots planted next to Patrick's hip. He looks up at me and raises one elegant eyebrow, so arched that I laugh.

"Shh," he says mildly, but he's got one hand wrapped around my calf and he's tugging and then I'm down on the couch cushions with him, my knee bent and brushing his thigh. "Hi."

"Hi." I huff a breath. "This can't keep happening."

"It can't, huh," Patrick says, not even really a question. His gray eyes are latched on mine.

"No," I insist, shaking my head. "Patrick—"

"Did he just kiss you good night?" he interrupts me. "My brother?"

My eyes widen. "Why is that your business?"

"Because I want to know."

"Too bad," I say immediately—that's over the line, even for whatever Patrick and I have going on here. That's just over the line. I get up off the couch, but Patrick stops me, curling his familiar hand around my wrist.

"Wait," he says, and he sounds so sincere I stop and look at him. "I'm sorry," he says. "You're right; that was fucked up. I'm sorry."

I let him tug me back onto the sofa, curling one leg up underneath. "I mean it," I tell him quietly. "We gotta stop."

Patrick nods without saying anything. He picks at a loose seam on the back of the couch. "I got into another program for the fall," he tells me quietly. "This Outward Bound–type thing, in Michigan. Rangering-type stuff, running parks tours." He shrugs. "It's a gap year, for if your grades aren't great."

"Your grades are fine," I say automatically.

Patrick frowns. "Not this year."

"I'm sorry." I think of what Tess said when she told me they got back together, all this stuff about the future. "Did you tell Tess?" I ask. "That you're going?"

"No."

"Why not?"

Patrick's head comes up, looks me square in my face.

275

"Because I wanted to tell you," he says.

I'm not sure which one of us leans in first.

It's not like the other night against the tree trunk, that desperate scrabbling—this is slow and measured, his long eyelashes brushing my cheeks. I make a quiet sound against his mouth. *"Shh,"* he says again, warm hands wandering up inside my T-shirt, skimming along the stretchy band of my bra until I'm shaking. Finally, I pull away.

"What *is* this?" I demand. It's worse that it wasn't a fast, messy blur this time. Somehow that makes it even worse. "What are you doing with me, Patrick? Tess is my *friend*."

"And Gabe is my brother," Patrick says, mild as milk toast. "But here we are."

"Should I break up with him?" I blurt, then immediately feel my cheeks flame. It feels horrifying to articulate the idea out loud—just as horrifying as it feels to be doing this to begin with. I care about Gabe. I'm falling in *love* with Gabe. So what the hell am I doing here? "Should I?"

Patrick shakes his head. "I'm not breaking up with Tess," he says decisively. "Not again."

I stare at him, pulse fluttering like the inside of a hive at my wrists and my collarbone. The damp summer air presses down. He leans forward to kiss me again, eases me back against the arm of the sofa. I close my eyes and sink in.

DAY 67

Gabe's the only one home when I come to pick him up for a double date with Kelsey and Steve the next evening: "In here," he calls when I rap my knuckles against the screen door. His bedroom's off the kitchen, a smallish afterthought of a space that used to be the servants' quarters a hundred years ago when the farm had horses and pigs and cows to milk. Gabe got it when he turned thirteen, on account of he was the oldest.

"Hey," I tell him cautiously, leaning against the doorway: It's the same as I remember it, the blue-and-green plaid bedspread, the pine dresser—everything almost preternaturally neat for a teenage boy, like maybe nobody even lives here. Patrick's room was always a disaster.

"Hey," Gabe says, pulling a frayed gray polo over his head. I haven't been in here all summer—haven't been in here at all since everything first happened between us, actually, the night in May of sophomore year when Patrick dumped me.

I remember stumbling down the back staircase and into the kitchen, physically disoriented—it felt like a canyon had opened up between us, like in some old cartoon where a crack appears in the earth and the ground breaks apart all in the space of five seconds. Like strolling blithely off a cliff and not noticing until you look down. I stood there in a numb haze, barely registering the sound of the side door slamming shut, then the rev of the Bronco's noisy engine as Patrick took off.

I didn't realize I was crying until I saw Gabe.

"Hey, Molly Barlow," he said, glancing at me once and then again more closely; he was making a turkey sandwich at the beat-up butcher block counter, twin slices of bread already laid out on a plate. His graduation was in a week and a half. "What's wrong?"

I shook my head. "No, nothing," I said, wiping my face and thinking for a minute of claiming allergies before realizing he'd never believe me and that it didn't really matter anyway. It was, after all, just Gabe. "Had a fight with your brother, we'll work it out, it's fine."

"*You* people, had another fight?" Gabe put the knife down and licked mustard off his thumb. He looked genuinely surprised. "What the hell, huh? Like, are the rivers turning to blood?"

"Shut up." I laughed a little, sniffled. "I mean, kind of. It's the same fight, I don't know."

"About boarding school?" Gabe asked, then hesitated. "I mean, sorry, I'm not trying to crawl up your ass or anything."

"No, no," I said, shaking my head. "It's fine."

"Okay," Gabe said, crossing the kitchen to stand beside me at the sink. This close he was taller than I'd realized, my head just about level with his sternum. It was rare for us to be alone. "So . . . what?"

And I told him.

I told Gabe everything, about the recruiter and about Bristol, how all of a sudden Patrick and I had started speaking different languages out of nowhere like the freaking Tower of Babel or the French tapes Connie liked to listen to while she weeded her garden. How I didn't know how to say anything to him anymore, didn't know how to make him hear me. How I felt more alone than I'd ever, ever felt. "I didn't even *want* to go to freaking Tempe at first," I finished. "What's in Tempe? Nothing. But I just. I just wanted to *talk*. And instead he, like . . . *broke up with me*."

Gabe listened wordlessly, arms crossed and blue eyes focused. When I was finished, wrung out like a washcloth, he sighed.

"Look," he said finally. "You know my brother. You know him better than anybody else, maybe. You know how

279

he is. He gets something in his head and that's the end of it, you know? He's a fucking donkey. He decides something's not good for somebody—especially him—and that's it. And you moving across the country, even for something awesome, even if it was something you really wanted to do? Definitely wouldn't be good for him." Gabe stopped then, just for a beat, and then he said it. "And I mean. For what it's worth, Molly Barlow? It wouldn't be so good for me, either."

I stared at him for a second, not comprehending. "I—"

Right away, Gabe shook his head. "Forget it," he said, looking shyer than I'd ever seen him—actually blushing, like he couldn't believe what he'd said. "That was out of line, you're my brother's—"

"I'm not anyone's," I blurted. God, that was the problem, wasn't it—like Patrick and I were one person, one soul or brain or *whatever* living in two bodies, so that whatever either one of us did had to be decided by committee. It felt suffocating, all of a sudden, or maybe it had felt suffocating for a long time and I'd just never noticed: *You're my brother's.* Like Patrick owned me. Like if he didn't like something that meant I couldn't do it, period. Bristol or anything else. "I'm mine, I mean. I don't belong to—"

"No, of course, I know that." Gabe shook his head. "You're his girlfriend, I meant. Or, you were, I guess. Look, this is getting messed up. I just meant—"

"I know what you meant," I told him, realizing in that moment that I did, just from the way he was looking at me. I glanced at the short hallway that led to his small, neat bedroom. I felt reckless and brave.

"Molly," Gabe said, and his voice was so quiet. Down near the pocket of my denim shorts his fingertips brushed mine. His eyes had flecks of brown in them I noticed. I'd never been close enough to tell. When he ducked his head down to kiss me, his mouth was plush and friendly and warm.

"Holy shit," I said, pulling back a minute or twenty later; my thoughts were careening everywhere, Gabe's hands creeping up under my T-shirt right there in the kitchen of his house. I had never known that before, that having my stomach touched was a thing that could feel that good. I had never known I was this kind of person. "Okay, we should—" God, this was wrong, it wasn't supposed to happen like this; it was supposed to be me and Patrick, a perfect moment right out of one of my mother's dumb books. Not like this. Already I'd come too far to ever go back. "*Holy shit*, Gabe."

"You want to stop?" he asked, a little breathless. His lips looked very red. "We can stop, fuck, we should probably . . ." He trailed off, nervous and almost panicky. I'd never seen Gabe anything less than sure. "What do we do?"

I looked one more time toward his bedroom, back up

the stairs to where I'd left Patrick what seemed like a lifetime ago. Everything felt inevitable all of a sudden, a book
that had already been written. I shook my head. "Let's go,"
I muttered softly. Gabe nodded, took my hand.

DAY 68

The next day it storms, which matches the state of my humid brain almost exactly; I wake up early to the wicked flash of lightning, to thunder so noisy I feel it rumble in my bones. There's no way I'm getting back to sleep, so I drag the quilt off my bed and head down to the living room, opening every window I pass to the hissing gush of rain. The trees rustle uneasily under the force of it, the green smell of water and the brown smell of mud.

Petrichor is the word for the scent of rain as it hits the blacktop. Patrick taught me that, a really long time ago.

I jab at the coffeemaker until it brews and take my mug into the living room with no real plan other than to sit there and listen to the rain, to let it wash me clean if there's any conceivable way. I've felt like crying since the moment I opened my eyes. I settle myself onto the big leather couch, blow on the coffee until it's cool enough to drink without scalding the inside of my body. There's a copy of *Driftwood* sitting with a stack of magazines on the table, a curling Post-it marking the place my mom reads from when she does events at libraries and bookstores.

I glance over my shoulder at the doorway, which is empty. Vita snores quietly on the rug. I'm alone here, just me and the book my mother wrote about me, the mystery words I've never been able to look at for more than a few seconds at a time. I've skimmed paragraphs here and there, with the guilty, shameful feeling of looking at something illicit and dirty.

Now I take a deep breath, pick it up, and read.

It's *good* is the worst part of everything; in my head it was hackneyed and nasty, like a cheap daytime soap on the page. The truth is it's . . . kind of compelling. I get why it did so well. The boys aren't Patrick or Gabe, not exactly, and while reading about Emily Green makes me supremely, squirmingly uncomfortable, I have to admit I'm rooting for her stupid coin-flipping self by the time I near the end.

I'm almost finished, turning the pages faster and faster, and the rain long since calmed to a steady drizzle when I hear the creak of the floorboards behind me: There's my mom in the doorway with Oscar, and I am unmistakably caught.

"Morning," is all she says, though, setting the dog down on the floor so he can trot over to where I'm curled under the blanket, toenails clicking on the floor. She looks from me to her book and back again, her face impassive. "You been up awhile?"

Long enough to read the best seller you penned about my love life, I think, but for the first time I can't bring myself to get worked up about it. "For a bit," I say. "Yeah."

My mom nods. "You want more coffee?"

I almost tell her something else then. I *want* to tell her something else—that reading this book was like spending three hours with her, that I miss her, that she's talented and even if I don't forgive her I'm still proud that she's my mom. The cover feels like it's gone hot inside my hands.

"Coffee would be great," I finally tell her, and smile. My mom nods at me slowly, smiles back.

Once she's gone I dig around in the couch cushions for a moment, come up with a fistful of crumbs but also exactly what I'm after—a tarnished, gummy nickel, cool and heavy in the palm of my hand. I squeeze it tightly for a moment, like I can give it special powers that way, like I can infuse a whole year's worth of questions into the metal.

Then I flip.

DAY 69

I'm down in the kitchen feeding Oscar his expensive, locally produced kibble when my phone starts buzzing in my pocket. When I fish it out I've got a new Facebook notification: *Julia Donnelly has tagged you in a photo.*

I tense, a low, greasy roll of dread rumbling through me before I can quell it, like too much questionable not-quite-Mexican food from the dining hall at Bristol. Julia did this a lot before I left: tagging pictures of me with bad angles that made it look like I had a double chin, ones with my eyes closed where I was making a stupid face. Once she posted a picture of a literal pig with my name on it. I'm not sure which of her brothers finally made her take it down. We're friendly again now, sure—at least, I *think* we're friendly—but as I click VIEW POST I flinch anyway, that feeling like the moment between when you stub your toe and when the pain hits. I'm sure this is going to hurt.

Which is why I'm surprised when I see what she's tagged this morning, that it's not a porn star with my face Photoshopped in or a blown-out close-up of me with a bad breakout. What she's posted is a throwback shot—the same one that's shoved in my desk drawer at this very moment, that I pulled off the bulletin board when I got back to Star Lake: the four of us, Gabe and Patrick and Julia and me, sitting in the hayloft, Patrick's arm wrapped tight around my rib cage. No mean caption, no cartoon penis drawn helpfully on my face. Just us, how we used to be. Before.

I look at our faces in the photo, grinning and silly. I smile at the screen in reply.

DAY 70

I'm looping the lake early the following morning, legs burning and swallowing giant mouthfuls of air, when I spy a familiar figure heading in the opposite direction. "We gotta stop meeting like this," I tell him as he slows to greet me, and Patrick raises his eyebrows.

"It's early," he says, and it is, still—the sky just getting light around the edges, all that smudgy pink and gray. It's going to be nice out today. I can hear the waking calls of the birds up in the pine trees.

"Uh-huh." I nod as he falls in step beside me, him doubling back in the direction he came from. The back of my warm, damp hand brushes his for a moment before he takes it, lacing his fingers through mine.

"Patrick," I tell him, low and warning. It occurs to me that possibly we aren't meeting here by chance.

Patrick ignores me. "You know what we haven't done yet?" he asks instead, grinning like a little kid with a secret.

"I can think of a lot of things," I retort without thinking, and Patrick tilts his head like, *Fair enough*, before inclining it toward the placid surface of the lake, morning-tranquil and empty. Right away I pick up what he's putting down.

"No way." It's a thing we used to joke about constantly, half-kidding and half-serious—both of us testing each other's boundaries or something, both of us feeling it out. Neither one of us ever called the bluff. "I'm not skinny-dipping in this lake with you right now."

"Why not?"

"Because we're not on *Dawson's Creek*! Like, to start with."

"And to end with?"

"Shut up."

"You don't have to take everything off," he tells me.

"Oh, how generous of you," I snap, and Patrick wrinkles his pretty nose.

"You know that's not what I meant," he says, a flash of flinty anger in his deep gray eyes. "I'm not some gross guy who wants to—" He breaks off.

Get naked with his brother's girlfriend? I almost supply. Not like we're not both thinking it. On top of which Patrick is that guy, clearly. He's exactly that guy.

And I guess I'm exactly that girl.

He can feel me considering it, he knows me that well; we've stopped moving entirely, standing here beside somebody's rotting old dock. There's not a soul here to stop us. There's not a soul here to know. "Mols," Patrick says, and his voice is so quiet. "Get in the water with me."

I look at him for a moment. Then I sigh.

"I'm not losing all my clothes right now," I tell him firmly.

"Noted." Patrick nods.

"And neither are you."

That makes him laugh. "Noted."

We don't talk a whole lot as we pull our various clothes off, my shorts and tank top and Patrick's T-shirt hitting the weathered wood of the dock in a cascade of quiet swishing. All I want in the world is to stare. My heart is thudding away inside my chest, the animal build of anticipation, the feeling of finishing what we started before everything crumbled away like wet sand. I swallow a breath down, trying not to shiver. Goose bumps prickle up and down my arms. When I glance up I see Patrick's staring back at me, watching, curious and overt.

"Sorry," he mutters when I catch him, rolling his eyes a bit.

"S'okay," I reply, gazing back at him evenly, both of us standing there in our underwear. It occurs to me that this is the first time since I got back from Bristol that I don't feel self-conscious about how I might look.

You can stare, I want to say to Patrick. *It's fine, it's me; I promise you can look.*

He shrugs, rubbing at his neck a little, looking out at the chilly black water. "You ready?" he asks.

"Uh-huh." I clear my throat, swallow once. "If you are."

"Yeah, Mols," Patrick says. "I'm ready."

We jump.

It's exhilarating, hurtling through the air like that—the sensation of flying just for a second, the chilly morning air buffeting my skin. We smash through the placid surface of the lake like twin explosions.

"Holy *shit*," Patrick swears once we've surfaced—it's freezing, he's not wrong about that, the cold sharp and immediate and aching. He barks out a frigid-sounding laugh. "Whose fucking idea was this again?"

"Some dummy's, certainly," I tell him, voice shaking a bit with the force of my shivering. I swim a few strokes toward the center, splashing around to try and warm up. Patrick turns a fast somersault, flecks of water sticking to his eyelashes. His bare collarbone juts in a way that makes me want to trace it with one gentle finger. I wonder what would happen if I did. I can feel my chest moving underneath the surface of the water. God, it is so, so cold.

"Now what?" I ask, a little breathless.

"I don't know," Patrick says, water dripping from his hair and skimming over his cheekbones, and puts his surprising mouth on mine.

It's a good kiss. God, it's the *best* kiss, it's the kiss I've been waiting for all summer and maybe my whole life, Patrick's warm mouth and the slickness of his wet shoulders sliding under my palms, his neck and the damp hair at the base of his skull. Every inch of my skin feels like it's on fire, the prickle and pop of nerve endings coming to life all over my body. I swear I can hear the steady hum of my blood inside my veins.

"Hi," Patrick mumbles against my jaw, licking at the pulse point just underneath it. I can feel the mossy floor of the lake underneath my toes. He's fumbling for the band of my sports bra, my arms coming up to help him as he peels the whole soaking thing off, the water cold and black and all the warm places where he's pressed against me. My legs come up like a reflex to wrap around his waist.

"Hi," I tell him quietly, and kiss him again.

It goes on for a long time out there in the murky water, nobody around to stop or see us, his solid body and his hands carding through my wet, tangled hair. Patrick pulls back for a moment to look at me, intentional. For a second he only just stares. "Mols," he says, in this voice like I'm a precious thing, in a voice like I'm rare. *"Molly."*

I shake my head, blushing even as the water feels like it's getting colder, how I'm freezing and burning up all over the place. "Patrick."

"I meant it, what I said that day it was raining," he murmurs, swallowing audibly. "About you being beautiful. I know you weren't fishing. But you are."

I get my hands on his face and kiss him again then, not

wanting to think about anything but this moment, like the sound of our own quick breathing can keep everything else at bay. Still, though, I can't keep myself from asking again: "What are we doing?" His mouth tastes like water, the zing of this morning's Colgate behind his teeth. "Huh? Patrick? You gotta tell me here, what are we—"

"I don't *know*," Patrick tells me, urgent, more vulnerable than he's sounded all summer long. His face is so close I can see his eye freckle, that dark fleck I've always thought of as just mine. Like you could get into his soul that way. "I don't *know*. We're going different places, aren't we? You're going to Boston with my brother."

"I'm not—" I begin to protest, but Patrick cuts me off.

"It doesn't matter," he says, his hands wandering, me arching into his touch before I can stop myself. "It's still here, isn't it? Between you and me. I loved you, Molly, I *love*—"

Patrick catches himself just then, doesn't finish. I wrap my arms around his neck and hold on.

DAY 71

I'm useless at work the next day. I have to recalculate payroll three different times before the numbers check out. I can't stop thinking about Patrick.

I remember finally telling my mom about me and Gabe at the very end of sophomore year—two weeks after it happened, graduation come and gone, Gabe headed off to be a camp counselor in the Berkshires, and Patrick and I still not speaking. Everything burbled up out of me like some long-dormant volcano: "Tell me," my mom urged, looking at me hard and searchingly. It felt like a purifying fire.

After that I ran to the Donnellys' before it was even light out, let myself in with the spare key Connie kept hidden underneath a clay frog in the garden. "Wake up," I said to Patrick, crawling across his bed in the blue still-darkness. He smelled like sleep, and like home. I felt like I'd dodged the most deadly of bullets, like one of those people that gets hit by a train but somehow manages to walk away unscathed. I felt guilty and lucky, a full helping of both. "Wake up, it's me."

"What?" Patrick blinked awake, startled, reaching for my arm. "Mols, what's wrong? What are you doing here?"

"I don't want to be broken up anymore," I blurted. "I'm not going anywhere, I'm never going anywhere; I was being an idiot." I shook my head. "I can run here, I want to stay here. I decided, and I wanted to tell you as soon as—" I broke off. "Please. Let's just forget about it and be normal again, okay?"

"Hey, hey." Patrick sat up then, looking at me curiously. His curly hair was crazy with sleep. "You all right?"

"I'm fine," I promised. "I'm perfect. I was being an asshole, I was just—"

"You weren't being an asshole," Patrick told me, "*I* was. I don't want to hold you back. I *love* you; that's the last thing I want. I'd fucking hate myself, if that's what I was."

"It's *not*," I insisted, looking at him urgently. "It's not. I want to stay here, I want to be with you."

"I want that, too." Patrick nodded. "Come here, hey. Of course I want that, too."

I climbed underneath the covers then, the cotton sheets warm with their time against his body. I'd made a *huge* mistake, doing what I'd done with Gabe, the weight of it like a grizzly settling down right on my chest. I'd never kept a secret from Patrick before. Still, in the moment it almost felt like a small price to pay to figure out what I really wanted: I was going to fix us. I was going to make it all right.

And nobody but me, my mom, and Gabe would ever, *ever* have to know.

"What're you doing?" Fabian demands, banging through the door of the office with a plastic Captain America in one hand and the Falcon in the other, yanking me out of the memory. I click SAVE on the computer, glance at the clock on the screen—Gabe's due to pick me up from work in twenty minutes.

Fabian's still waiting on an answer, impatient; I take the action figure he proffers, shake my head. "I'll tell you, buddy: That's a really good question."

DAY 72

Imogen and Handsome Jay seal the deal at the beginning of August at his tiny student apartment; two days later he surprises her with tickets to a sculpture park in Woodstock, a place she told him she wanted to visit on their very first date.

"Good on *you*, lady," I tell her, sitting cross-legged on the carpeted floor of her bedroom as she organizes the pieces for her art show at French Roast, which is coming up two weeks from now—I offered to help her, but she's got a complicated vision, she says. "You *should* be with somebody who knows you that well, you know?"

Imogen raises her eyebrows, glancing over her shoulder at me—she's holding up two small canvases with birds on them, scrutinizing how they look side by side. "You mean like you and Patrick?" she asks distractedly.

My internal temperature drops roughly fifteen degrees. "I—what?"

"Oh my God," Imogen says, whirling around to face me completely, dropping one of the canvases onto the carpet and clapping a hand over her mouth. She huffs out an awkward giggle, eyes wide. "I totally just meant to say you and Gabe. I legit wasn't even trying to heckle you just then, I'm so sorry. You and Gabe, you and Gabe."

"Jerk." I'm blushing and laughing, relief and embarrassment washing through my body in equal measure, hot and cold. "Me and Gabe, yes. Like me and Gabe."

"God, sorry. Let's just be thankful Tess wasn't here, too." Imogen picks the second canvas back up off the floor, holding them out for my inspection. "What do you think, which way?"

"Um," I manage, swallowing audibly, relieved at her willingness to drop it. I haven't told a soul about what happened—what's *happening*?—with Patrick. The smart thing to do is to let him alone. "Side by side."

"I think I like them stacked," Imogen says, and I don't answer. My head thuds softly back against the wall.

DAY 73

I'm almost asleep, that foggy in-between that's not quite dreaming, when my phone buzzes loudly on the nightstand: *You home?* Patrick wants to know.

I push my hair out of my face, sit up on the mattress. *Yeah*, I key in, trying to ignore the dark thrill in my stomach that tells me this can't possibly lead to anything good. *Where are you?*

In your driveway.

I creep downstairs and let him in the back door wordlessly, lead him up to my third-floor tower with his warm hand tucked in mine. As soon as the door's shut, he presses me up against it. My T-shirt hits the carpet with a barely audible whoosh. I never turned a light on and it's dark in here, nothing but a silver puddle of moonlight on the carpet and the feel of his warm mouth wandering over my collar-bone and ribs.

We stumble back toward my mattress, a tangle of arms and ankles. Still neither one of us has said a single word. His weight presses me down into the sheets for half a second, mouth glancing clumsily off mine before he's gone again, fingers hooked in the elastic of the boxers I went to bed in, pulling my bottoms down my legs.

"What are you doing?" I ask, popping up on my elbows to look at him. *"Patrick."*

"I wanna try something." His rough cheek scrapes against my inner thigh, gentle. "Will you let me try something?"

"Uh-huh," I say, more of a gasp than anything. I reach down and scratch my short nails through his hair. It feels *insane*; it feels like my bones have come apart and only my skin is keeping them from flying away entirely. I make a damp fist in the sheets.

"Come up here," I say finally, pulling at his shoulders until he listens. I'm shaking everywhere, needing something to hang on to. I think my nails are digging into his skin. "Come here."

Patrick crawls up my body, presses his mouth against mine. "Are we doing this?" he asks me quietly, an echo of two years ago in his family room, the way it was all meant to happen before everything fell apart. "Mols. Are we—?"

"Yeah," I say, nodding into his shoulder. He wants to, I

can feel that he wants to. I want to do it, too. "Yeah, yes. We're doing this."

Patrick exhales in what sounds like pure relief to me, like he thought I was going to send him away. "I wanted it to be with you," he mutters, tugging me up on top of him, my leg slung across his hips. "That's always how I pictured it, you know? It's corny as shit, but . . . the first time, I just, I always—me and you."

I—*what?*

I freeze in his grip, this horrifying coldness running through me, like there's lake water in my veins instead of blood.

He thinks—

He doesn't know—

Oh, *shit.*

For a moment, I just stay there, rigid, wanting more than anything to get up and out of here—to run barefoot to Bristol or Boston, hair streaming behind me like a flag of retreat. How can I not tell him? I owe him the truth, after all this time. I owe him that.

"Patrick," I tell him, sitting back awkwardly, one hand on his naked chest. I can feel his heart through the vellum skin there, and I swear it stops for a beat as he figures it out.

"It's not the first time, is it?" he says slowly, staring at me in the darkness, his eyes like a midnight cat's. "Not for you."

"Patrick," I repeat, trying to keep my voice quiet, the

way you'd calm an animal or a little kid. "Listen to me. I thought—because of *Driftwood*, I thought you—"

"I thought it was just part of the book," he says, jerking away so fast I land back on the mattress with a bounce; I reach for the sheet like an instinct, wanting so badly to cover up. "Because I'm a fucking moron, evidently. *Dammit*, Molly. Are you kidding me?"

"I—*no*," I tell him, stumbling over my words, a hundred different responses ricocheting around in my brain all at once. *You hated me that much, and you didn't even think we had sex? I want to ask him, or maybe: Don't you know I've loved you my whole entire life?* "You told Gabe he should go to Boston," I finally sputter, these hot ashamed tears burning in my face like I swallowed a mouthful of pool water, like I'm drowning. "You told me not to break up with him. You got back together with Tess, you've been messing with me *all summer*, you said—"

"I'm not *talking* about that, Molly," Patrick snaps at me, up off the bed and flicking the lamp on, the room flooded with harsh white light. I pull the sheet more tightly around me. "I'm talking about sophomore year, when *you fucked my goddamn brother* like some kind of filthy whore."

Like some kind of—

Okay.

Patrick shakes his head and we're both on the verge of tears then, like we've finally destroyed each other, finally eaten each other alive. We're never coming back from this; I know it. Both of us have finally gone too far.

Patrick knows it, too—I see it on his face then, my Patrick, whom I've loved my entire life. "I gotta go," he says, reaching for his crumpled T-shirt. He slams my bedroom door so hard I wince.

DAY 74

I get to work the next morning and find Desi and Fabian
sprawled out on the floor in the office playing Candy Land,
Penn digging her way through a pile of invoices at her desk.
Desi jumps up when she sees me, wordlessly scrabbling halfway up my body like a silent, skinny squirrel climbing a tree.
"Hey, Desi-girl," I tell her, lifting her the rest of the way and
smiling as she hooks her twig legs tightly around my waist.
I'm hugely grateful for the affection this morning, honestly,
my face puffy and tender from crying. I plant a smacking
kiss on top of her head. "Hi, guys."

Penn isn't amused, though. "Get down from there, Des,"
she snaps, more sharply than I've heard her speak to either
of her kids since I've worked here. She stands up from
behind the desk, arms out. "Come on."

"It's fine," I promise, shaking my head and shifting

Desi's lanky body to one hip. "She can come with me on rounds if she wants; it's totally okay."

"It's really not," Penn counters, reaching out and peeling Desi off me. "I'll take my kid, you take your notebook, how about that?" She hands me the pad I carry when I walk the Lodge and grounds at the start of every shift to see who and what needs attention. "Before you go, though, I want to talk to you about something. I want to send you up to Hudson, to scope out some club chairs for the lobby. An antiques dealer I know is holding them for me, and they're cheap, but I can't tell if he's screwing me or not and I can't face putting the kids in the car for that long to go check it out myself."

"I—okay," I tell her slowly, trying to figure out what's happening here. It seems like I'm being punished for something, like I'm being sent to my room, and I can't tell exactly why. In my head I know there's no way it has anything to do with Patrick and Gabe, but it feels like that anyway, like the whole world can see the blackest parts of me, like there's shame and scandal radiating off me in cartoon waves. Like even Penn can't bear to look at me right now. "Sure. When?"

"Tomorrow, day after?" Penn sets Desi's sandaled feet down on the rug, looks at me coolly. "It's a long drive, probably an overnight, so check it with your mom, obviously. You can take Tess with you. I'll give you my credit card to get a motel room."

That's all she's got to say about it, apparently—no *I trust you*, no *I'm sending you 'cause I know you're the right girl for the job*. I glance down at Desi, who's watching me silently. "Sure," I say, stuffing the notebook in my jeans pocket and wiping my clammy hands on my legs. "No problem."

DAY 75

"Okay, okay," Imogen says, squinting at the sun in her rearview and changing lanes on the sparsely populated highway. "I've got one." She had a couple days off in a row and decided to tag along on our Lodge Girls field trip to Hudson to check out the furniture, unknowingly saving me from an overnight solo excursion with Tess. The three of us are piled into her Fiat, embroiled in a super-intense round of Fuck Marry Kill as the dark fragrant pine trees whiz by on either side of the car. "Harrison Ford, Robert Redford, Paul Newman."

"We always knew Imogen liked 'em older," I tease, just as Tess asks, "From the salad dressing?"

"And the popcorn," I remind her from my perch in the backseat. She's been quiet all afternoon, a mumbled mention earlier of Patrick being weird and distant over text the last couple days. I murmured sympathetic noises in response, looked away. It's over for good now, whatever warped, twisted, *horrible* thing I had going with her boyfriend. It's finished, no need for her to ever get hurt. "Also lemonade."

"And, like, a million classic movies!" Imogen protests.

"But mostly the salad dressing," I point out.

"I do like salad dressing," Tess says diplomatically. "Or, okay, though, what about the kid from One Direction—"

"Which kid from One Direction?" I interrupt.

"The floppy one."

"They're all floppy."

"The floppiest one!" Tess says, laughing, swearing as we hit a pothole and she splashes water from her Nalgene all over herself. "The kid from One Direction, Justin Bieber, and the Backstreet Boy of your choice."

"Kill Justin Bieber," Imogen and I say in perfect unison, then dissolve into giggles. I was dreading this trip, but I'm surprised by how light I feel here in this car with them, legs stretched across the backseat and my hair knotted sloppily at the very top of my head. It feels like it doesn't matter, everything that's happened before now. It feels like maybe I can start clean.

"No, no, wait, I've got the best one," Imogen says, pushing her sunglasses up on her nose and pausing dramatically. "Fuck, Marry, Kill: Gabe Donnelly, Patrick Donnelly, Julia Donnelly."

For a second, the car is totally silent, just the hum of the little Italian motor and static cutting in and out on the radio as we pass through the mountains.

Then we all crack the hell up.

DAY 76

Tess sacks out around midnight, the cheery purple glow of a *Friends* rerun on the old tube TV in our motel room; she's an easy sleeper, our Tess, limbs starfished sloppily across the bed. I'm not tired, though, not even a little: "I'm going to check out the vending machine," I tell Imogen, slipping outside and down the concrete staircase, humid night pressing in from all sides.

I dig a dollar out of my shorts and get myself a pack of Twizzlers—not Red Vines, but they'll do in a pinch—then wander back up to where our room is. Instead of going back inside, I lean over the concrete railing for a minute, staring blankly at the neon light of the motel sign and the Burger King across the street and trying to ignore the chorus of voices—Julia's, Connie's, Penn's, Patrick's loudest of all—echoing endlessly through my skull. I don't know how long I'm out there before the door opens behind me.

"You're right here?" Imogen asks, flipping the deadbolt so the door won't lock behind her and joining me on the catwalk. The faint scent of cigarettes lurks in the air. "I thought you got murdered."

"Sorry," I tell her, holding out the package of Twizzlers. She's in her pajamas, these crisp old-fashioned looking things with pink and white stripes. "Was just thinking."

"About what, huh?" Imogen asks, fishing a strand of licorice out of the plastic. "You're been emo all day."

"I have not!" I protest. Have I? I've been trying to act normal—thought I *was* acting normal—but could be she knows me better than I give her credit for, even after all this time.

"Okay," Imogen says, making a face like, *nice try*. "You and Tess both, a pair of Mopey Mopersons."

Yeah. "That's what my driver's license says, actually," I tell her, leaning against the railing. There's a scatter of moths flinging themselves at the yellow light mounted to the wall.

"Mm-hmm," Imogen says, smiling a little. "What's up?"

I don't answer for a minute, debating. I tuck my messy hair behind my ears. I remember that I didn't tell her last time, that I carried my secret like a rock in my shoe and in the end it came tumbling out anyhow.

This time, I tell her everything.

Imogen looks at me for a moment once I'm finished, unreadable. Then she shakes her head. "That's fucked up," Imogen tells me. "Crap, why the hell did you just tell me that, Molly?"

I blink. "I thought—" I start, that same horrible sinking feeling as I got the other night with Patrick, like I've totally misread everything and everyone. "Should I not have?"

Imogen shakes her head again. "No, no, I take it back, of *course* I want you to tell me, but . . ." She glances over her shoulder at the door to our motel room, open just the tiniest crack. She moved over a little, sits right down on the grubby cement floor. Like an instinct, I sit down across from her, our bent knees making twin pyramids so that anyone walking by would have to spelunk over us. "Tess is my friend, too. Tess is *your* friend, too, I thought."

"She is!"

"Really?" Imogen raises her eyebrows. "Because that was, like, a serious breach of the Ovary Code."

"I know," I say miserably, thumping my head back against the wall. "I know. I messed up. I really messed up, Imogen."

"You did," she says matter-of-factly. "You messed up huge. But so did Patrick. On top of which, I think virginity is kind of an antiquated concept, right? Like some boy sticking it in you changes who you are as a human being?"

"I don't know if it was so much about the concept of my

virginity as it was about me losing it to Gabe," I point out.

"I mean, fair." Imogen sighs. "Look, you know I never thought it was so bad, what you did with Gabe to begin with. I mean, it was *bad*, but it's not like you killed anybody. But the point is that the moment it gets to be about doing messed-up stuff to other girls is the moment I get off the train."

"I know," I tell her honestly. She's always been that way, Imogen, some combination of her own achingly compassionate temperament and seventeen years spent praying to the Goddess. "I want to get off the train, too. It's done now; it's over. I am officially off the train."

"You promise?" Imogen asks me, and holds up her pinky for linking. I hook our fingers tight together, and I swear.

DAY 77

You home? I text Gabe as soon as I'm back in Star Lake, jumping into my car and heading down the treelined road to the farmhouse; over the last decade I've traveled its winding curves on foot and by bike and once in a pair of vintage roller skates of Connie's that Patrick and I found in the Donnellys' attic.

Today, I speed.

Sure thing, Gabe texts back just as I'm pulling into the driveway. *You coming over?*

Already here.

He comes out the side door fresh from the shower, hair damp and curling down over his ears. "What'd you, miss me or someth—" he starts to ask me, then gets cut off as I jump up right into his arms.

"I did," I tell him firmly, arms monkeyed tight around his broad back and the stamp of my lips against his. "But I'm back now."

DAY 78

"Can I talk to you for a minute?" Penn asks when I get in the next morning, shutting the door to the office behind us. She's wearing a pale pink blouse with three-quarter sleeves, a man's watch around one wrist.

"Sure," I tell her, with a little trepidation—we checked in over the phone about the club chairs while I was in Hudson, but other than that we haven't really talked since she was sharp with me the other day. "What's up?"

"I owe you an apology, I think."

I blink at her. Penn's office is basically the only room in the Lodge that didn't benefit from the rustic-chic makeover: The chairs are all covered in pink flowered cushions, and there's an ugly print of a cluster of sailboats along one wall. Fabian's coloring stuff is heaped on the cheap pressboard bookshelf. "You do?"

Penn nods. "I was a weirdo to you about Des the other

day," she says, taking a sip of her coffee. She perches on the edge of the cluttered desk instead of sitting behind it. "Before I sent you off like that. She's attached to you, and it just tweaked me out a little, I'm sorry."

"No, no." I shake my head, surprised. "I mean, I'm attached to her, too, obviously. I'm really sorry if I overstepped."

"You didn't," Penn says flatly. "Look, it was a bad divorce, me and the kids' dad. I bought this place because I needed a fresh start, and I thought the kids needed one, too, but then we got here and Des just completely stopped talking." She waves her hand like she's trying to clear cigarette smoke away, like there's something poison in the air keeping her from breathing it properly. "Maybe I was wrong, I don't know. But I just wasn't crazy about the idea of Des getting close to another person who's leaving, and I was trying to protect her from that. And maybe I was trying to protect myself, too." She rolls her eyes. "I rely on you for a lot here, you know? You help me run this place, and you're not going to be here forever." She drains the coffee, sets the empty mug back down on the desk. "Not the most emotionally intelligent moment of my life, maybe, but there you have it. That's why I was short with you the other day." Penn sighs. "Anyway. I hope I didn't scare you off from hanging with Des.

Ultimately, my kid needs as many people that care about her as possible, right?"

I smile at that, then step forward impulsively to hug her. "Yeah," I say finally. "Yeah, I think she does."

DAY 79

I get an email from the housing office alerting me that my roommate is one Roisin O'Malley from Savannah, Georgia.

"Does that say *Raisin*?" Tess asks, peering over my shoulder at the computer in the office, her braid damp from the pool and dripping onto my back. "Raisin O'Malley?"

"Yes," I tell her, laughing, closing down the browser. We're almost done for the day, and have a plan to get dinner at Bunchie's. "That's exactly what it says. My roommate is a sun-dried grape."

DAY 80

The next morning when I get into the office, there's a giant package of California Raisins sitting on my desk chair.

"You girls are very strange," Penn says.

DAY 81

After dinner I bring a cup of coffee up to my bedroom, sit down at the desk beneath the bulletin board and the cheerful *Golly, Molly*. I log into my incoming student account, click through the pages until I find the drop-down menu full of majors: Architecture and Art History, Education and Engineering. I scroll through the list until I get to Business, my fingers hovering over the track pad on the laptop.

I take a deep breath, and declare.

DAY 82

I head over to the Donnellys' the next evening to watch
some weird Canadian import show Gabe can't get enough
of, everybody dressed in plaid and saying "aboot" all the
time. His long fingers play idly in my hair. The episode's
just ended when the screen door in the kitchen slaps open,
Julia's giggle ringing out through the house. She appears
in the doorway of the family room a moment later. I hear
a set of footsteps behind her, and I'm terrified it's going to
be Patrick, but instead it's Elizabeth at her heels, holding a
pint of Ben & Jerry's. "Oh, hey," Julia says, her eyes flicking
from Gabe to me and back again. "I didn't know you guys
were here."

"Here we are," Gabe says mildly, but I wonder if he can
feel the muscles in my arms and back and shoulders seizing

up, how self-conscious I feel about the way I'm sacked out across the cushions. How many times has Julia walked in on this exact tableau over the course of our lifetimes—but with me tucked into the crook of Patrick's arm instead of Gabe's?

If she thinks it's weird, though, she doesn't say anything about it. "You want ice cream?" she asks instead. Then, without waiting for us to answer: "Lizzie, you wanna get two more spoons?"

Which is how I wind up splitting a pint of Phish Food with Gabe, Julia, and Julia's girlfriend, the two of them sitting on the floor and scrolling through the channels for close to an hour, all of us making fun of lame car insurance commercials and passing the ice cream back and forth. Elizabeth, randomly, does a really good William Shatner impression.

"I heard you talked Penn into throwing an end-of-summer staff party," she says as she's getting ready to leave later, sliding her feet back into her Sperrys. "That was pretty cool of you."

It's not exactly *Sorry I tormented you at our place of business*, but I'll take what I can get. Gabe nudges me in the back with all the subtlety of a big brass band. "Yeah," I tell her, ignoring him and smiling a little. "It should be fun."

Gabe walks me out not long after, the smell of coming rain wet and heavy in the air. "*Thaaaaaat* was something out of an alternate universe," I say, disbelieving. "Like, in all seriousness, did I just hallucinate this whole night?"

Gabe shrugs. "Face it, Molly Barlow. We're old news."

"I guess so." I smile in wonder. None of us talked about anything important, nothing was awkward or heavy or weird. It felt . . . normal.

Gabe's not interested in processing the events of the night with me, though: "So, hey," he begins, and right away it's clear he's got something else entirely on his mind. "You know my buddy Ryan, the one who had the party? He's at some music festival in Nashville the next couple days." Gabe shrugs a little then, too casual to actually be nonchalant. "He said the camper's empty, if we wanted to use it for a night or two."

I raise my eyebrows at him, unable to hide a grin even as my stomach's flipping over at the notion. "I'm sorry," I tease, glancing instinctively at the barn, which is dark and shuttered. "If we wanted to use it for *what* exactly?"

Gabe shakes his head at me, all that fake coolness melting away like ice cream on a sun-warmed sidewalk. "Shut up," he mutters, smiling.

"No, really, tell me," I nudge, bumping my bare ankle at his. "I want to know what exactly you were imagining we'd be using Ryan's super-swank camper to *do*."

Gabe rolls his eyes, rubs at his jaw a little. "You're the worst."

"I know," I tell him, still grinning. "Tell me."

He changes tactics then, slips a finger into my belt loop, gets closer. "To be alone," he says.

"Oh, to be *alone*." I pretend to consider it—as if there's anything left to consider at this point. I pop up onto my tiptoes to press a kiss against his mouth, gentle. "I see."

DAY 83

The carpet in Ryan's decrepit camper by the lake is this truly hideous green shag number, the kind I feel sure must be housing some kind of wildlife; Gabe and I sit on it anyway, my legs canted open over his and an ancient checkerboard on the floor between us. He traces patterns on my ankle with one finger, the skin prickling there.

"My dad used to love checkers," Gabe tells me, skipping his red checker over two of mine. There's a Young the Giant song on his iPhone, quiet and slow. "We used to have these epic tournaments every time it snowed."

I smile at him, remembering. "I know."

"Shit, of course you do." Gabe shakes his head. "I love that you knew my dad, you know that? I love *you*." Then, as my surprised gaze comes up away from the board to look at him: "I do. I mean it. I know I kind of said it at Falling Star, but I mean it."

"I love you, too." It's tumbling out of my mouth before I even think about it, maybe the first thing I've done or said all summer without worrying about how it's going to look or sound. It's true, though; I know as soon as I hear it. It feels like everything that happened since I got back to Star Lake—including, *especially* what happened with Patrick—has led me here. "Hey. Gabe." I grin, the feeling of it breaking open inside me, molten and real. "I love you, too."

"Yeah?" He looks surprised at that, and so happy—it feels good and powerful, to make someone so glad. He leans across the board and he kisses me. I hold on as tight as I possibly can.

DAY 84

I wake up in the camper's tiny bed the next morning and find Gabe rummaging through Ryan's mini fridge, the kind you'd find tucked under a lofted bed in a college dorm. Pale yellow sunlight trickles through the tiny windows, making kaleidoscope patterns on the rug. "Hi," I say around a yawn, rolling over onto my side to see him more clearly, his tan unblemished skin and the T-shirt he slept in. "Whatcha doing?"

"Scoping out the breakfast situation," Gabe tells me, smiling at my presumably sleepy expression. "There's eggs. And, like, gross instant coffee. Or we could drive into town and go to French Roast, if you want."

I look at him for a beat longer, a package of questionable Kraft Singles in one hand and his easy morning grin. Last night's *I love you* echoes inside my head like the refrain of my favorite new song. I take a deep breath.

"I don't," I tell him, reaching my hand out across the tiny camper. "Come back here."

Gabe doesn't move for a second, head cocked to the side and his face a quiet question. "Okay," he says after a moment, and laces his fingers through mine. He gets both knees up on the narrow mattress, hair falling across his forehead as he gazes down at me. "You sure?" he asks, barely more than a murmur. I look up at him in wonder, and I nod.

DAY 85

Imogen's art show is a roaring success, French Roast packed to bursting with friends and strangers alike: She pushed this event *hard* on Twitter and Instagram, put up fliers in every shop in town, and it paid off in a crazy, crazy way. Nearly everywhere I look I spy pieces with little red SOLD stickers on them, the collages and the brush script, the series of the lake in the fading light. A lot of people love Imogen: It's a trip watching her make the rounds and talk to everyone, Handsome Jay's arm slung casually around her shoulders. I'm proud of her.

"She's good, huh?" Gabe asks me, in front of a line drawing of Tess in profile, her expression mysterious and wry. He's right—it's a gorgeous piece, the texture of her braid just right and the rich way the ink's soaked into the thick paper. I can hardly do more than mumble my vague agreement, though, because just then the door to French Roast opens and Tess herself walks in, Patrick's long fingers hooked through the belt loop on her jeans. He catches my eye for a moment, and stares.

I swallow. It's the first time I've seen him since the awful night in my bedroom, both of us beaten to wreckage like ships—we've avoided each other carefully, orbiting around each other in our little social circle like magnets with repelling poles.

"What's his problem?" Gabe asks, following my sight line to Patrick's stony expression.

I shrug, turning purposefully away. I'm surprised he can't smell it on me, the sweaty sheen of guilt coating my skin. "I dunno."

"Deep existential angst no layman could understand," Gabe diagnoses. "You want food?"

I don't. It seems like it should be easy to get lost in the crowd milling around in the coffee shop, the big tables of pastries and drinks and so many things to look at and people to chat to, but instead from the moment Patrick turns up it feels like he and I are the only two people in here, this weird animal awareness of him no matter where he goes. He's tracking me, too; I can tell he is, can feel his gaze on my body like a constant, low-grade hum. I stick close by Gabe's side and try not to look.

Afterward there's a party at Handsome Jay's tiny apartment, all of us crammed onto couches and in his little galley kitchen, a fridge full of Bud Light and a few cheap bottles of liquor on the counter. I step over Jake and Annie, who are making out on the futon, and mix myself a vodka cranberry that's mostly juice.

When I see Patrick duck out onto Jay's balcony, I glance over my shoulder to make sure Gabe and Tess are both distracted before I follow. "I *am* a champion of the world," Imogen is saying, holding up her beer bottle with a giggle in a tipsy toast to her own success. Tess clinks, and they both take long gulps.

Patrick's leaning over the railing staring out at the patchy woods beside the apartment complex, a bunch of anemic-looking pine trees ringing the economy-filled parking lot. "Got a minute?" I ask quietly.

Patrick shrugs. "It's a free country, I guess," he tells me, which is a thing we used to tell each other real snotty-like when we were little. Then he sighs. "What do you want, Mols?" he asks, and he sounds so tired of me. "I mean it, what could you possibly want from me?"

He's drunk, I can tell by the way his gaze is slightly slow to focus. Not exactly ideal conditions for a resolution, but I have to try anyway. I have to see if I can get this out.

"Look, will you talk to me for a second?" I ask him, still trying to keep my voice low—the party's noisy inside the apartment, but the sliding door's still open a bit. I feel like I've spent this whole entire summer worried someone's going to overhear. "The summer's almost done, you know?

And I don't—I *love* you, and I care about you, and I don't want—"

"You love me, and you care about me." Patrick snorts. "Okay."

"I do!" I protest, stung by the dismissal. "Why the hell else would I have done what I did with you all summer, huh? Why would I have risked hurting Gabe like that—?"

"I don't know; why did you do it last time?" Patrick demands. "Because you like the attention. That's what it is with you. You're a poison, you want—"

"Can you keep your voice down?" I hiss, but it's too late—here's Tess sliding the glass door all the way open, fresh beer in her hand.

"Everything okay out here?" she asks.

And Gabe on her heels: "What's going on?" he asks.

Patrick focuses his reply on his brother: "Why don't you ask your girlfriend?" he suggests nastily. "And while you're at it, why don't you ask her what the fuck else she's been doing, the whole time she's been fucking you?"

I freeze in total horror. Patrick moves to shove his way past us all. Gabe grabs his arm to keep him from going, though, and just like that Patrick whirls on him, his fist connecting with the side of Gabe's face with a sick crack like something out of a movie. Tess screams. Gabe hits back. And I do the only thing I can think of, the only thing I've ever been any good at in my whole entire life:

I run.

332

DAY 86

I can't—
   I didn't mean—
   Oh God oh God oh God

DAY 87

Overnight it's like something heavy and poisonous bursts open inside me, a cyst or a tumor: I wake up sobbing into the mattress, and I can't for the breathing life of me stop.

I ruined everything; I destroyed it.

You're a poison.

dirty slut.

I lie there for a while, curled in a ball and wracked with it like some stupid Shakespearean tragedy character, crazy Ophelia eating her own hair, but eventually crying that hard makes me feel grossly like I'm going to barf, so I force myself into the bathroom, which is where my mom finds me when she comes upstairs what could be minutes or hours later, I'm not sure.

"What's wrong?" she asks urgently, flying through the doorway and dropping right down onto the tile beside me, getting her arms around my shoulders and squeezing tight. She smells like sandalwood, her flowy cardigan soft and cool against my damp, blotchy skin. "Molly, babe, what happened? What's wrong?"

I blink at her through my tears, surprised: Even back before communication went solidly to crap in our house, the two of us weren't really huggers. It's basically the sum total of the physical contact we've had all summer and right now it only makes me cry more, way too hard to answer her with words. My breath is this awful shuddering wheeze, this feeling of being physically crushed like how they used to kill witches in Massachusetts, slabs of rock piled one after another on my chest. I feel like I'm running a marathon I haven't trained for at all.

"Molly, babe," she says again, warm breath at my temple. It's like some weird dormant instinct is taking over for her, stroking through my hair and rubbing my back like I can't remember her doing since I was really, really little. "*Shh.* You're okay," she promises. "I'm here; your mom's here. You're okay."

Your mom's here. You're okay.

It's the same thing she said the night I told her about Gabe, I remember suddenly—me breaking down and coming to her in her office, the feeling like I was the last person on Earth. I used to think that was what set this whole awful game of dominoes in motion to begin with, that none of this would have happened if she hadn't gone and used me like she did.

Now? I'm not so sure.

We must think of it at the same time, though, because my mom draws back and shakes her head. "You don't have to tell me," she promises quietly, and it sounds like an absolution. "We can just sit here. You don't."

So that's what we do, the two Barlow women, on the floor beside the bathtub, the tile cool and clean. Eventually, the tears stop coming. Neither one of us says a word.

DAY 88

I drag my sad, sluggish self downstairs for a run the next morning, the fog rolling off the lake like clouds of milky chowder. I've barely made it out the door when I freeze.

It's not eggs this time, coating my mother's house all slick and sludge-slimy.

It's toilet paper.

Toilet paper that got rained on overnight.

I sit right down on the lawn when I see it, rolls upon rolls of super-absorbent two-ply soaked through and cling-ing to the shingles and shutters and gingerbread scrollwork in mushy, sodden clumps. It's clogging all the gutters. It's hanging from the trees.

"Well," my mother says, sipping her coffee; she came outside when she heard my laughter through the open win-dow, a deranged cackle that didn't sound anything like my normal laugh. I sobbed once as she stepped through the front door to investigate, then pulled it together. The wet grass is seeping through my shorts. "You have to give her points for narrative consistency, I suppose."

"Mom," I snap, and this time she softens. She offers a hand to help me up. "You can call Alex," I tell her miserably. "You can call Alex to fix it this time. I give up."

My mom looks at me with something like compassion, her slim hands surprisingly strong. "You know what you gotta decide when you're a writer?" she asks when I'm standing, damp green grass sticking to the backs of my legs.

"Whether or not to turn your teenage daughter's sex life into a best seller?" I reply. It's an instinct, but a vestigial one, and my mom can tell. She rolls her eyes, but kindly, still holding on to both my hands.

"Which stories to tie up at the ending, Molly," she tells me. "And which ones you have to let go."

I look at her for a moment, at this woman who chose me eighteen years ago. Who raised me and broke me and just lifted me off the ground. "Can I ask you something?" I begin, feeling stupid and embarrassed but also like this is a vital piece of information, something I should have known long before today. "What's your favorite flower?"

My mom looks surprised—that I'm asking, I guess, or maybe that I care. "My favorite—lilies, I guess. I like lilies."

I nod slowly. "Lilies," I repeat, like it's a word I've never heard before. "Okay."

DAY 89

I find Tess hosing off the rubber lounge chairs in the morning, a dozen of them lined up like soldiers in the sunshine along the pool deck. I have to force myself down the stairs from the porch. Up close she looks terrible, face swollen and shiny and tender from crying, a zit sprouting on one cheek. Her hair is lank and greasy. I think I probably look way worse.

"Hey," I say, one hand up in an awkward wave like it's the beginning of the summer all over again, like she's a stranger I'm vaguely afraid of. Like I'm a stranger she probably hates. "Can I talk to you a sec?"

I'm not far off: Tess looks at me for a moment, something like wonder passing over her puffy, distorted features. "No," she says.

"Tess—"

"Don't, Molly," she interrupts, shaking her head at me. She drags the hose across the concrete, begins to wind it up. "I mean it. I don't want to hear it, I really can't."

"I'm so sorry," I try anyway. "Tess, seriously, please just listen for a sec—"

"You listen for a sec!" she explodes. It's the first time I've heard her raise her voice all summer. "I was nice to you when nobody else was, do you get that? Everyone said to watch out for you, but I liked you, so I didn't care." She shakes her head, eyes filling. I feel like the worst person in the world. "Is that why you were friends with me to begin with?" she asks me, voice high and brittle. "To, like, misdirect?"

"No!" I exclaim. "No, I swear. I liked you, too, right away. You've been such a good friend to me this summer, and I—"

"Thought you'd pay me back by screwing around with my boyfriend?" she asks.

"I—" I break off, helpless, glancing around like an instinct to see if anyone has heard her, like I did when I first found Julia's note on my car. I'm ashamed of myself, truly. It's inexcusable, what I did to Tess.

"Please leave," Tess tells me, trying unsuccessfully to undo a stubborn kink in the hose. "Seriously. Just—if you ever wanted to do something in your life that wasn't selfish. I mean it. Please, please leave."

Back in June, I watched a documentary about ghost

hearts, which doctors prep for transplant by scrubbing all the cells until all that's left is connective tissue, empty and white and bloodless. I don't know why I'm thinking about that right now.

"Of course," I say finally, nodding ever so slightly. I turn around and get out of her way.

DAY 90

I sit in bed with my arms wrapped tight around my knees and watch a documentary about Mary Shelley, who kept her husband's heart in her dresser drawer for years after he died. I cry for a while. I hide.

DAY 91

I haven't heard a word from Gabe or Patrick—not that I was expecting to, I guess, but there's a small part of me that held out hope Gabe would reply to one of the thousand *I'm so sorry* texts I've sent him. I've called, but he hasn't picked up. Late last night I gathered up all my courage and drove out to Ryan's camper, where Imogen told me he's staying, but even though the station wagon was parked in the clearing nobody answered my knocks on the door. I sat there for hours, in the cold and the dark, waiting and waiting, but he never came. Now I type his name into the search bar on Facebook, stare at his tan, smiling face.

I friend Roommate Roisin while I'm on there, then lose an hour snooping idly through a bunch of her photo albums. *Raisin has a super hot boyfriend!* I'd text Tess, if I thought Tess ever wanted to hear from me again in this lifetime. Instead

I keep clicking: Roisin and her softball team in Savannah, Roisin in a prom dress last May. She looks well adjusted and popular and nice and friendly.

I wouldn't want a thing to do with me if I were her.

DAY 92

I haul myself out for a run the next morning, a blessedly solitary loop around the lake. A cool breeze is blowing, the first one I've felt all summer, it seems—that reminder that fall is on her way. I round a copse of trees and stop short where I'm standing—the Donnelly Bronco is rattling down the road in my direction, gleaming in the late-summer sun.

For a second, this incredibly strange, incredibly *real* fear flickers through me, this cold knowledge that I'm all by myself out here. And of course in my head I know none of the Donnellys would ever physically hurt me—the very thought of that is insane—but I *don't* know that for sure about Mean Michaela or even Elizabeth really, and people do crazy things in groups. I don't know if I was always the kind of person whose first instinct is to run, or if this summer has made me that way. It's not a quality I like in myself.

In any event, it's not Julia and her coven of nasties behind the wheel of the Bronco, waiting to hock something from the window or jump out and beat me up.

It's Connie.

"Thought that was you," she says, slowing to a stop where I'm hovering frozen and stupid, peering at me through the passenger side window. Her gray hair is in its usual stubby ponytail at the back of her head. "You wanna hop in, I'll drive you home?"

That would kind of defeat the purpose of my run, on top of which it feels like I've pretty much hit my quota of Donnelly time for one summer, but it doesn't exactly seem as if she's asking. "Um . . . sure," I hear myself tell her, opening the passenger door and climbing up onto the bench seat. I can smell the sweat clinging to my skin. "Thanks."

"No problem," Connie says as we head back around the lake in the direction that I came from. We ride in silence for a moment, just the crackle of the oldies station she and Chuck always used to listen to when they dropped us off or picked us up. "Just a few more days, *hm*?" she asks, pausing for the traffic light at the intersection of the lake road and Route 4. "I'm driving Julia out to Binghamton next week."

"Yeah," I say vaguely—it feels weird to the point of distracting to be in the car with her, to wonder what she's heard and thinks and feels. "We talked about that, a little."

Neither of us says anything after that, this echoing silence that feels like it stretches on for days. The sun bounces off the wide wooden dashboard. Connie speaks first. "Listen, Molly," she says, sighing a little. "I don't know what went on between you and my boys this summer. I don't really want to know. They're my boys, all right? I'm always, always going to stick up for my boys. But honestly—" Connie breaks off. "Honestly, kiddo, you didn't exactly have an easy go of it either the last few months, did you."

"I—" I have absolutely no idea how to respond to that; it's not a question. I feel like the top of my head's been blown off. "I'm okay," I tell her finally, because it seems like the best answer even if it's maybe not the truest. "I made it through."

"You did." Connie nods. "I used to be able to give you guys Band-Aids and Popsicles," she tells me. "That used to be all it took."

I don't know what to say to that, either, exactly. It feels like she's trying to tell me something, but I don't know what. We're approaching my house now, the long ribbon of driveway; I probably could have made it home just as fast on my own. Connie stops at the bottom, doesn't bring me all the way up. "Thanks for the ride," I say.

"You're welcome," she says, nodding. "Take care of yourself, Molly."

I stand there until her taillights disappear, just watching.

That's when I remember.

———

It was before Patrick broke up with me, before anything happened with Gabe: I stopped by the Donnellys' on the way back from my run after school and found Connie in the kitchen making breakfast for dinner. "They're out in the barn, I think," she said, sneaking me a piece of bacon off the paper towel. "Tell them this is almost ready, okay?"

"Sure," I promised, but I hadn't even made it all the way across the yard when I heard their raised voices.

"—can't just let it alone, can you?" Patrick was asking. "Just back the fuck off, bro, I mean it."

"It's not really up to you, is it?" That was Gabe. I stopped outside the barn, still flushed from my run and feet sinking into the fragrant muck of the yard. What were they fighting about? It felt like things had been building between them for months now—or longer, maybe, ever since Chuck died.

"It's not up to me?" Patrick countered, disbelieving. I couldn't see him inside the barn, but I could picture him fine, his limbs sprawled across the sagging plaid sofa. "What is that, a challenge?"

"Call it whatever you want," Gabe said. "She's a big girl. She can make her own choices."

I stand there at the foot of the driveway, not quite home and not quite gone. For so long I've felt like the one who came between Patrick and Gabe, this horrifying destroyer who busted up their otherwise perfect family. And maybe I am.

But maybe—

What is that, a challenge?

I take a deep breath and head up the driveway. I unlock the door and go inside.

That night I don't sleep, I just lie there, brain raging like a hurricane: Patrick and Gabe and my own bad judgment, that quiet argument in the barn in the winter chill.

dirty slut dirty slut dirty—

Enough.

I lift my head up off the pillow, actually open my eyes in the dark: At first it sounds like Penn's voice, or possibly my mother's. For a moment I think it might be Imogen.

Then I realize: It's only me.

Enough.

Enough.

Enough.

DAY 93

I'm fully intending to skip the Lodge's end-of-summer staff send-off—it's pretty clearly suicide to show up—but Penn stops me on my way out the door specifically to make sure I'm going to be there, and I don't have the heart (or the courage) to tell her no. The stupid party was my idea to begin with, back when this summer seemed like it might somehow work out after all. I don't want Penn's last memory of me to be as someone who bailed.

As soon as I turn up poolside, though, I know it was a mistake of epic proportions: Here are Tess and Mean Michaela with their feet in the water, Julia by the food table with Elizabeth Reese. I was hoping Jay might bring Imogen for a buffer—even texted her a frantic *SOS*—but she's working late tonight at French Roast, which means I'm totally on my own. I swallow and square my shoulders, trying not to feel like a zebra smack-dab in the middle of a hungry pride of lions. I have as much right to be here as they do after all.

That's what I try to tell myself, anyway.

The waitstaff is playing a noisy game of Marco Polo over in the deep end, and after I say hi to Jay and the rest of the kitchen guys I watch them for a while, trying to act like I'm really interested. I fish my phone out of my pocket, attempting to ignore an overheard snatch of conversation from Julia's corner that night or might not include the word *ho*. I feel my face flush scarlet anyhow. I can feel everybody's eyes on me like physical touches, like I'm being grabbed from all sides. *Twenty minutes*, I promise myself firmly, going far enough to set an alarm on my phone—like there's any way I might miss it. *You have to stay for twenty more minutes, and then you can go.*

I'm pouring myself a plastic cup of Diet Coke, not because I actually want it but because at least it's something to do, when a shove from behind jostles me forward, the sticky soda splashing all over my flip-flops: My head whips up and there's Michaela and Julia passing by.

"Better watch where you're going, Mols," Julia says, her voice more artificially sweet than the cola coating my feet and ankles. Then, more quietly: "Skank."

I whirl on her then, spine straightening, drawing myself up to my full height. All at once I've had it. Suddenly, I'm mad enough to spit blood. "You know what, Julia?" I snap. "Shut *up*."

She looks at me, surprised, stopping in the middle of the concrete. "Excuse me?"

"You heard me." There's something hot and acidic running through my veins and it takes me a moment to realize it might be bravery, that for once—for the first time all summer, maybe—the urge to fight is stronger than the urge to run away. "I'm sick to death of you and everybody else acting like your brothers are some perfect angels that I defiled or something. That's not what happened. And even if it *was* what happened, it's not your business." I turn to Mean Michaela: "And it's *definitely* not your business. So I don't want to hear it." My hands are shaking, but my voice is steady and clear. "Enough," I say, echoing the words I heard late last night in my bedroom. "I've had enough."

Julia's just staring at me, pink mouth gaping. Tess is staring at me, too. I focus my attention on Julia and Michaela, eyebrows raised in challenge: *Come at me*, I want to tell them. *I'm not going to let you hurt me anymore*. And maybe that's true and maybe it isn't, but in this moment I feel invincible, I feel full of strength and steel.

I'm about to say something else when I feel my phone alarm vibrate in my pocket—time is up, then. I'm allowed to go home. I'm not running, I know as I set my cup down and head for the lobby, a quilt of silence around the pool deck that somehow doesn't rattle me at all.

I'm done. And I'm walking away.

DAY 94

"*Sooo*, I heard you laid the smackdown on Julia at the Lodge party last night," Imogen tells me. We're up on wobbly stepladders at French Roast after closing, taking down the pieces from her show so we can wrap them and send them off to their new homes. She sold more than half of what she exhibited. I'm as proud as if she were my kid.

"I didn't lay the smackdown!" I protest, lifting a canvas collaged with magazine cutouts to look like the lakefront at night off the wall and setting it carefully on the bowed wooden floor. She's got Bon Iver on the stereo. "Or, like, okay. I laid the smackdown a little bit."

"*Mm-hmm,*" she replies, prying a nail out of the wall with the claw end of a hammer and dropping it into a coffee mug along with the others. "That's what I thought."

"It's not that I don't think they all deserve to hate me,"

I tell her truthfully. "I mean, Tess definitely does, and probably Julia, too. But I'm not the only one they deserve to hate. It just felt like such a gross double standard, I don't know. I got mad about it; I got word vomit."

"It *is* a double standard," Imogen says, reaching for the giant roll of bubble wrap. "And I'm glad you said something. Equal opportunity hate, or no hate at all."

"Exactly!" I giggle at the dark absurdity. Six days until I leave for Boston, and it seems like that's all that's left to do about it.

Or, okay, not *all* that's left to do about it.

But close.

"Anyway, I'm proud of you," Imogen tells me now. "It was gutsy, what you said to them. I think Emily Green would be proud, too."

I reply with a loud, theatrical retching sound. "Oh my *God*, gross."

"I mean . . . the book was good," Imogen defends herself. "You gotta admit that."

I shake my head and move the ladder over, climbing to the top to reach a canvas hung way up high. "I don't, actually," I counter. "Or at least, not out loud."

Imogen laughs at that, trilling and familiar. Even after everything, I'm glad I came back. It's strange to think in a few weeks we'll have completely different lives again, that we refound each other this summer just in time to say goodbye for good.

"Uh-uh, don't get mushy on me now," Imogen says, like she can tell exactly what I'm thinking. "You said it yourself, Boston and Providence aren't that far." She reaches over and gently tugs the back of my flannel, so I know she's behind me.

"We'll be neighbors," I tell her, and grin.

DAY 95

"Don't," Patrick says immediately when I come into the shop the next day, bells above the door ringing out and my wild hair pulled back off my face with an enamel comb I filched off my mom. I wanted to look serious or something. This felt too important for messy hair. Patrick's standing behind the counter, his whole body tense and rigid like the bars on a birdcage. There's a green-yellow bruise healing on his face.

"Patrick." I gasp when I see it even though I knew it would be there, the difference between hearing about a natural disaster and seeing the wreckage yourself. "Is that from——?"

"I said *don't*, Molly." Patrick shakes his head, voice lower than I've ever heard it. There's a bunch of middle school boys scarfing slices at the table by the window, a middle-aged couple lined up side by side on the stools. "It's done now, okay? It's finished. You shouldn't have come here."

"It's not, though." I take a deep breath. It's all I've been able to think about since Connie picked me up by the lakefront. I have to get an answer from him once and for all. "Was this even about me?" I ask, and it feels like all the air is rushing out of me. "This whole summer, everything that happened? Or was it all some kind of messed-up contest with Gabe?"

Patrick looks at me like I've lost my mind. "Everything that *happened*?" he parrots back incredulously. "Like you had no part in it."

"That's not what I'm saying!" I'm loud enough that the middle-aged couple looks up, but I'm too far gone to be embarrassed. I'm too far gone for anything but this. *I'm the girl from the book*, I want to tell them. *Go ahead and stare.* "That's not what I'm saying at all. I'm a big kid," I tell him, echoing his mom without meaning to. "I made my choices. But what we did—admit it, Patrick. It wasn't 'cause you missed me, it wasn't because we're us and you wanted to try to make this work, whatever it is. It was just 'cause you wanted to take me away from your brother. You wanted to win."

"I wanted *you*," Patrick counters, and the way he says it sounds worse than any curse he's ever uttered. "I fucking loved you, Mols, how do you not get that?"

"Loved me so much that you messed with me all

summer and humiliated me in front of everyone we know?"

Patrick looks at me for a beat across the counter. Then he sighs. Like he's got nothing left. "I didn't know how to let you go."

I stare back at him for a moment—farther away than he ever was the whole time I was in Tempe, my heart leaking something so pungent I feel like he'll be able to smell it over the sauce and pepperoni. I search his pretty face and his gray-storm eyes, the cut of his angry jaw, but he's just—he's not there. My Patrick—the Patrick I know and remember and love—is gone. I broke it, this thing between us. Both of us did. I used to think we could fix it—that what was happening between us all summer was fixing it, bringing us back together in some messed-up way. But some things can't be repaired. I don't know if I ever really believed that, not until now. The realization makes me feel as if my ribs have parted ways.

"I shouldn't have said what I said to you," he says finally. "In your room that night, I shouldn't have called you—" The bells above the door jingle then, interrupting; a family of five traipses in. Patrick makes a face and winces, the livid yellow and green on his face. When he speaks again, the spell is broken. "Look, Molly," he says, like I'm just another customer. Like I'm a stranger right off the street. "I gotta work."

I feel the air go out of me, like a valve's been released

somewhere. All at once I'm so tired I can hardly stand. "I leave in a few days," I tell him finally. I take a deep breath. "I'll miss you."

Patrick nods. "Yeah, Mols," he says, and it sounds like the end of the summer. "I'll miss you back."

DAY 96

I've got a ton of packing left to do after dinner, my same old duffel openmouthed and gaping on the bed. I made myself more at home here than I ever meant to: clothes spilling out of drawers, and crinkled Lodge stationery scattered across the desktop.

I think of the last time I packed up like this, grabbing huge handfuls of socks and underwear and shoving them into my bag to bring to Arizona, the whole affair taking roughly twenty minutes and completed in total silence: I'd turned off my phone and computer to dam the incessant ping of text and email and Facebook, one nasty message piling up on top of another and never a single word from Patrick himself. The Bristol track team didn't need me anymore, they'd told me primly—though I was welcome to try out in the fall—but they'd agreed to take me anyway, the only new senior girl in a class of sixty-five.

One year later and I take my careful time with it, packing up my jeans and my boots and my hair ties; I take the *Golly, Molly* artwork and the collage of the lakefront Imogen sent me home with the other night. It made me cry when she handed it over. After a minute, it made her cry, too.

I've got Netflix for company, the same low drone that's ferried me through this whole summer, and I'm halfway through a documentary about the secret lives of birds when my phone rings, a number I don't recognize appearing on the screen. I answer with some trepidation, wondering briefly if it's someone new and different calling to whisper something poison in my ear: "Hello?"

"Molly?"

"Yes?"

"It's Roisin," an unfamiliar girl's voice says, pronouncing it *RO-sheen*, and it's only after she adds, "Your roommate?" before I put things together.

"Oh my God, Roisin!" I exclaim. Then, not wanting to explain *I've been pronouncing your name like* Raisin *in my head all summer*: "Sorry. I had, like, a brain fart there, I don't know."

"The name thing?" she guesses, laughing a little. "You're . . . definitely not the only one. I couldn't spell it until I was in, like, seventh grade."

We spend a few minutes small-talking about our parents

and if we have any brothers and sisters, the logistics of who's going to bring a TV (me) and mini fridge (her). "Do you know what you're going to major in?" she asks me.

"Business, I think." It's the first time that anyone's asked me that question and I've had a answer ready. "I think business."

"Yeah?" Roisin asks. "I always think that's so neat, when people can just answer that question. I have no freaking idea what I want to do with my life, so those emails the dean was sending out every three seconds about declaring a major were, like, super appreciated."

"Ugh, I know," I say, laughing. She has a Southern accent, Roisin from Georgia. It's nice. "He's eager, for sure."

"I told myself I was going to figure it out this summer," she continues, "but instead I got bogged down in all this drama with my boyfriend. I'll bore you with the details of that mess during orientation, I guess, but basically it's just really hard to remember your hometown isn't the only place in the world, you know?"

That lands for me, sharp and sudden. I look at the lush green trees outside. In five days I'll be in Boston, someplace where I've got no reputation. Where everyone, not just me, will be fresh and clean and new. "Yeah," I say slowly, pressing my forehead against the cool glass of the windowpane. "Yeah, I know."

DAY 97

I stay way past the end of my shift putting paperwork together, a bible for whoever comes next. The sun's already setting, and Penn and the kids are long gone by the time I head out to the lot and realize with a sharp, fast intake of breath that there's somebody sitting on the hood of my car, waiting.

Gabe.

"Hi," I say, my eyes filling up unexpectedly at the sight of him, how every day this summer his face has been my good, good thing. I want to hug him, want to hold tight and keep on holding. I wrap my arms around myself instead. "What are you doing here?"

"I don't know." Gabe shakes his head, crossing his own arms and looking annoyed at himself, or maybe at me. He's got his baseball cap on, that handsome face shaded in the gold-purple light. "I wanted to see you. I'm an idiot, but I did."

"You're not an idiot," I say, my voice breaking a little. There's a cut at the corner of his mouth, his lip a little swollen, the physical damage right there for all the world to see. Something sharp and painful twists inside my chest. "I'm sorry. I'm sorry, I messed up."

Gabe shrugs. "You could have told me," he says, and, God, he sounds so *disappointed*. "All summer, we've been— you could have—I said I *loved* you, Molly." He huffs out a frustrated laugh. "And, like, I'm not a lunatic, I know how fast that was, but—"

"Did you, though?" I interrupt suddenly. "I mean, did you actually love me? Or did you just need to beat Patrick at this, too?"

"Molly." Gabe touches his tongue to the split place on his mouth, looks at something over my shoulder. "Maybe it started that way."

"That's gross," I say immediately, stepping backward, feeling my face go hot and prickly with building tears. "That's *gross*, Gabe."

"You don't think I know that?" Gabe asks me. "Walking around with a bunch of feelings for my little brother's girlfriend, like he had one thing I didn't and I—"

"I'm not a *thing*!" I burst out, shocked at the unfairness of it. "For fuck's sake, Gabe, I'm a *person*, and there were these huge consequences for me, and you just—"

"I know you are," Gabe interrupts. "Of *course* I know that. And it might have been about my brother in the beginning, in a way. But the fact is I did, I spent this whole summer falling in love with you, and if you knew this whole time you were never gonna love me back, then—"

"I *do* love you, though," I tell him. "That's the worst part, don't you get that? I do." I climb up onto the hood beside him then, the metal warm from sitting in the sun all day. I take a deep breath. "Patrick was the first person I ever loved, but you . . . I've spent this summer wondering what it would have been like if I'd been with you from the very beginning," I tell him honestly.

Gabe sighs. "Me too," is all he says.

We sit there for a while, watching the sunset. I can hear the crickets beeping in the trees. It's the end of August now, the world gone heavy and expectant. It doesn't feel as awkward as it should. "When do you leave?" I ask him finally. "For Indiana?"

"Day after tomorrow," he says. "I didn't get the MGH thing. Not that it matters, I guess." He shrugs. "They say I can reapply for next spring."

I think of the fantasies I had earlier this summer, the two of us piggybacking through the New England leaves. I'll miss him, I realize, something like homesickness setting up residence behind my rib cage. "I think you should," I tell him. "Reapply, I mean."

Gabe raises his eyebrows, a flicker of interest passing across his handsome face. "You do, huh?"

"Yeah," I say. "I do."

Gabe nods slightly like maybe he'll think about it. Slides off the hood of the car. "Be seeing you, Molly Barlow," he says softly. Kisses me on the cheek before he goes.

DAY 98

The next day is my last shift at the Lodge, everything wrapping up for the season and a walk through the grounds with my replacement, a community college bro named Hal. Penn and the kids get me a memo book as a going-away gift, already filled with half-sensical Penn-flavored notes-to-self like, *Watch out for dining-hall meat products* and *Floss your brain.*

"I love you," I tell her, standing on my tiptoes to squeeze her tight and not realizing how true it is until the words are out of my mouth. The thought of leaving the Lodge makes my chest feel tight, like the band of my bra's a size too small.

"Love you back, Molly," Penn promises quietly. She gets both hands on my face and plants a kiss there. "Go do good."

I smooch Fabian good-bye and turn to Desi, who's standing in the corner with one thumb shoved thoughtfully in her mouth, watching me with those big dark eyes.

"What do you say, Des?" I ask her, squatting down on the carpet so we're at eye level. "You wanna tell me bye?"

Desi looks at me solemnly and for one heart-stopping moment I think we're about to get there, that she'll finally open her mouth after months and months of silence. I hold my breath and wait for it. She kisses me once and wordlessly on the end of my nose.

I'm in my car on the way out of the parking lot before I realize I forgot my last check in the office, and I let out a quiet swear under my breath. I managed to make it all the way to the end of my shift without running into anyone who hates me. The last thing I need is one more *screw you* for the road.

Instead of driving all the way back around to the employee door, I pull up in front of the main entrance and leave my hazards on—I'll grab my check and get out of here ASAP, I promise myself, sweaty palms slipping on the brass handle of the Lodge door. After that, I'll be gone for good.

Shit.

Julia and Elizabeth are all hanging out around the fireplace in the lobby, ankles crossed and fountain sodas sweating in their hands. Penn doesn't like us to park ourselves here, she says it's off-putting to guests, but Penn's long gone for the day and here they both are, folded into the same club chairs Tess, Imogen, and I went to check out a couple of weeks ago. It feels like a lot longer than that. As soon as they spot me they fall completely, abruptly silent, like a record coming to a screeching halt in some old movie.

"I'm just getting my check," I tell them, hands up in surrender, feeling my face flush—none of that piss-off, don't-mess-with-me vinegar I felt coursing through my veins the other night at the party. "You don't—I'll be out of here in a second."

"Thank fuck," Julia says, in a voice exactly loud enough for me to hear her. So much for laying the smackdown, I guess. I think of what Roisin said on the phone the other night, *It's easy to forget that your hometown isn't the entire universe.* I wish there were a way to convince myself that's true.

I slip into the office and fish my check out of my mailbox, which is already retagged with a label reading HAL. It's crazy how fast things can change. I stuff it in my pocket and head for the doorway—

And that's when I see Tess.

She's standing in the hallway waiting, smooth braid and Barnard T-shirt, looking a thousand times more pulled together than she did the other day by the pool. "Hi!" I blurt, some weird muscle memory, that feeling of *my friend is here.* Then I blush some more. "I mean. Hi."

Tess doesn't smile. "I broke up with Patrick," she tells me flatly, crossing her arms across her chest. "For good this time."

"You did?" I echo her posture without totally meaning to, then drop my arms to my sides. I think of how guiltily my heart leaped when I heard that news the last time. All I can call up now is numbness and exhaustion. "I'm really sorry."

Tess shakes her head. "No," she says, sounding a little impatient. "That's not why I'm telling you. I just—" She breaks off for a moment. "You and me are never going to be friends again, Molly, okay? We're not. But I just wanted to tell you, I guess, that you were right. What you said at the party. That you're not the only one who screwed up, and it sucked for us all to act like you were." She raises her eyebrows. "Me included."

For a moment, I just gape at her, uncomprehending. It sounds like something Imogen would say. It probably *was* something Imogen told her, as a matter of fact, but wherever it came from, hearing it feels like being hit with a wrecking ball, like my heart actually breaking in half. I didn't always deserve them, friends like Tess and Imogen. From now on I'm going to make sure I do.

"Thanks," I tell her finally, swallowing down the sharp press of tears—it feels like there shouldn't be any more left in me by this point. My insides should be dried up like a prune. "I mean it. Thank you."

Tess shrugs. "Take care of yourself, Molly," she tells me. She waves to me once before she walks away.

DAY 99

My mom and I leave for Boston in the morning, the two of us hefting my packed duffel into the trunk of her car, plus the TV and my shower shoes and starchy extra-long sheets printed with tiny dots. "Oh, one more thing," my mom says, then runs back into the house and returns with the biggest box of Red Vines I've ever seen in this lifetime, enough to keep me in candy for the entire semester at least.

"I went to Costco," she says, and she grins.

I say bye to Vita and scratch Oscar under his doggie chin, then zip up my hoodie—it's colder in the mornings now, the lake breeze tempting fall—and pick up my shoulder bag, doing one last mental double check for anything I might have missed. There were two texts on my phone when I woke up today: a pattern from this summer, maybe, but instead of twin missives from either Donnelly brother this morning, they were from Imogen and Roisin—*good luck!* and *can't wait!*

"Ready to go?" my mom asks me, a hand on my arm as we stand in the driveway. I glance up at the lilac Victorian, then higher at the treetops. The sun is warm and yellow-feeling on the back of my neck.

"I am," I tell her, and smile. I squeeze her hand once before we get into the car.

ACKNOWLEDGMENTS

Oh, *hey*, this does not get any easier the second time. So many people make it possible for me to do this thing that I love so hugely, and every last one of you holds my heart and truest gratitude:

To Alessandra Balzer, for your keen vision and steady guidance—you make me want to be a better man, and by "man," I mean "writer who is not in fact a man." To Emilie Polster, Jenna Lisanti, Nellie Kurtzman, Caroline Sun, Ali Lisnow, Bethany Reis, Alison Klapthor, Andrea Pappenheimer, Kerry Moynagh, Kathy Faber, Ruiko Tokunaga, Susan Katz, Kate Jackson, and every other gorgeous soul at Balzer + Bray/HarperCollins for your unflagging support and general wonderfulness. I'm so honored to play for this team.

To Josh Bank, Joelle Hobeika, and Sara Shandler: I honestly just love the shit out of you. To everyone at Alloy—especially Les Morgenstein, Natalie Sousa, Liz Dresner, Romy Golan, Heather David, Lauren Metz, and Theo Guliadis—*thank you*. You're champions of the world.

To Christa Desir and Julie Murphy, for your fearlessness; to Court Stevens, for your heart; to Jasmine Warga, for your insight and encouragement on these pages.

To the Fourteenery, who make sure I am never alone.

To Rachel Hutchinson, best and most, always and always.

To all the Cotugnos, for launching me onto this delicious, unbelievable flight path, and all the Collerans, for giving me a safe place to land.

For special offers,
chapter samplers,
competitions
and more,
visit …

www.quercusbooks.co.uk

@quercuskids